The horse he couldn't buy . . .

took Ev Winton away from his family ranch at Savage Creek. It set him on the road without a penny in his pocket. It triggered the betrayal of the man he most admired. It forced him into a bargain with the gunman, Timberlake. For the love of a horse, an honest young man had galloped into a life of crime.

Could he ever get back again?

WARNER BOOKS
By Max Brand

MAN
FROM
SAVAGE CREEK

Max Brand

WARNER BOOKS

A Warner Communications Company

1

AT THE TABLE in the Winton ranch house sat three men and a woman. All the men were more or less formidable outside the house, but inside it they were all in fear of that one woman. Ned Winton feared his wife a little more than did his twenty-year-old son, Everard. Ned's brother Clay Winton, who had been a paying guest of the ranch at Savage Creek for four years, was so accustomed to being the target of his sister-in-law's attacks that he had developed a good deal of skill in making retreats from such battles.

A charge was about to be made now, and all three men knew it. They could tell by the fixed smile on Mrs. Winton's face that trouble was in the air.

Mrs. Winton wore a mask of pleasantness which, she felt, was a perfect disguise, but which flecked the blood of all the others in the family with cold. She might have been carved in ice, and the dim blue eyes of the three Winton men were fixed upon her.

"How was your day, Everard?" she began.

He was working every day in town, in the blacksmith shop.

"Oh, it was a good day enough," said the son. "Plenty to do. We had to weld a break in the coupling of Tom Walter's big iron wagon. It was heavy to handle, but we managed it."

"Was that the job that made you so late coming home?" asked the mother.

Uncle Clay Winton glided in swiftly and gently. He said:

"That was one of the biggest two-man jobs of welding that I have ever seen. Reminds me of a time in Dodge City when a new prairie schooner outfit was getting ready

5

for the plains, and along come some bohunks with wagons with iron frames. One of 'em took and tumbled over the edge of the creek where—"

"Dodge City again!" sighed Mrs. Winton.

Her glance was as bright as fire; it might have burned the very soul of a person less callous than Clay Winton.

"Well, Dodge City was Dodge City, in the old days," said Clay Winton. "Mighty few things that didn't happen there, one time or another. The days when Wild Bill Hickok was town marshal—"

"Seems to me," said Mrs. Winton, "that you talk as though you were there yourself! You weren't even born when Wild Bill Hickok was murderin' his poor victims!"

"Now, Martha!" said Clay Winton. "You ought to be a little kinder and milder when you refer to a man like Wild Bill, that was a hero. I've known plenty of men who were friends of his. A finer gentleman and a truer man there never was none!"

"He murdered a hundred men. Ain't that one of your boasts about him?" demanded the mother.

Uncle Clay leaned back in his chair as though overcome by despair. Then he rallied, shrugged his shoulders, and returned to the defense, saying:

"He never murdered anybody, Martha. Nobody ever dared to say that Wild Bill done murder. He was on the side of the law. That's what he was!"

"I have it out of your own mouth—and if you know anything you ought to know the history of Hickok; how he shot one of his own best friends in the street!"

"Why, Martha," said Uncle Clay, "it happened this way—"

"I don't want to hear how it happened! Murder is murder," said she.

Uncle Clay looked to the ceiling and made a two-handed gesture of surrender that was almost Oriental in its expressiveness.

The mother turned upon her son.

"Everard," she said, "what would *you* be callin' it?"

Said the boy, "Wild Bill was incapable of a dishonorable act."

"Incapable, fiddlesticks!" said Mrs. Winton. "You got

just a lot of Clay's nonsense into your mind, is what you've got. Murder! Red murder is what it was!"

"Mother," said the boy, "Bill Hickok never took an advantage—"

"What else did he take?" exclaimed Mrs. Winton. "The devil that loved him taught him to be a dead shot. Ordinary men didn't have a chance against him. It was murder—not duelling! He wouldn't of had the nerve for a real stand-up fight with a man that was his equal!"

"There was no fear in him," answered her son, his face darkening, and a gleam coming in those misty eyes.

He would have said more, but Clay Winton caught his eye and made a warning gesture. Everard looked back to his plate.

"You don't need to shut up my boy at his own table, Clay," snapped Mrs. Winton. "He can speak his mind for himself, I hope—unless the only mind he's got is what *you've* put into his head!"

Clay looked at his brother and Ned Winton stirred uneasily and put up a hand to stroke his long mustaches. Then he said:

"The fact is, Martha, you're bearin' down pretty hard, ain't you?"

"It would make a saint bear down!" said Mrs. Winton, flushing with anger.

Uncle Clay put in genially, smoothly, "Speaking of the old times, I saw a sight today that would have stirred the blood of Dodge City—every man and woman in it. Harry Lawson has come back from his horse hunt, and he has the horse with him!"

Mrs. Winton parted her lips to continue the flow of her harangue, but the family was familiar with her fits of temper and by long practice they had worked up perfect team-play; so now Ned Winton hastily broke in.

"You mean that red stallion—the pacer?"

"I mean the Red Pacer," said Clay. "*What* a horse!"

"It's not one of those pretty things that the ladies love the minute they clap eyes on it," he went on. "It's an inch over sixteen hands, and you can see the whole machine. You can see the frame of that horse and the muscles that pull on the bones, is what you can see. He could take a

7

standing jump and sail over the moon, is what he looks like."

"Nacheral pacer, ain't he?" asked Ned Winton.

"He is," said Clay. "And a nacheral bunch of dynamite, too. I seen Buck Sanders and a puncher by name of Miraflores, and they both tried to ride him, today. There wasn't nothing to it. He just exploded 'em into the air, and then he went sailing off to the far end of the corral and looked through the bars and cocked his ears at the mountains. They've built up the corral fence to nine feet. He'll jump anything up to eight!"

"If he can't be rode how was he caught?" asked Ned Winton.

"They trapped him. A dozen of 'em snagged him," said Clay. "Harry Lawson spent about every penny that he's got in the world to land that stallion."

"A pile of use it'll be!" said Mrs. Winton. "A hoss that can't be rode!"

"There's a worth in things that can't be used," said Clay. "I reckon that Harry'd give that hoss away to anybody that could ride it, fair and square, without pullin' leather. But there's a worth in things that can't be used."

"What worth?" snapped Mrs. Winton. "I'd like to know what worth!"

"Why," said Clay, "you can't eat a diamond necklace, can you? But it's good to look at, all the same. He had the fun of hunting the red hoss down. I reckon a thousand punchers have seen the Red Pacer on the edge of the sky, and wished their hearts out to have him. But it was like chasing lightning to chase him."

"I'd like to put a saddle on him. I'd like to try him," said Everard Winton slowly.

He spoke so quietly that his mother barely heard him. "What's that you say?" she snapped.

He shrugged his shoulders. "I'd like to try my luck with the Red Pacer," he answered.

"And get your neck broke?" she inquired angrily.

"I hope not," said the boy.

Again he looked to his uncle, and received the warning sign. But Mrs. Winton also had seen the check of the shaken head, and she was more furious than ever.

8

"You can waste your time ridin' wild hosses—you can't waste your time comin' home and helpin' with the chores, like a right-minded boy would do," she exclaimed. "D'you say that you were kept late in the blacksmith shop, this afternoon?"

Before Everard could answer, and he was habitually slow in speech, his uncle replied:

"Well, Martha, if you'd seen your boy wrestling with that iron beam and treating it like a stove poker, you wouldn't be asking questions. Tom said he never seen a finer piece of welding done by nobody."

Mrs. Winton raised a forefinger.

"Everard!" she said.

"Yes, Mother?"

"If you was down there in the shop, weldin' iron beams together, then was it the ghost of you that I seen fightin' that big hulk of a Berner boy behind the barn? And your precious uncle standin' by and lookin' on—encouragin' you to a brutal waste of your time?"

2

THE SILENCE of disaster settled coldly over the four at the table. Mr. Ned Winton looked gloomily down at his plate, and shook his head wearily. Only his wife was on fire with the cruel triumph.

Everard spoke first. He said:

"I didn't lie to you. I didn't say that I was in the shop all the time."

"You'd of sat and let me think so, though," cried his mother. "That's what you'd of done. Your precious uncle there, could talk about the weldin' work as though that had kept you. It wasn't weldin'; it was *breakin'* that you were doing. Tryin' to break heads and bones with

9

your fists—wastin' your time—fightin' like a regular animal."

Her emotion and lack of breath stopped her.

"What in thunderation is all this about, anyway?" demanded the father. "It ain't that big Rudie Berner that Ever was fighting, was it? Why, Rudie's six three, and made like an ox."

"Fightin'! Fist fightin'!" stormed Mrs. Winton, the shrillness of her voice sending the blood up to swell and redden in her face. "Right out behind the barn—right when I needed help in the milkin' and in gettin' in the wood—right out there behind the barn I peeked around and *seen* Ever fightin' Rudie Berner with his fists."

"We were only boxing, Mother," said Ever Winton, looking at her with a strangely cold eye. "We had on six-ounce gloves."

"Fightin'!" she insisted. "With your Uncle Clay Winton standin' by and encouragin' *both* of you. D'you think you can hoodwink me, Clay Winton? D'you think you can say it wasn't fightin'?"

Clay Winton, who had said nothing, canted his head to the side and endured the assault.

"You can't bamboozle me!" exclaimed Mrs. Winton. "I got the eyes that God gave me. Didn't I see Rudie Berner beat my boy to his knees? Didn't I see Ever jump up and whang Rudie till Rudie Berner lay against the side of the barn with his hands down?"

"It was a right hook," murmured Clay Winton dreamily. "A beauty, on the button! That turned the trick."

"Ever," demanded Ned Winton, with a grin, "did you lick that big whale of a Rudie Berner?"

The grin maddened Mrs. Winton.

"And you're *praisin'* him for slackin' his chores and fightin' and lyin' to me!" she cried.

Everard pushed back his chair from the table. Again his uncle made the negative sign, and again Mrs. Winton saw it. This time the slender remainder of her patience was entirely exhausted and she cried out:

"Clay, don't you go to shuttin' up my boy in his own house! Let him talk out!"

"I'll talk out," said Everard, as deliberately as before.

10

"Clay Winton!" shrilled Mrs. Winton. "I'll have you know—"

Everard lifted his hand, and the pain in his face stopped her at last.

"Maybe you're right, Uncle Clay," said he. "I won't say anything. I'll just go out and take a walk."

"Go out and take a walk? You set down right this minute and finish your supper!" commanded Mrs. Winton.

"I'll go take a walk, I think," said the son insistently.

"Ned!" she cried out. "Are you gonna let that boy defy you like this?"

Everard was already through the screen door and stepping onto the back porch as his father answered:

"He's twenty, and growed up. I can't treat him like a baby no more."

Mrs. Winton turned on her brother-in-law.

"It's you!" she exclaimed. "It's you that has done it all! It's you that's taking him away from his own flesh and blood!"

Clay Winton was a long-suffering man where women were concerned, and particularly with his brother's wife. But now even his patience gave way a little. He said:

"You gotta remember, Martha, that half his blood is Winton blood, and that's what runs in me."

He stood up in turn.

"I'll be stepping out," said he.

"And go and walk with my boy? And raise up his heart agin me?" cried Mrs. Winton. "Ned, are you just gonna set there and see things like this happen under your own roof?"

Ned Winton sighed and leaned back in his chair with his eyes closed.

"Oh, Martha, Martha!" said he. "Wouldn't you leave it be for a while? Wouldn't you let it drop?"

Clay Winton passed through the door in his turn, and his footfall went across the porch and down the steps, sounded hollowly along the board walk, and then disappeared from hearing.

A silence came over the dining room. Mrs. Winton was still red-faced and panting, but there was alarm in her eyes.

11

"There had to be a time," she said. "There had to be a time. It's just what I've suspected for a couple of years. Clay's corruptin' our boy."

"Martha," said her husband, "a boy that can be corrupted ain't worth the saving. That's all I've got to say. I'm gonna go and cool off."

He stood up from the table, but she ran around it and stood before him, gripping him by both sleeves.

"Oh, Ned!" she said. "Suppose that something would happen to him. I'd die. I wouldn't live none, if anything happened to him; an' neither would you. We're all wrapped up in him. And now—it's shootin' and fist-fightin'. And next thing you know he'll go and take and ride that Red Pacer—and have his neck broke!"

He put his hand on her head and waited until he was no longer choked by the pain in his throat. Then he said:

"Well, Martha, I'll tell you what I'll do. I'll forbid him from riding the Red Pacer."

"That's something!" she said eagerly. "It'd be somethin' more if Clay'd decide to take and live in another place."

"I'm goin' out on the front porch," said Winton. "I'll wait there and speak to Ever when he comes back in."

He left the dining room, as he spoke, and Mrs. Winton sat down at her place, with the tears working down her face unheeded. At last she sighed, gave her shoulders a short, quick shrug, and settled down to finish her supper.

After she had washed the supper dishes and dried them —a task which Everard generally performed—she went out to the front porch and sat for a moment beside her husband.

"Ned," she said, "I want to ask you somethin'."

"Yes?" he said, wearily.

"I wanta ask you where Clay really got all his money."

"Mining."

"That's what *he* says."

"Are you going to doubt his word every time he speaks?" asked Ned Winton.

"You know, Ned," she answered, "that lying comes dead easy and nacherel to lots of folks. And I notice little things—I notice a pile of little things."

"I know you do," he replied sourly.

"Ten years ago," she said, "Clay went West, smooth-shaved. Four years ago he came back, and started to grow a beard and a mustache. Then a year ago he shaved off the beard."

"Can't a man please himself, wearing his face rough or smooth?" asked the husband.

"I'm not a fool, talkin' to hear myself talk. In the old days Clay always was wild. He had to have girls, dancin', liquor. And now he lives like an old man."

"He's sowed his wild oats," said her husband sadly.

"Hot blood never grows cold," she answered. "But now Clay lives like a rat in a hole—just like that! He don't leave the ranch once a year hardly."

"What about it?" demanded her husband irritably. "He's lazy, maybe. But he's made his pile and he can afford to be lazy, all right. That's his business. What are you upset about?—His sitting around and his mustache?"

"You don't put things together," she objected.

"What do *you* make out of it?" he asked.

"You remember when Clay came back the first time, full of money? He'd made it prospectin' and minin', didn't he?"

"Yes."

"Done it for years, and finally hit it rich?"

"Yes, that's true."

"Well, Ned, you ever look at the hands of a miner?"

"Sure I have."

"What about 'em?"

"Calloused like leather. Why?"

"You remember the hands of Clay when he came back?"

"Can't say I do."

"Well, *I* remember them, though," said she. "They were as white and soft as the hands of a girl."

"Humph!" muttered her husband.

"Can you put two and two together?" she demanded.

"I ain't a suspicious sort of a fellow, Martha," he answered uneasily.

"Maybe not," she replied, "but it's as plain as the nose on your face. It's been plain to me all the while, Clay

13

never dug a penny out of the ground. Faster and easier pay was what he was after. That's the kind of money he's got, and that's the kind of money he'll send our boy after!"

3

NED WINTON considered this idea for a moment. Then he replied:

"I dunno, Martha. It's hard to know what's on the inside of a man like Clay, that don't talk nothing except what he wants to talk. I've always noticed that. But leave him be. People like Clay—you're always best off to leave 'em be. Even when he was a kid, we all of us noticed that it was best to let him alone. He'd set as quiet as a mouse till somebody came and riled him. Then he'd raise trouble. Nobody ever raised as much trouble as he could raise."

"Hush!" said Mrs. Winton. "I guess they're comin' back now. There they are, beyond the oak tree. Now, Ned, I don't ask you to do nothin' except about the ridin' of that Red Pacer. That's all I ask. You lay down the law there. You tell Everard that he don't dare to try to ride that horse. There's gotta be a time when a boy learns that what his parents say is law."

"The Pacer is a murderin' beast," declared the father. "I know that, all right. I'll tell Ever not to go and try to ride him."

"Lay down the law!" whispered Mrs. Winton. "Go and tell him that—that he's gotta obey—or get somethin' that'll bring him to his senses. Somethin' that'll show him that his Uncle Clay is leadin' him all wrong."

She hurried back into the house and left Ned Winton squirming a little. He disliked the duty that had been laid upon him; on the other hand, he was not one to

14

shirk responsibilities. Like most men, he felt that his wife knew more than he did about the proper raising of youngsters.

Through the gate that opened on the road came the figures of his brother—easily recognized, even in silhouette, by his slouching walk—and the erect, light-stepping form of his son. They moved down the path, and Ned hastily packed a pipe and lighted it, as a means of letting them know he was there.

"Hello, Father," said Everard, in the quiet voice of one who has been thinking of important things.

"Hello, Ever," said he. "Come here a minute, will you?"

The boy came to the foot of the steps and paused there. It was hard to see him by the dimness of the night light, for there was no moon in the sky; but it seemed to the father that his features stood out more clearly than if the sun had been beating all about him. From his infancy, there had been something clean and fresh and radiant about the lad. Sometimes Ned Winton thought it was because he was their only child; that all their love and yearning for a family had been poured into this one mold.

"It's about that Red Pacer," said the father. "You know, Ever, that's a damn dangerous hoss."

"I've heard that," said the boy, his tone constrained. "But you know the saying?"

"What saying?"

" 'Every horse can be rode—every man can be throwed.' "

"I've heard that," said the father, "and there's sense in it, too—which is more than there is in a lot of things. Speakin' about throwin', you know what the Pacer done to Indian Murphy? He broke six or seven ribs and smashed a leg and a collar bone.

"You know what kind of a collar bone Murphy's got now? Silver, or something. That bone was busted so bad that it couldn't be hitched together again. They had to splice up the pieces with a silver tube, is what they had to do. Murphy, every time he has a fall nowadays, he gets a dent in his chest—and the dent don't go away. He's gonna die of consumption before long, I hear."

"I'm sorry for that," said Everard Winton.

"Well," remarked his father, "I was just leading up to a point. Don't you go and be a fool and try to ride that stallion."

"But you see, Father," the boy replied, "I sent word to Harry Lawson I'd be sure to come over and try my hand with the Pacer."

"Then you send him word that you've changed your mind," said Winton.

He noticed that his brother was saying nothing, his head turning a little from side to side, as he marked the conversation.

Then the boy was saying, "It's hard to send him word I've changed my mind. He'd think—"

"It ain't no matter what he thinks," said the father. "What *I* think and what your ma thinks is what you oughta do, just now. There's no good in a wild-caught mustang stallion. Sometimes they've been rode, but I dunno one that ever gave no satisfaction to his master. Likely to turn any minute and put a hoof through you. Likely to get you off and savage you. Ever seen a man savaged?"

"No," said Everard.

"Well, you don't want to see it—and no more do you wanta *be* it. Don't you go near that hoss and make a fool of yourself, Ever."

He settled back in his chair and sighed. He drew out a bandanna and mopped his wet brow. He was sorry, afterwards, that he had done this. It showed that he was too worked up over the matter. He wanted to make it a casual affair and not underline its importance.

The boy answered. "It wouldn't matter, Father, very much, except that I've said I'd be there. And besides—"

"Besides what?" snapped Ned Winton. "I'll drop by the Lawson place, tomorrow. And I'll tell him that I wouldn't let you go. I reckon I'm old enough to know what's right for you to do."

"But you haven't seen the Red Pacer," remarked the boy quietly.

"I've seen plenty of hosses," said the father. "One's as good as another—pretty mean."

The boy did not answer at once. These pauses that he made was somehow characteristic. They made all of his words seem to come from his heart.

"A man on that horse," he said, "would be like a king on a throne, Father!"

Ned Winton struck his fist into his open palm.

"I tell you," he said, "that it's come to a point where you got to know that you ain't your own master till you're of age. Don't you go near that damn hoss! Understand? Don't you dare to go near it!"

He waited. He could hear his heart thumping. The wind stirred and the moist, warm breath from the fields of spring reached him with the scents of growing grass and the kind, fruitful earth.

"Wait a minute, Ever," murmured Clay Winton, as the boy turned to leave.

"It's no good waiting," replied the boy. "I'm afraid I know already that I have to ride the Red Pacer—or break my neck trying!"

4

WORDS BROKE OUT from the father in a rush.

"Everard, if you won't obey me, then I'm through with you! You can go your own way, is what I mean. Either you're my boy or you *ain't* my boy. You been four years followin' Clay like a dog at the heel. You been his shadow. He's been more than teacher, father, mother and friends to you. I don't like it, and I ain't gonna have it. You hear me talk?"

"I hear you," said the boy coldly.

He waited for more words, but his father had run out of them. Those the older man had spoken remained to ring in his ears, and he could hardly believe that the stern utterances had been his own.

"You go on to bed," he muttered in conclusion, and heard the voice of his son coldly bid him good night. Everard passed from view around the corner of the house.

With a sore heart, Ned Winton said to his brother, "This is some of your doings, Clay."

"Why?" asked the other. "What have I had to do with it, Ned?"

"You know what you've had to do with it," insisted Ned. "He's been around with you all the time. He's got your wild ideas."

"You figure," said Clay, "that the only way to live is to work till your bones ache. You get the ache in the bones, all right, but you don't get much life."

"I've got a farm and cows on it and plenty of saddle-stock. Everything's fenced up and fixed right, and I started with nothing," boasted Ned.

"You work like a dog every day of your life," said Clay. "But what's the good of owning a thing that makes a slave of you? You don't own the place; the place owns you! I have enough to live on, as far as that goes."

"How'd you get it?" snapped Ned.

"Why, out of the mines."

"You never was a miner!" declared Ned.

"Hello!" murmured Clay Winton.

"You've never been a miner," continued Ned. "You never had hands that were that hard."

"Martha's been talking to you, Ned," said Clay.

True accusations annoy us, always, far more than idle ones. Ned Winton grew hot at the mention of his wife.

"Leave Martha out of it!" he exclaimed.

"I'm glad to leave her out," answered Clay.

"She ain't good enough to please you, maybe?" demanded Ned.

"She's all right," said Clay. "I'm going on to bed."

"All right, go to bed," said Ned Winton. "Only—leave your hands off of Ever, will you?"

"No," said Clay Winton suddenly.

He turned and came quickly back to his brother, climbing the steps of the veranda. They stood face to face, each watching the glimmering eyes of the other.

18

"You won't, eh?" said Ned.

"As long as I stay here," said Clay, "I'm gonna keep on doin' what I can for him."

"Teach him to make a fortune the way you did? You dug it out of wallets. A six-shooter was the tool you used for breaking your ground."

Clay paid no attention to the accusation. He said:

"What a fellow does with his money is just as important as how he gets it. You've worked like a dog; you'll have to keep on working. You'll go into the grave like a tired old hoss that ain't ever known a thing but harness and blinders and the furrows ahead of it. God, what a life for a human being! Wintons are meant for better things than that. They're meant to fly higher and freer. In the old days the Wintons were gentlemen."

"You think a man with callouses on his hands can't be a gentleman, eh?" declared Ned Winton. "Because your own damn lazy hands are soft, maybe you're a gentleman, are you?"

"I'm lazy and worthless," said Clay with surprising frankness. "I never done anything worth while, and I know it. I had a bit of fun, but I never knew enough to enjoy life the way it oughta be enjoyed. I never studied or read enough; I never worked hard enough with my brain. There's only one good thing that I've started; but I'm gonna finish it—in spite of you!"

"What have you started?" asked the other.

"I've started Ever. And I've worked on him for four years."

"And what good have you done him, I'd like to know?"

"I came back and looked at him," said Clay, "and I seen that he was a thoroughbred hitched to a plough. I walked him right out of the ploughing field; I put him into training. I've got him almost ready for the race track and the big stakes!"

"You want to make him like yourself!" said the father, savagely. "A hell of a thoroughbred you ever were!"

"Youn're only calling me names," said Clay Winton, "and the names you throw won't break my skin. I say that when I came back here I found Ever a poor lump of a kid, a little bit dull and sad, and not knowing what was the matter with him. I tell you what I've done for him; I've started him working at books—every evening he's been workin' in 'em. I couldn't tell him where to start, but he went out and got the right advice. I started him to watchin' his language, till now he speaks a good clean English. I've made him watch out for his clothes, too, and now he *looks* like something. I've taught him that whisky is poison, but that it can be handled. I've taught him not to boast or talk big or loud or to swear or to use slang.

"I've used myself as a model of what *not* to be. I've worked on his training, too. He can jump higher, run faster, box better, ride cleaner, shoot quicker and straighter than anybody around here. A man that he can't throw he can knock down. He's fit to stand anywhere in the world and to be taken for a gentleman, which is what his blood calls for him to be. For three generations the Wintons have been rooting in the ground like pigs. I've fitted Everard for something better."

It was a very considerable speech, and Ned Winton grew more and more angry as he felt the justice and truth of some of Clay's remarks. At last Ned said:

"I'll tell you how it is. You're satisfied with your own ideas, you think they're fine. Well, I don't. I tell you just this—keep your hands off Ever from this minute on."

"I won't," said Clay.

"Then get out of my house and get out of my life," said Ned Winton.

"You mean that?" said Clay.

"I ain't gonna have Ever dragged down and thrown away by following your example," said Ned Winton. "Besides, you're upsetting the whole family," he muttered.

"All right," said Clay. "I'll leave in the morning. And if Ever leaves with me, I'll be sorry for you."

He walked straight through the front door and disappeared in the house, leaving the father frozen in his place in the darkness of the outer night. Ned's hand was raised in expostulation. The next word was still hanging on his lips as he was about to reply, but it seemed that that final speech of his brother had robbed him of all utterance.

20

For a moment he remained like this, staring blankly before him until the distant stars seemed to dance together. Then he turned and went into the house.

He opened the screen door with care and carefully shut it behind him, like a guilty husband returning too late at night. The warm, close air of the house closed about him and made the perspiration start on his face. There was a smell of stale cookery in the hall; it was always there.

He went to the bedroom and was about to light the lamp when he remembered his wife's weary face as he had last seen her. He wanted her advice now, but he decided it would be better to wait until the morning. To rouse her now and tell her the recent threat of Clay would be to send her into a fury, and he dreaded those paroxysms of anger more than anything else in the world.

He himself sat down by the window, knitting his fingers together. It seemed to him that the world was a flat and savorless plain, a limitless waste of labor and joyless death.

A mosquito sang suddenly at his ear; another droned not far away. A shudder ran through Ned Winton's body, but he remained motionless in his chair, staring at the obscure night outside.

5

IT WAS the very rose of the morning, when young Everard Winton rode over the hill and down to the shack of Harry Lawson.

Early as it was, Harry Lawson was already up. He was in front of his house, with his face toward the sun, seated on a sagging cracker box and whittling at thin sticks from which he was constructing stretchers on which pelts could be dried. It was said that Harry Lawson had spent his every penny on that long, long hunt for the red horse. In that quest he had hired many a man; many a horse had been ridden to death; many a month had been consumed relentlessly. He had been almost rich. All was spent to capture the red stallion—which he could not ride!

To eke out a living, Harry Lawson was trapping wolves and coyotes for the bounty and for the value of the pelts.

The time had been when Harry Lawson had bet five thousand dollars on the single ruffle of a faro pack—and lost—and shrugged his shoulders at the loss. Now he had fewer dollars than he formerly had thousands. On the other hand, in the old days he was merely "Half-breed Harry" or "That Lawson Injun." And now he was a revered figure. Men rode scores of miles to look at his splendid horse. The legend of the long pursuit of the Red Pacer filled the range.

Lawson remained the same dusty-faced, sawed-off, bowlegged specimen of an unpretentious cowpuncher that he had always been. He looked very much what he was—a cross between a stubby Comanche squaw and a hardy Highlander.

He looked up as the boy jogged the mustang nearer, but continued his whittling, merely reducing the size of his shavings as he stared at Everard Winton with fixed eyes.

The latter approached, dismounted, and waved to the Indian.

"I'm Ned Winton's son, Lawson," he said.

He went over and held out his hand. The Indian took it without rising. His curiously impersonal eyes wandered steadily over the face of the boy, as though he looked at a picture rather than a human being.

"I'll take a look at the Red Pacer, if I may," said Everard.

The Indian shrugged his shoulders.

Winton stepped to the corral fence. He went with his eyes to the ground. Only when he reached the bars did he look up, suddenly; and then he blinked and gripped the nearest bar with both hands. His eyes dimmed; he heard a singing in his ears, and his heart rose like a bubble in his breast.

He blinked the moisture out of his eyes and looked again. There was a glow, a light, about the stallion. It was not the sheen of his eyes or the shimmer of the sunshine down his flanks; that was not the light that the boy saw around the horse. Dark red chestnut, the name was not hard to understand. There were three white marks—a splash in the tail, a star between the eyes, and one silken white stocking drawn up almost to the knee.

The boy went back to Harry Lawson, who remained on the cracker box, whittling.

"Suppose somebody could ride that horse, what price would you put on him?" asked Everard.

The Indian looked away toward the sky, considered for a long moment with dim eyes, and then shrugged his shoulders.

The boy caught his breath with impatience.

"Suppose I put a saddle on him? May I try him?" he asked, at last.

Harry Lawson nodded.

When the stallion saw young Winton enter the corral he came to life and swung around the big corral with a flourish. He made the place look small, as a circus seal makes its foolish tub look small. It seemed to the boy that with every stride the monster horse rode high enough to clear the fence, had he been of a mind to do so. Winton snared the red horse around the neck at the first cast. To his delighted amazement the stallion stood still at once. One lesson he had learned perfectly—not to pull against a rope. The saddle and bridle were worked on with equal ease, and there was not even a protest when Winton swung himself into the saddle. But when he hit home in it, the action began.

It seemed to him, a minute later, that the great horse had risen under him, turned into a fountain of fire, and dissolved as it struck the earth, dropping its rider into a cloud of darkness.

Then Everard Winton was sitting up in the depth of the corral dust and spitting dust from his mouth. Blood came with the dust. He put up a hand and found that red was trickling from both mouth and nose. There was a rip in his trouser leg and a cut in the skin beneath the

23

rip. Blood trickled down that leg, also, the wound burned like fire. That was where he had grazed the fence.

He dragged himself to his feet, but he was so dizzy that he had to sit down again, at once. He felt as though a club had struck him at the base of the brain.

When his wits cleared again, he saw that the saddle was lying in the middle of the enclosure. The stallion had bucked it cleanly off, and he was in a far corner now, nibbling at the grass that extended a little distance under the fence, his ears pricking. The very contented switching of his tail was like the gesture of one who has done a task well.

The boy waited for a full half hour before the misery was out of his brain and the sickness out of his heart. Then he stood up and turned to see that the Indian was moving away from him, working busily to fit together the pieces of a stretcher. Harry Lawson was not excited, it appeared, by the proceedings of this new aspirant.

The Winton blood and the pride of the Wintons stood up in the boy. Again he caught the horse by the trailing lariat, and saddled it as easily as before. Mounted again, he was once more hurled up into the sky. But this time he hit the saddle when he came down. He stuck through that and half a dozen skyrocketings. Then the big horse spun around in a sudden circle and Everard went off, stretched flat out in the air and whirled as he shot forward. He clicked his head against a corral post and lay face down in the dust for half an hour.

When he awakened, he was almost suffocating, and the increasing heat of the sun was burning the back of his neck.

He sat up in a world that rocked about him as if he had been in a small boat in a heavy sea. He had to close his eyes, and it was another half hour before he ventured to get to his feet. But he could not stay on them; he had to sit down again. Only much later did he manage to get to the watering trough, turn on the tap, and drink deep. That refreshed him.

He looked toward the house and saw that the Indian was still whittling sticks. Again Harry Lawson's back was toward the corral. For all he knew, a dead man lay

24

in the corral—dead with a broken neck or a cracked skull. But that did not trouble the Indian.

The saddle, too, was lying in the middle of the corral once more, though it had been cinched up with redoubled care.

Winton went to pick it up, and found it a loose, pulpy wreck. The stallion must have rubbed it against the fence posts when he found that he could not simply shake it off. Winton's riding was ended for that day, but he was glad of it. Nothing but the fact that the Indian was there to look on would have induced him to make even another trial.

So, with bowed head, he went toward the corral gate, trailing the ruined saddle under his arm. He did not look up until he had reached the gate itself; and then he saw that Harry Lawson was facing toward him, at last, and regarding him and the horse. It was with amusement that the Indian looked upon him; it was with a smile that turned into the heartiest, but most silent of laughter.

The boy ground his teeth together! If he had been a little older, he would have controlled himself. But at the sight of that mockery, a madness fired his brain. The nausea left him, all at once, and he whirled about, fairly running to the stallion. Saddle or not, he would try again, for the sake of manhood.

He sprang onto the bare back of the great horse and waited for the explosion that would hurl him at the blue sky. But the Red Pacer merely turned his head. Without alarm, with what seemed an air of curious surprise, he regarded the first man ever to sit on his naked back.

6

HARRY LAWSON was seated on top of the corral fence. He was like a stuffed bird; there was not a trace of emotion on his face.

Ever dismounted and then tried the stallion on the lead. It was as though the horse had learned, long, long ago, in the days of its colthood, all the lessons that can be taught. For it now responded quite readily to the pull on the reins and to the pressure on the side of the neck.

Until noon the boy led the great horse up and down. Then he went to the shack, hoping for lunch. But the Indian remained sitting on top of the corral fence, his arms folded on his knees, studying the stallion with a blank face.

That made little difference. In the West, on the range, one may take it for granted that there is a certain hospitality. And young Everard Winton sliced up potatoes with bacon, put on a pot of coffee, and banged on a tin pan when the meal was ready.

Harry Lawson had not moved from his perch all that while, but now he climbed down to the ground and went to the house. He pumped some water into a basin and took off his felt hat, time-altered from black to green. Above the rim his hair was shining black, but below the line of the rim it was gray with dust. In the cold water, without soap, he washed his hands and face with a few brief gestures. Then he dried his face by slicking off the water with the edge of the hand, and dried his hands by flicking them together a few times and giving them a final wipe on his greasy overalls. He removed his felt hat from the nail on which he had hung it, replaced it on his head, and sat down to lunch.

He ate slowly. Most of the time he spent in carefully

loading his knife. The fork, though he preferred his fingers, was used to build up a high stack of food along the length of the knife blade, and after the load was built the knife was slowly raised, the mouth opened so wide that the eyes were reduced to glimmering slits, and the knife-load disappeared. Once the whole load fell off just as it reached his lips, but that was the only mishap; and after that accident he built the heaps more recklessly high than ever, and never made a mistake.

Ever's own appetite was good, but the Indian fairly beat him, consuming at least two-thirds of the amount of food Ever had cooked. Still Harry Lawson had not spoken. But at the end of the bacon and fried potatoes, he winked, grinned all on one side of his leathery face, rose from the table, and from a hidden shelf brought down two cans of blackberry jam. He cut off the tops of both cans, put one in front of his guest and took the other for himself. He used no bread with the conserve. Instead, he simply raised the can above his face and shook clotted lumps of the sweetness into his vast mouth.

Young Everard finished his meal and his coffee with haste, and went outside to take the air.

He could still feel the effects of the falls he had had that morning, but no pain of body could match or master the joy that was in his soul.

After a time, while he was smoking a cigarette, Harry Lawson came out and sat beside him.

"How much you want for that Red Pacer?" asked Winton.

The other held up five grimy fingers. And a swift, fiery hope rushed through the soul of the boy.

"Five hundred dollars?" he asked.

Harry Lawson shook his head, and a cold hopelessness filled the boy.

"Five thousand?" he demanded.

The other nodded, and put down his hand again while Everard Winton looked desperately ahead of him, his eyes straining as though he were trying to make out obscure print. Five thousand dollars! The sum rang and beat against his ear like a death bell.

"That's a lot of money, Lawson," he argued. "You've

got to remember that the mustang's not a thoroughbred."

The Indian shrugged his shoulders, seemed to consider, and held up three fingers.

The world, for Harry Lawson, had suddenly shrunk to the shape of that silken monster; and the price of the horse was three thousand dollars. Not a very great price for a man's entire world! But an impossible price for young Winton.

Winton picked up the wreckage of the saddle and returned to the corral. For hours he worked steadily, and at four o'clock sharp he climbed tentatively, gently, into the saddle. This time the stallion did not strike for the sky. Instead, he sank almost to his knees, trembled, and gradually straightened. With loose rein, Winton kept his place, talking constantly to the great horse soothingly. And down from his hand, through the leather of the reins to the steel bit and to the brain of the horse, he felt an electric current running.

It was not a conquest.

Not as a fighter was Ever winning the Red Pacer, but as a companion and a friend.

He dismounted, undid the cinches, and carried the saddle back to his mustang. Harry Lawson was again at work on the stretchers, making them with wonderful handicraft, binding the joints with waxed twine. Hundreds of years before, perhaps, Comanches had made stretchers just like these!

"Three thousand dollars, eh, Lawson?" Ever asked wearily.

The half-breed shook his head, and lifted two fingers.

"Two thousand?" exclaimed the boy.

The other nodded.

Two thousand dollars seemed to Ever so little, by contrast, that it seemed for a burning instant that the red horse was already in his hands. And then he remembered; he had not twenty dollars in the world. His father had plenty in the bank, perhaps; but his father had forbidden him to come near the horse.

Only Uncle Clay Winton might have ideas.

Everard went to his own horse. It was not necessary to waste an adieu on that brutally silent man; so he mounted and rode back over the trail toward home. And his heart was like red-hot steel in his breast.

7

IT WAS after supper time when young Everard Winton put up his mustang and came to the house.

He went into the kitchen and found his mother washing dishes. She merely turned her head over her shoulder, offering him no food, only the stern greeting:

"Your pa wants to see you on the front porch."

The son looked back at her curiously. Her head was bowed lower over the dishpan, and she worked her elbows furiously, as though she were over a washtub.

He went to her and laid a hand on her shoulder; her whole body trembled.

"What's the matter, Mother?" said he. "Are you going to take it as hard as all this?"

She stiffened at that, and whirled around to face him.

"It ain't me that you're to wheedle! It's your pa that wants to talk to you," she said.

He looked again into her angry face. Fear was in it, too, but he saw that his advance was taken in the wrong spirit entirely. She felt that he was trying to break ground with her before he went out to see the head of the family.

But that was mere pretense, for *she* was the head of the family, as he very well knew.

He was ravenously hungry, so he picked up a crust of bread, spread it with butter from a dish on the kitchen table, and paused at the door to munch.

"You didn't go to the blacksmith shop at all," she exclaimed, without turning her head. "Don't lie and say you did. Pa went and inquired, and you wasn't there!"

"I wasn't going to lie about it," he answered simply.

29

Anger jumped up in his breast. "What sort of a fellow d'you think I am, anyway?" he asked her.

"Go and talk to your pa!" she retorted.

He went out of the kitchen and through the dining room and down the narrow darkness of the hall, very slowly. He was finishing the heel of the loaf as he stepped onto the front porch.

There were two spots of light in the dusk; one was from his father's pipe, one from his uncle's cigarette.

"Hello, Clay. Hello, Father," said Ever.

"How are things?" asked Clay Winton.

The father merely grunted.

"Mother says you want to talk to me, Father," said the boy.

"I do," said Ned Winton gruffly.

Now that the time had come, the words came out with a surprising ease. Ned Winton added:

"Were you at the blacksmith shop, today?"

"No," said the boy.

"Why not?"

"I was busy at something else."

"What was it?"

"I rode the Red Pacer," answered Everard frankly.

"You *rode* him, eh?" exclaimed Clay Winton. "Good boy, Ever!"

Ned leaned forward to face his brother. "Are you gonna keep your mouth out of this?" he asked with a dangerous softness.

"Yeah. I'll keep out of it," answered Clay.

"So you rode the hoss, eh?" said the father.

The boy was silent. It was a question he had already answered.

"I told you not to and you went and did it?" questioned the father.

"I said that I pretty near had to," replied Everard. "You know how a thing gets into you—and burns."

"But I told you not to!" insisted the father.

"That's true," said the boy.

"And still you went and done it?"

"Yes."

"What had I ought to do about a thing like that?"

30

"I don't know."

"*I* know," said the father savagely. "I'd oughta throw you out of this house and into the road! That's what I oughta do—and I got a mind to do it."

The boy lifted his head.

"It's easily done," he said. "One word will turn the trick. Just one word more is all you need to use."

Ned Winton leaped from his chair and stamped until the boards creaked under him.

"Sassing me back, are you?" he shouted.

"I don't want to," said Everard. "I don't want to make you angry, either."

"All you want is to have your own way, eh?"

"Father," said the boy, "I know you're angry—and I don't blame you, either. You told me there was something I mustn't do, and I did it. That was wrong of me, but I just couldn't help myself. I want to make a business deal with you. You've always wanted me to stay and work more on the ranch. You never wanted me to go into the blacksmith shop, for instance. It was only that I thought that I couldn't be interested in the ranch, you see. Well, I'll change my mind, if I can. I'll come back here and work on the ranch; I'll be a hired hand. I'll show you how I can pitch in and work for you."

"What makes you say all of this, so unexpectedly?" asked the farmer. "What makes you so doggone eager to get to work on the ranch?"

"I'm not eager to do that," answered Everard. "But I want to please you and I want to please myself. I've got a chance to get a thing that means more to me than anything else in the world. You can help me get it. And if you'll do it, I'll work out what I want you to give me. I'll work without any pay—as common puncher, plough-hand, anything you say."

"What is it that you want?" asked the father.

"Two thousand dollars!"

"Hey?—What?"

The boy was silent.

The father exclaimed again. "What you done that you need two thousand dollars?"

"That's the price of the Red Pacer."

"My God!" cried Ned Winton. "I could buy twenty good hosses—I could buy a whole herd of 'em—for that price. Are you clean crazy, Ever?"

"Well, after seeing the Pacer twice, I'll about die unless I have him; and Harry Lawson wants two thousand dollars for him."

Said Ned Winton, "I ain't that kind of a fool!"

Said the boy, "Would I be worth five hundred dollars a year to you, and keep, as a regular ranch hand—and to run things, too, while you're away from the place, now and then?"

"Five hundred dollars!" said the father, scenting a bargain, and beginning to cavil. "While you have boxing matches behind the barn?"

"I'll stop that," said the boy. "I promise."

"And burn up ammunition with revolvers and rifles —and never shoot no game—just practice?"

"I'll stop that, also," said Everard. "I'll stop it all. I'll be what you want me to be. I'll throw myself into the job. I'll study the cattle business day and night, when I'm not riding range or doing other things. I'll work out of books and take notes on everything that the old-timers say to me. I'll never look at a gun or anything like that. It'll be work—work—work—for me. I'll give you four years of work like that, if you'll advance the two thousand dollars now."

The father sighed.

"To think of a son of mine actually wantin' to blow in two thousand dollars on a hoss!"

"I'll work six years for you," said the boy, steadily and quietly. "I'll spend no more time making things in the blacksmith shop, or fiddling around with the locksmith, or shooting, or hunting, or playing foolish games. I'll toe the line every minute of those years. I'll do that for the two thousand dollars."

"You will?" muttered the father.

There was a long silence. Then the parent whispered, "Two thousand dollars for a worthless hoss! You'd be the laughin' stock of the range, and so would I. Folks would just laugh at us. Two thousand dollars? You could get that hoss for five hundred!"

"Harry Lawson spent fifteen or twenty thousand dollars to catch that mustang," said the boy. "What with the hire of men and the burning up of horseflesh, he spent at least that much. And his place went to pieces while he was away. He was pretty well heeled a few years ago, and he's broke now. But he did that for the horse. He asked five thousand at first; but afterwards he came down to two thousand—after I'd ridden the Pacer. That's his lowest price. I saw in his face that it was the lowest."

"Harry Lawson is a half-breed fool!" said the father.

Clay Winton broke in. "Ned, do it. Ever offers you six years of his life. By the end of that time he'll be a cattleman in spite of himself, and that's what you want him to be. Let him have the money. I'll advance it to you if you're short on hard cash."

That word from his brother simply happened to strike Ned Winton at the wrong moment and in the wrong place.

"I want none of your stolen money in my hands!" he shouted.

His brother stood up and leaned a hand against a wooden pillar. He felt the eyes of the boy on him, through the darkness.

"You've said a hard thing to me," said Clay.

"I've said a true thing. Tell Ever if it's true or not. On your word of honor, tell him true—if you dare!"

"It's true," said Clay Winton. "I live on stolen money."

After a deadly pause Ned Winton muttered, "I didn't want to kick you in the face like this—only—"

His voice faded into an obscure mumbling that had little or no meaning.

Clay said, "I might of guessed from last night that it would pan out this way. Well, I'll be rolling my blankets."

He stepped through the doorway and into the house.

"Hadn't you better call him back?" asked Everard of his father.

Ned Winton exploded again. He felt that he had done something brutally wrong, for he loved Clay and always had. It had been a stunning shock to him to learn that his wife's suspicions, after all, were correct. Now he turned and poured his rage on the boy.

"Are *you* gonna give me advice now?" he demanded. "You, that has been the cause of it all?"

"No," said Everard. "I'll give you no more advice."

8

Mrs. winton was not the most tactful person in the world, but never had she chosen a more tactless moment than this for coming to the front porch. Her husband badgered and desperate and feeling that he wanted support from some one, turned to her eagerly.

"Here's our Ever, that wants two thousand dollars for a hoss!"

"Two—thousand dollars—for a hoss!" she cried, throwing up her hands. "Where's your brain, Ever? Where's your brain?"

The boy stepped back to the door. His parents thought that the argument was just beginning; they did not know that in reality it was ending.

He expounded his proposal again.

"I've just been telling father that I'd work six years for nothing—as hard as I can work, and I know that I can work hard. I've been a fool of a kid, but I can be a man now. I'm not boasting, but something's happened to me. I know I can be a man now, and do a man's work. I've offered to work six years for the two thousand dollars."

"For a hoss, eh?" said the mother. "The craziest idea that I ever heard in all my born days!"

Her son pulled the door open.

"Well," he said, "I know that you're the boss here, and that what you say goes."

He stepped inside and closed the door after him. Even from his childhood his ways had always been those of silence. The door made no sound now, and they hardly realized that he was gone.

Then said the mother, "You been layin' down the law to him?"

"Clay's leavin' the house," said her husband abruptly.

She made half an exclamation of pleasure, but something told her to cut it short. Her husband rarely overawed her, but this was one of the occasions.

"Well," she said, "sometime he was bound to go. I guess that's the only way to look at it."

"I told him," said her husband, "right in front of Ever. I told him that he was livin' on stolen money."

"What did he say?" breathed the wife.

"He said that he was," replied Ned Winton.

"He *said it?*" she echoed. "His own self, he said it?"

"Yes," he replied. His voice was stifled as he added with effort. "He's a man, Clay is. I always told you that—Clay's a man. He up and said it, in front of me. That don't matter much. But he said it in front of Ever, too—and he loves Ever. He loves him better than God loves little apples. But he admitted in front of Ever that he had been a thief."

"It's a terrible thing!" she whispered.

Then, with Everard's slowness, and with his voice, she heard her husband saying, "You had to talk. I wish you hadn't talked about it. You put the idea in my head."

A rush of anger flushed her face, brought a thousand words to her lips; but she was silent. She realized, suddenly, that she had put in motion wheels that she could not stop.

Everard, when he entered the house, paused at the door of his uncle's room, where the light slid out across the faded pattern of the matting that covered the hall floor. He tapped lightly.

"Hello!" said his uncle's clear, quiet voice.

Everard admired the purity of the sound, with no choke of emotion in it.

"It's Ever," said he.

"Come in, Ever," said Clay Winton as he came to the door and opened it. Clay Winton offered, now and again, little touches of courtesy of which most people in that part of the world were incapable. He held the door open now, and smiled at the boy. But Everard did not fail to see that the face of the other was pale as stone.

"May I come in?" the boy asked.

"Why, come in, Ever. Of course," said Clay.

He waved his nephew to a chair; then he closed the door softly behind his guest.

Everard went to the chest of drawers and leaned his back against it. He lifted his chin, and from an altitude looked down on the work of the packing. He had been sixteen years old when this man came to the house, but he felt as though the last four years had composed nine-tenths of his life. He said nothing; he merely watched. Everything had been taken from the drawers and piled on the bed. On the floor beside the bed lay a tarpaulin; and in it shirts, underwear and other odds and ends of apparel were being laid with great rapidity. It was as though Clay Winton had planned long before a quick departure such as this, and knew exactly what he would want.

He said, bending to build the pack, "You can wear my things, Ever. You take what I leave behind, will you?"

Emotion, with a cold and terribly unexpected hand, gripped Everard by the throat. He could not answer. He could only be thankful that his uncle did not look up at that moment.

"I guess that's about all," said Clay, after a time, looking carelessly about the room.

He folded the outer edges of the tarpaulin over, and with a swift twisting of rope, made his bundle into one that would fit behind a saddle. Then he crossed to the table, opened a drawer, and took out a Colt revolver which he broke open, examining its loaded cylinder, and held out to the boy.

"I want you to have the old gat," said Uncle Clay. "She's never missed, for me. I guess she'll never miss for you, either."

Everard took it, gripped it hard, and then put it away in his clothes. He had used it before. He knew how Clay Winton trusted that gun.

Again, swift emotion choked him and he could say nothing.

His uncle sat down, rolled a cigarette and lighted it.

"Don't you make any mistake, Ever," he remarked. "Your mother's right. I wouldn't be good for you—in the long run."

He stopped speaking. Sitting in silence, he finished the cigarette with long, slow inhalations. Then he walked to the window and threw out the butt. It made a little arc of sparks through the darkness of the night.

"I'll be saying so long, Ever," he said.

Everard paid no heed, but with lowered head began to pace rapidly back and forth.

Clay Winton went on, "Four years and a half ago, I walked into the Green River First National Bank and pulled a gun on the cashier. It was just noon, and everybody was hurrying out. Nobody but the cashier noticed me and the gun. I made him open the safe; the others were mostly out for lunch, by that time. He brought me the boxes. There was a lot of cash, and there was a lot more in convertible securities. It was worth about half a million. No, four hundred thousand would be nearer. I dropped the stuff in three saddle bags and got away. They only shot me once. I still have the bullet in the left leg. You know how I limp when the first frosts come?"

"I know," said Everard, as he stopped his walking.

"So long, Ever," said his uncle quietly.

"What horse are you riding?" asked the boy.

"The only hoss I have," said the older man. "That roan bronc."

"All right," said Everard. "When you get outside the corral gate, will you wait for five minutes?"

"Yes," said Clay Winton.

"All right. You wait for five minutes, that's all. Before you ride on."

"I'll do that."

Clay Winton went to the door, picked his sombrero off a nail, shouldered his pack, and left the room.

Then, on the front porch, Everard could hear the spoken good-byes, very brief and stilted. It was an amazing thing to the boy, the ease with which the ties of blood could be broken all in a moment.

37

Immediately afterwards he heard his mother enter the house.

Then, in his turn, he went out to the porch.

9

IT WAS his father's bedtime, but he was lighting up a fresh pipe, and a shower of sparks blew down the lazy wind.

Everard waited until the preliminary puffing had ended and the red glow had died from his father's face. Then he said:

"Uncle Clay has gone?"

"Yeah," muttered Ned Winton. "Clay's gone."

"He couldn't stand it," insisted the boy. "That's why he's gone."

There was no answer.

"I'm going, too," said the boy.

He waited.

"Are you?" asked his father.

"Yes, I'm going," he said.

He waited again.

"All right," said Ned Winton.

"About Mother—" began the boy.

"It's Clay that's making you go," said the father.

"No, that isn't so," insisted the boy. "Uncle Clay said that you were right; and he said that Mother was right. He doesn't even know that I'm going."

"Well, it's all right," remarked Ned Winton. "You're going because I wouldn't give you the two thousand dollars."

"Because you wouldn't trust me for the two thousand dollars," Everard corrected him.

The boy smiled to himself.

"Your mother, she says it's the craziest idea that she

ever heard of—two thousand bucks for a twenty-year-old kid."

"Perhaps it is a crazy idea. I don't know. But I've got to have that horse."

"How you gonna get it? Steal it?"

"Maybe," said the boy.

"My God!" muttered Ned Winton.

He turned in his chair, suddenly, and started to speak. Then he checked himself.

"My mother," said Everard, "is behind all this. But she's not as swift and bitter as you think. She loves me, and I love her. If I went to say good-bye to her now, she'd raise the roof. I couldn't stand it, and she couldn't stand it. We understand each other. That's why she's always been afraid that I'd go wrong.—I'm not going near her, but I want you to say two things to her, for me."

"I'll say them," said the father.

His voice was a whisper. There was nothing in his heart; it was an empty space. Pain would come later.

"Tell her that I love her, and tell her good-bye for me," said the boy. "She'll raise the roof, mind you, but you can stand it. For you could stand calling your own brother a thief."

His father puffed at his pipe, leisurely. He could not answer for a minute, so terrible was the pain that was beginning to creep inside his breast.

"Yeah," he said, "I called Clay a thief. He is. Clay's a thief."

"Yes," said the boy. "Uncle Clay's a thief. But do you know something?"

"Well?"

"He's the finest man I know," said the boy pointedly.

The father continued to smoke, and made no comment.

"I'll be going along now," said Everard. "Are you shaking hands, Father?"

He held out his hand.

"Why, sure," said Ned Winton. "I guess we're shaking hands."

He stood up and held out his hand. He said:

"Speaking of the six years' work, that would be all

right. The six years' contract and the two thousand dollars."

But his son answered, "If I were in hell and one penny would get me out, I wouldn't take that penny from you now."

"That's pretty clear," said Ned Winton.

"I hope it is clear," said Everard. "Good-bye."

He went down the steps. His footfall crunched on the long, straight, graveled path, and he passed out of the obscure shadows of the trees and into the pale starlight beyond; he opened the gate, closed it with his customary softness, and went up the road toward the corral gate.

His father smoked out his pipe and then went into the house.

At the door of the bedroom he waited for a moment, with his hand upon the knob, but finally he went inside. All the Wintons moved softly; so did Ned. Through the darkness he said:

"Martha!"

He had to repeat the call.

"Well?" she said, awakening.

"Clay's gone," he said.

"You needn't to wake me for that," she answered. "I know he's gone—and a good riddance."

He lighted the lamp and remained with his back turned toward her, his hands resting on the edge of the dresser, with the lamp before him, so that his shadow swallowed the white walls of the room.

Suddenly she sat bolt upright.

"Ned, what's the matter?" she asked.

"Aw, nothing much," said he.

She was awed by his very silence.

"It ain't that I didn't know you love Clay," she said.

"Did you know that?" he asked skeptically.

"Will you turn around and look at me?" she pleaded.

"Yeah. Pretty soon I will," said he.

A dreadful fear got hold of her; she could hear the thumping of her heart, and in the silence it seemed to her that strange little noises stole down the hall and paused at the door of the room.

"Clay said he was a thief," said the father. "He said it before Ever."

Still his wife made no answer, and a dim wonder stole over him. He had never known her to lack words before.

After a time, while he still considered the lifting of the yellow flame in the hot chimney of the lamp, he said:

"Ever's gone."

"Gone?" she asked, unable to comprehend.

Her voice had grown so thin and small that he stood up straight, with a start; but he could not bring himself to face her.

"You drove out Clay," he said.

"I drove out Clay," she answered. "God forgive me if I was wrong about it. I was only thinkin' of poor Ever. He's only twenty."

"But you went and drove out Ever, too," said he.

He heard a rustle of the bed clothes, and the fall of a bare foot on the floor. He said hastily:

"Don't come near me, Martha. Don't touch me!"

He shrank at the thought of her.

"I wouldn't bother you none, Ned," she said brokenly. "I'm only standin' here and askin' you something."

"All right," he answered. "That's all right. Whatcha wanta know?"

"Everard—" she began. "What about Everard? What about my boy?"

"You wanta know something?" he said.

"I wanta know anythin' you'll tell me, Ned," said she.

He wondered at her small and childlike voice now.

"Well," he said, "I was talkin' over about the two thousand dollars and the six years' contract. You said that was the craziest idea you ever heard of."

"Yes," said the new, small voice. "Maybe I said that." And, in a whisper she added, "Oh, God!—Oh, God! What's happened?"

"Well," said he, "Ever said that if he was in hell and only wanted a penny to get out, he'd stay right there in hell rather than take the penny from me now."

He felt her come nearer.

"Maybe you mean that Everard has left us for good?" she asked.

41

"He didn't take nothin' with him," said the father. "He didn't make up no pack; he didn't even take his new rifle. He just walked off the front path, and he opened the gate and turned up the road. He wanted me to say two things to you—that he loved you, and good-bye."

He added, hastily: "Don't touch me, Martha! I'm gonna go out and have another pipe. I was just telling you. He didn't take nothing. If he was in hell and a penny would buy him out, a penny from us wouldn't do him no good now."

10

EARLY the next morning, Mrs. Ned Winton drove to town in the buckboard with a cargo of fresh butter and eggs to be delivered at the grocery store. There she received part payment in trade and part in hard cash. She hurried through her business, for she had something else on her mind that had to be executed, and it was a thing which she did not wish her husband to know about.

She went, in fact, straight to the office of the sheriff— but not quite to it, for in fact she encountered Sheriff Lewis Darrow walking down the sidewalk with a big stride and she pulled up the buckboard beside him.

He took off his hat to her, lifting it so high that she saw the gleam of the bald spot on his head. He was not as trim about the waist as he had once been, and his long face was more like that of a horse than ever—an aging horse, but one with plenty of spirit still left to shine out of the eyes. Deep furrows ran down his cheeks, slanting from the temples toward the chin, and his eye was sunk under a sun-faded shrubbery of brows.

She had known him since her girlhood. That long acquaintance and the fact that he represented the law throughout the huge domain of that county made her feel and value highly the sense of possession with which she looked upon him.

"I wanted to talk to you a couple minutes, Lew," she said.

He stepped out from the sidewalk, raised his right foot, and rested the ball of it on the hub of the front wheel.

"All right, Martha," he said, with a smile. "You never let me take up much of your time. I'll stand here all day, if you'll keep on talkin'."

She smiled, and though the smile died quickly, a sense of pleasure remained long after. She had been a very pretty girl, in her time.

"It's about my boy," she said.

"Ever?" said he. "Oh, Ever's all right.—Been cutting up a little, has he?"

"He's got into bad company," said she, "with Clay Winton."

The sheriff did not so much as blink. He could face guns, also news like this.

"I always liked Clay a lot," said he.

"He's taken my son away from home," she answered.

"I'm sorry to hear that," answered the sheriff.

There was consideration and doubt in his eyes.

"I want him stopped!" she burst out.

A thousand times before, the sheriff had heard from women requests just as unreasonable as this one.

He met her eye gently and answered, "I'd stop Clay in a minute, but I ain't got the power. There's gotta be a cause for arrest, and a warrant's gotta be swore out."

She stared at the sheriff, and felt her face turning cold and her heart turning hot.

"I'm talkin' to you alone, Lew?" she said, finally.

"You are, Martha," he answered, with a start.

"If ever a whisper comes back to my husband that I've gone and told you, my life's a plumb ruined life, Lew!"

There was a note of desperation in her voice.

The sheriff took his foot from the hub of the wheel, for the mustangs had begun to stir uneasily, backing and then stepping forward. The wheel kept making quarter-turns.

"No whisper ever comes out of me, when things are told to me in private, Martha," he said. "But I'm a sworn-in officer of the law. Y'understand? When you talk to me, you're talkin' right to the law, in a manner of speakin'. Maybe you better not tell me what's in your mind—till you've gone and talked it over with Ned."

A moaning came suddenly from her throat.

"Oh, Lew," she said, "Ned blames me because both Clay and Ever are gone. But I bore down on Clay. I knew he wasn't good for my boy. I knew right well. And I knew that he never dug honest money out of the ground with those soft hands of his. Yesterday, it was put right up to him and he admitted that his money was stolen. Is that good enough to arrest him? But God help me if you bring me into it! Only, I want him stopped! He's gotta be stopped. I gotta have poor Ever back home again, or I'll die!"

Tears brimmed her eyes, but she set her teeth and would not surrender to the pain.

The sheriff let a moment pass. Then he said:

"Martha, I'll tell you what. If you wanta drive on home and forget about what you've told me—why, I'll forget about it, too!"

"And let Ever go with him?" she pleaded.

"You want me to arrest Clay, eh?"

"I do! Something's gotta be done. There's nothin' left but that!"

"All right," said the sheriff slowly. "Where did he steal the money?"

"I don't know that. All I know is that he stole it. It must of been a whale of a lot, too, because he has everything that he wants, and he never has to turn a tap with his hands. He's got it all invested, somewheres. He's just livin' on the interest, all this while.—Is that enough to arrest him on?"

"I'm going back to the office and see," said the sheriff. "I'll try to trace it. I guess I oughta say that I'm glad you told me—but I ain't. I'm sorry. I always liked Clay a lot!"

"You never knew him," said the woman, trembling.

44

"You never seen him workin' on a son of yours, an' stealin' the boy's heart away from you."

"No, never saw that," admitted the sheriff.

"I'm gonna drive on," she said. "Mind you, Lew, my life's murdered for me if ever Ned finds out that I've told you. He'd never forgive me; he'll never forgive me anyway, unless Everard comes back—and I—"

The tears suddenly overbrimmed her eyes. She slapped the mustangs with the reins and drove off without a word of farewell.

11

THE SHERIFF walked on into his office, full of thought. There in the office, waiting for him, was Jim Butler, his deputy. Jim was far too old to ride with a posse, and his hands were far too slow and uncertain to wield a revolver. Sometimes he took a week off and devoted the time to serious drinking. Nevertheless, he was worth his weight in gold to the sheriff.

"Lookit, Jim," said Lew Darrow, seating himself on the sill of the open window. "How long's Clay Winton been around town, lately?"

"He ain't been around town ever. He's always out to Ned Winton's ranch."

"Mighty lively boy, Clay used to be," said the sheriff. "But he's quieted down a lot.—Never sees nobody, lately."

"No, he never does," said the other.

"That's a funny thing," remarked the sheriff. "Lookit here, Jim—how long has Clay been back—back from his mining?"

"Lemme see.—Four years. Past four years," said the all-knowing Butler.

He saw that other questions were about to be asked

him, and puckering his brows, he buried both fists in the length of his white beard. He was like one submitting to torment. He hated to disturb the vast accumulation of facts which had piled up in his brain, with or without his will.

The sheriff pointed a brown forefinger at him and frowned, demanding absolute concentration.

"Where was Clay Winton when he was away from home?" he demanded.

The face of the other was stirred by the effort of recollection.

"He said he was off in Old Mexico, most of the time," said the other, relaxing with a faint sigh because of the ease of answering this question.

"Think!" ordered the sheriff. "Away back there, four-five years ago, did anything big happen in the line of robberies?"

"There was the Denver and Q. R. Express that was held up by the Townley gang."

"Leave gangs out of it," said the sheriff. "No Winton is likely to work with a gang. Gangs leave tracks that are too broad, an' Wintons are all folks that move silent and careful."

"Did Clay Winton rob something?" asked the other.

"Never mind that. You just keep on remembering. Pick out some big job—most likely a one- or two-man job."

The other sighed. "Wait a minute, Lew, and I'll get it sure," said he.

He pulled open a drawer of the desk and produced a whisky bottle and a glass.

"Leave that be!" commanded the sheriff. "You don't touch no drop till you hit on something."

The old man groaned faintly. He pushed the bottle and the glass reluctantly to the side, though his eyes dwelt on them still.

"About five years back," he said, "there was a pair of gents that stuck up the Cripple Gulch Stage."

"There was red-handed murder in that job. Wintons are not murderous. Try again."

"Up in Lassiter Falls there was one day when the

46

town woke up and found that the safe of the biggest bank in town was blowed."

"That was another gang job," said the sheriff. "Try again."

"There was the Green River First National job, too. That was a beauty."

"How was that?"

"It was one noon, that a gent walks into the bank—"

"Alone?"

"Yeah, alone."

The eye of the sheriff brightened. "Go on!" he ordered.

"He walks in alone, and there was still some people in the bank. Well, this gent steps to the cashier's window and slides a revolver under a stack of papers and just lets the muzzle shine at the cashier. Somehow, it didn't look like news from home to that cashier, neither. So the cashier forked the dough out of the safe. He sees that the robber is cold and cool as ice.

"The guy who done it is pretty well toward six feet, kind of lean, clean-shaven, and he's got a pair of blue eyes that look different from most. So he passes over the loot, and the other drops it into three saddle bags and backs toward the door. And as he gets to the door the cashier gets his courage back and grabs his gun. He shoots that gent through the leg; he even seen the blood fly, he says. But the robber, he was right at the door. He dragged through it, and pulled himself right onto a horse. Away he goes, and he turns into one alley and up another, gettin' clean away, though he must of bled a terrible pile."

The sheriff sat transfixed.

"Does Clay Winton ever limp?" he asked.

"Yeah. I've heard sometimes in the winter he does."

The sheriff leaped to his feet.

"Jim," he cried, "you can take that drink now! You've done a year's work in a day!"

And he fled from his office to the street.

12

IT WAS midnight when Clay Winton and the boy came over the top of the last hill and looked down at the faint black spot which was the shack of Harry Lawson, the Indian.

There Clay Winton pulled in his horse.

"I don't like it, Ever," said he.

"What?" asked the boy.

"Arrivin' anywhere—even at a shack like that— with me on a hoss and you on foot."

"When I have a horse," said the boy, "I'll ride with you. And while you have a horse and I'm on foot, I'll do the traveling on foot, Indian style."

"What are you gonna say to old Harry?"

"I'm going to beg him to keep that horse for me as long as he will—a month, maybe—until I have a chance somehow to get hold of the right amount of money."

Clay Winton cleared his throat.

"You know, I've got more solid cash than that along with me, Ever?"

Ever was silent for a moment.

"Have you?"

"Yes. I'll pass out the price of that horse to you. You can pay me back later on."

The boy hesitated.

"I don't know," he said. "There's something in me against doing that."

"You're worried because it's stolen money? Well, Ever, suppose I hadn't told you what it is? You'd have taken it, then, wouldn't you?"

"Perhaps I would," he admitted.

"Then take it now. And as soon as you've paid it back,

you're free of trouble about it. Your hands are clean again."

The boy turned suddenly to him.

"Uncle Clay," said he, "we're partners, aren't we?"

"The best ever," said the other.

"Well, I can't touch your money, Uncle Clay. I'm sorry, but I can't."

He bowed his head.

"All right," said Clay Winton. "That's that. And I won't argue. In the long run, clean hands are the best hands, I suppose."

They started down the hill together. It had been a long march, but the step of Ever Winton was as easy and swaying as when he had started.

"That Green River business, Uncle Clay," he remarked. "You mind talking about it?"

"Not a whit—to you."

"Did they ever get after you?"

"I faded out of the picture, grew mustaches, and came home to your father to get older. They never bothered me any."

"Another thing—"

"Fire away, Ever."

"Anybody very badly damaged because of the money you took?"

"Why, I don't know," said the older man. "The bank didn't fail, if that's what you mean."

"That's the main part," muttered the boy.

"Make you feel pretty bad about me?" asked Clay.

His voice was solemn.

"No, not that," said Everard. "Only it makes me sorry, and rather down. But it doesn't change my main idea."

"What's the main idea?"

"Well, of all the men I've seen, I'd rather be like you than any of the rest."

There was a quick exclamation of protest.

"You think that now, Ever," said the other, "but you'll think better, later on. I've had the luck to be with you when you were learning things, and I had a few tricks to teach. That's all!"

Everard was silent for a moment as they entered the chilly air at the bottom of the hollow. The night was gloriously clear. Taking a quick, deep breath of the pure air, he looked up to the sheen of the stars.

"Let me tell you something," he said.

"Fire away, brother."

"You remember when I first started boxing?"

"Yes, I remember pretty well."

"And you had me box with that big redheaded Peg Wallace?"

"I was a fool to do that," said Clay Winton. "He was too big and too old for you. His strength had hardened on him a lot; he was a lot nigher to a man than a boy."

"That was all right," said the boy. "You remember how he kept slamming me in the side and the stomach?"

"I remember. I thought his fist was going through you, a coupla times."

"So did I," said Ever. "I could feel it jar right up against my backbone, it seemed to me. It kept me bending over, the pain of it."

"I remember," said Clay Winton.

"And then he would whang me in the body, and change to the head, and knock me flat."

"I remember that, too."

"And every time he knocked me flat, you stood over me and swung your arm up and down for the seconds. And every time, as I got up to my knee, you said that I'd done enough, and asked me if I wanted to give up."

"I did that. And I meant it."

"No," said the boy. "There's the point. You said it, but you didn't mean it."

Clay Winton was silent.

"You'd rather have seen me killed than to hear me give up," said Ever.

"Well—maybe," drawled the uncle.

"I thought I *was* going to die," said the boy. "And every time I got up, I looked at your face, and you looked so white and sick that I thought it would be a lot better to die than to shame you and the rest of the Wintons. So I kept on, until I managed to start left-handing him. Then I put a big red bump where one eye used to be."

"Aye, that was the old sharp-shooting," cried out the older man joyously. "That was hitting the target. Dog-gone me! I ain't gonna forget how he winced when you kept on whacking the spot. Remember how he backed up finally and said it wasn't fair to keep hitting on one spot?"

"That didn't matter," said the boy. "After he quit, I was pretty sick."

"Yes, I remember."

"I had to lie down on my back and you squatted be-side me and rubbed my sore stomach and my ribs. But I kept on groaning, and groaning. I couldn't help groan-ing."

"It was enough to groan over," said Clay.

"I didn't care much about the groaning," answered the boy. "I didn't care at all, because I knew after that fight that all the rest of the life that lay ahead of me, I'd always rather die than give up. That's no trick, and that's what you taught me. I owe it to you."

"It's a lot, and no mistake," said his uncle. "But you don't owe it to me. The Wintons are that way. They don't give up."

"Anyway," said the boy, "I had to get that out of my system. I had to try to tell you what you've done for me. And at the same time, I can't tell you that I'll take your money. I don't know why; it just goes against the grain."

"Don't worry about it any longer," replied Clay Winton. "Between you and me, Ever, there can't be any dispute. You don't want stolen money, and I don't blame you. And there it is."

"We'd better sing out to Harry Lawson," remarked Clay, as they drew near to the house. "If we walk in on that old-timer when he's in the middle of a bad dream, he's likely to wake up shooting." So he called out: "Harry Lawson! Hello!"

They came up to the shack in time to see a shadowy form appear in the black square of the doorway. A moment later a lantern was lighted, and Harry Lawson came out to meet them, with a grunt and a nod of welcome.

"I've come over to make you a proposition about the Red Pacer," said Ever.

The other grunted, nodded, handed the lantern to Clay Winton, took the pack from behind the saddle of the horse, and then led the mustang off toward the barn.

"He's dumb, today," said the boy. "I was here for hours. He made a few signs, but never spoke."

"He's an old-timer," answered Clay Winton. "They're likely to be queer. He's taken the pack off the horse and gone to put it up; he's given us the lantern so we can go inside and make ourselves at home. A coupla gestures like that are better than a flock of words."

13

BY THE TIME they had brought the pack into the shack and looked around them, at the few sticks of furniture and the two bunks, only one of which had blankets or a pallet on the boards, Harry Lawson was back again.

He pointed toward the stove with an inquiring air, as Winton unstrapped his blankets.

"We're not hungry," said Clay Winton.

At that the Indian picked one of the blankets from the stack out of which he had just rolled, twisted it around his body from head to foot, turning himself into a mummy with one arm outside the wrappings, and lay down on the hard boards of the floor. His greenish felt hat he pulled over his eyes to shut out the lantern light, and in half a minute he was snoring softly.

The boy had attempted to protest against this giving up of a bed but his uncle prevented him with a strong signal.

"No good," he remarked as the snoring began. "Harry

can't change his ways. He's making us comfortable, as well as he can. That's all. Don't try to interrupt him. Let him be as he is!"

He bedded down his own blankets on the opposite bunk, leaving Everard to stare with uncomfortable curiosity at the heap which the Indian had just left. However, it did not do to be too particular. He rolled into the warmth and presently he was asleep.

"The morning's a better time for you to talk hoss to old Harry, anyway," his uncle advised him, in saying good-night.

The two were awake at the same moment in the morning as the gray of the dawn began to turn golden. The sound of chopping roused them, and as they turned out they saw Harry Lawson swinging an ax beside a pile of tangled brush.

Clay Winton went out and took the ax from the half-breed.

"You know where the chuck is in the house," he said. "You start up the fire with what you've chopped and I'll bring in an armful."

Harry Lawson, instead of replying to this suggestion, turned his broad expressionless face down the hill toward the hollow, where the creek spread itself out in a considerable pool. Everard was running down the slope, loosening his clothes as he went. Now, on the bank, he flung the garments aside and flashed like a bolt of bronze into the icy water.

Not a ripple formed over the spot where he had disappeared, it seemed. Harry Lawson looked with a shudder of profound interest. His red-stained eyes looked aside toward the face of Clay Winton, and the latter, poising the ax above his shoulder for a stroke, nodded.

"He's all leather," he remarked. "He'd break ice to get his morning swim."

The head and shoulders of the diver broke water at a distance, in the pool; with powerfully swaying arms and shoulders, he drove himself across to the farther bank, climbed out, ran up the slanting trunk of a tree, and dived off again.

This time, well after he had disappeared, the sound of

the plunge came dimly up to their ears, like a very faint and far-away explosion.

Halfway across the face of the water, the head and arms of Everard Winton appeared again. He stood on the shore, whipping the water off his body. Then, squatting on his heels, while the wind blew him dry, he lathered his face and shaved.

The half-breed grunted.

"All that's not leather in him is iron," said Clay Winton, proudly. "Anybody else would ret rheumatism and double pneumonia. But there's no let-up in him. You can't dent him—not with bullets, you can't."

Harry Lawson went back to the shack, and presently smoke was curling out of the top of the chimney. At the same time the boy was dressed and back, making himself useful, rolling up his uncle's pack, laying out the tins and knives and forks on the table, and finally jogging out to the horse shed where he saddled Clay Winton's mustang and brought it back in front of the shack, prepared for an early start.

While he was away on this errand, as the bacon crisped in the pan, Clay Winton was saying to the veteran, "Look here, Harry. That nephew of mine wants the Red Pacer, and wants him bad. You got a high price stuck on the hoss. Two thousand, eh? Well, that's a lot, but I ain't here to bargain with you. What he wants to do is to make a bargain with you. If you'll guarantee not to sell the Pacer for a month or so, he'll come back and bring you the money—with interest, too. You understand?"

Harry Lawson nodded.

"Would you do that?" asked Clay Winton.

The half-breed shook his head.

"I thought you might not," said Winton, though he frowned a little at the gesture. "But he's dead set on having that horse. I don't mind telling you he's stepped out of his home and gone on the road without a penny in his pocket or a hoss to ride on, because he had trouble with his folks about the Red Pacer."

The coffee pot began to simmer. Harry Lawson, as though totally uninterested in this tale, pulled the pot

54

farther back on the stove and paid no heed to Clay Winton. The latter went on:

"But I'll tell what I'll do. I'll pay you the two thousand, cash. I have it on me, Harry. I'll pay you the money, and when he makes his talk to you, you tell him that you're willing to take his word for paying, later on. Say you'll let him have the stallion on trust. But don't tell him about my part in this. Does that sound good to you?"

He counted out a sheaf of bills as he spoke, and held them out.

But the other shook his head.

"Why not?" asked Winton, rather angrily. "That's money—that's the two thousand you asked for the hoss. Why won't you take it?"

Harry Lawson turned his back, took the pan of bacon off the stove, and began to serve it out, with stale, warmed-over pone on the plates. This, together with coffee, made up the breakfast.

The boy had come back by now, and his uncle held his peace; but there was a grim look in his eye. Terseness and bluntness may be forgiven in old sour-doughs, up to a certain point, but there are limits, always, which must not be passed.

They had finished eating and were on their second round of coffee when young Everard began his proposal to Lawson.

The latter sat back in his chair, expressionless as a carved Buddha, holding a cigarette between thumb and forefinger. Whether he listened or not could hardly be told, for his eyes were a blank.

So, with increasing difficulty, Ever stumbled through to an ending. Then he waited, intent, fairly crouched with eagerness.

Still there was no answer.

Clay Winton broke in, "It's no good, Ever. He won't let you have the hoss. I dunno why. I tell you what I did. I went behind your back and offered him two thousand dollars hard cash on the spot, if he'd turn that mustang over to you. But he won't do it."

Everard Winton jumped up from his chair, his face hard and his dim blue eyes utterly altered, as though a storm wind had blown over them and cleared the mist away. Then he cried out:

"Yesterday afternoon you were going to sell the Pacer to me for two thousand. What's come over you that's changed your mind? That's what I want to know."

Harry Lawson looked straight before him, with red, unconscious eyes. It was a though he had been facing for hours the very wind which had merely sharpened the vision of the boy.

Clay sat back and watched. There was trouble coming, perhaps—big trouble, it might be—unless Harry Lawson decided to speak. Every second the suspense grew, and nerves were tightened as the pressure increasd. And always the fire glinted more and more brightly in Everard's eyes as he waited.

At last the Indian muttered, "You're like that damn Harry Lawson. You want that damn hoss too much."

The other two stared at each other. Harry Lawson got up from his chair and stalked out of the shack.

"What's the meaning of it, Uncle Clay?" demanded the boy.

"I don't know," said the other. "Maybe Harry's lived alone too long. Sounds a bit batty, to me."

"That long hunt of the Red Pacer, and the way his place had gone to wreck," suggested Ever. "That may have had something to do with it."

The uncle nodded. Then, squinting his eyes, he repeated, "What was he driving at? What did you do with that horse the other day?"

"Nothing. He piled me a couple of times, that was all. Then I took a chance at him bareback, and the chance worked. It was the saddle that had been bothering him, and—"

"You took a chance bareback!"

"Yes. He'd bucked the saddle off twice. The second time he smashed it."

"So you took a chance on the Pacer bareback?" said Clay again.

"Yes. I was pretty dizzy, and old Harry Lawson was laughing at me. It made me a little mad."

"You tried him bareback, eh—and it worked? You

tried the Red Pacer bareback?—Well, Ever, it ain't old Harry Lawson that's batty; it's you! What were you thinkin' of?"

"I was thinking of riding the horse. That was all."

Everard got up from his chair and began to pace the floor.

"Don't be worrying about it," said his uncle. "You can't figure it out. Something's got stuck in Old Harry's superstitious mind, and you can't budge him away from his ideas. Here comes somebody, riding up. Let's go and see who it is."

He went to the door and saw three riders swinging rapidly up the slope from the hollow toward the house. One rode in the lead and two others kept a little back.

14

EVEN from a distance, it is easy to tell how a man is riding, whether carelessly or grimly or in slovenly or businesslike fashion.

There was a swing and rhythm to the galloping of this trio; the very beat of the hoofs made a cadence that for a moment drew the boy away from his half gloomy, half savage thoughts.

He joined his uncle outside the door of the cabin.

"They want something, those boys," declared Clay Winton.

The dust they raised was now blown away, and the riders emerged clearly and drew up near the house; three cowpunchers from the range, as it seemed, but—

"They've got some hossflesh under 'em—for plain cowhands," said Clay.

So they had. In fact, they had plenty of daylight under them. Their mounts had legs, and they had bone, too.

They were no better groomed than ordinary cowponies,

but the quality was there and it showed through the dust.

The riders dismounted. Two of them stayed with the horses; the third rider strode forward, demanding:

"Where's Harry Lawson?"

"At the corral, there," said Clay Winton.

His eyes followed the stranger as he walked away. A curious calm had come upon Clay's face, and his eyes, of the Winton blue, were mistier than ever and more gentle. But the boy was not deceived. He knew that his uncle had seen something that was of the utmost interest.

As a matter of fact, the stranger was a man to be marked in a thousand. He had the carriage and the voice of one accustomed to command, and though he was only of average height, his bearing made him seem taller. The sunken eyes, the deeply marked features, made him seem one who had lived through many a busy decade; but second thought declared him to be no more than in his middle twenties. The two who followed him were older by years, in fact, but it was plain that they were under his control. They stood back, talking quietly to one another, until their leader drew away.

Harry Lawson sat on the top rail of the corral fence, bunched up like a buzzard on a perch. He was watching the stallion. Nothing about him moved except his head, whenever the Red Pacer stepped to another bunch of grass and tore at it or whirled, with a flash of fire along his silken flanks to defy the half-breed with his eye. So might an Indian worshipper in the old days have squatted at the door of a temple and adored the golden god of the sun.

Everard Winton saw and understood now why mere money could hardly buy this treasure from Harry Lawson. It would be almost miraculous if many, many thousands of dollars could induce the half-breed to part with the great horse. Something more than money would be needed.

Then one of the strangers asked, "That the Pacer, over yonder?"

"That's the Pacer," nodded Everard Winton.

"He looks like a *hoss*," said the stranger.

"He *is* a horse," said Everard.

"He stands over some ground," said the second stranger, shading his eyes and peering at the glistening form of the stallion in the corral.

"He's got a middle-piece, too," declared the first speaker, likewise shading his eyes.

"Think Lawson would sell him?" asked the first.

"Maybe. To a man that can ride him," said Clay Winton.

"The chief'll ride him if anybody can," said the second stranger, with confidence.

"The chief'll ride him," said the first.

The chief, in the meantime, with long, swift strides had come to the Indian. They spoke together for a moment, Harry Lawson gestured briefly toward the horse, and the chief turned and sang out briskly:

"Get a saddle on the Pacer, boys. Jump to it!"

In an instant, they had a saddle off one of their horses, and on the run they went for the corral.

"You know that first man?" asked the boy.

"Got an idea," murmured Clay Winton. "Only an idea, that may not be worth a rap. I'd put him down—"

He paused, his voice trailing away, while he frowned. The boy waited. He knew his uncle well enough to understand that he was not to be pressed.

"Timberline, I guess," said Clay Winton. "Probably the one called Timberline."

The boy started. He had heard that name many times. A thousand wild exploits were connected with the name of Timberline, so-called because he was constantly crossing and recrossing the naked heights of the mountains; was constantly appearing where he was least expected.

As to the man's character, he was believed to be one of those who hover on the verge of the law, sometimes inside it and sometimes outside. He had been town marshal half a dozen times, in this or that little wild frontier camp which some gold rush had filled for the moment with adventurous, lawless men. On such occasions he enforced the law, not because he loved the law, but because he was given such a free hand with his guns. Again, when the Cavendish band had established themselves as the most successful large-scale rustlers in the West, Timberline had taken the job in hand and fairly run the band to the ground.

But he had not always been a supporter of law and order. Not once but many times he had been tried on the ugly charge of murder, and though in each instance he had been cleared for "self defense," even the liberal Western interpretation of that term which made a "hip motion" equivalent to the drawing of a gun could not entirely cover up the stigma that began to attach to the name of Timberline. A man may be cornered once, twice, or even three times, and have to fight for his life. But rarely on more occasions than that. And though the law may clear him, public opinion will not.

Besides, it was often wondered how Timberline got his income. He was never without funds, it was said, and he was generally to be seen riding with companions who were often of dubious character. Once or twice, crimes other than gun fighting had been laid to him, but he had freed himself from these with equal ease.

Finally, the range split wide open on the question, one-half taking Timberline's side, and the other half declaring that he was no better than a sheer adventurer who lived by the keenness of his wits and the accuracy of his talented six-shooters.

All of these things flowed through Everard Winton's mind as he heard the man's name.

"Timberline will ride the Pacer," said Clay Winton. "If anybody can, he will."

"Timberline will ride him," said the boy gloomily. "Timberline was the fellow who rode that circus devil of a no-good pinto man-killer, down in Texas. Wasn't that Timberline?"

"He's the one who did it. He rode the famous Baldy," said Clay Winton. "And if he could ride Baldy, he can ride about anything, I suppose. I saw Baldy pile three of the best bronc busters in the world—all in twenty minutes, and him taking it easy."

The stallion was calmly submitting to rope and bridle and saddle.

"He ought to be easy today," said Clay Winton. "My

nephew, here, took the edge off him yesterday, Timberline."

At the word, the other spun about.

"Who are you?" he demanded.

"My name is Clay Winton."

"And you say your nephew rode the Pacer?"

"Yes."

Timberline turned to the Indian.

"What about it?" he asked.

Harry Lawson nodded, and at that Timberline looked squarely at Ever. For the boy that glance was a colder plunge than that which young Winton had taken in the icy water of the pool that morning. He felt himself being measured and weighed.

"You could ride him but you couldn't ride him away, eh?" said Timberline.

"Lawson wouldn't sell," said Ever.

He was surprised at the violence with which he spoke. He could feel the outthrust of his chin, and the tightening of his brow in a frown.

Timberline looked him up and down with some surprise, and then turned away with a smile.

A haze of black anger swept across Ever's eyes. Then he remembered, like the dinning of a bell in his ears, the voice of his uncle saying, years ago: "Always see clear! Always see clear."

It was a bad time, now, to allow his vision to be clouded.

He saw the glance of Harry Lawson fixed upon him. It was almost impossible to guess at anything in the mind of the half-breed by trying to read his face, but it seemed to Everard Winton that he could detect a sort of dim, savage curiosity in the solitary's eyes. It made Ever want to fight for his rights, but he was in such a position that there was nothing to fight against.

The stallion was saddled at last, and Timberline went up to it with a quick step, as though he was about to fling himself into the saddle. He seemed accustomed to hurling himself at difficulties and sweeping them quickly out of the way. The greater the wall, Ever guessed, the more furiously he would attack it.

61

However, he was not as headlong as all that. He first looked to the fit of the bridle, had the cheek pieces let out, and then the throat latch tightened. After that he carefully tested the tautness of the girths, found nothing wrong there.

Then he was suddenly in the saddle, and the horse was loosed.

Up it bounded, and plunged away across the corral, bucking like an inspired fiend.

15

WELL and nobly did Timberline then live up to his great reputation as a rider. It seemed that he was reading the mind of the stallion and forestalling its moves and plunges whole seconds before they were made. He lost a stirrup in the first mad circling of the corral, but he caught it again in a moment.

"Look at him, Al!" cried the smaller and darker of Timberline's two followers.

"Look at him, Garry!" cried the larger man, slapping his thigh. "The horse ain't born that can throw that gent. Not even a sun-fishin' fence rowin' son of trouble like the Pacer! He's gonna make that hoss eat out of his hand —*hai!*"

The last loud yell was an unexpected termination of his speech. The Red Pacer spun in a sudden circle, checked in an equally sudden reverse, and the rider shot sidelong through the air and landed rolling.

The stallion whirled about and raced for the fallen man, with a savagery that amazed Everard Winton. He had seen nothing of this sort in the fight of the day before. On that occasion, the Pacer had fought as though he understood the rules of the game!

"He'll get the chief!" grunted big Al, and snatched out a gun.

Everard reached swiftly out and struck up the hand of the other. Al had not had time to fire. He saw his master roll and scramble to safety underneath the rails of the fence; nevertheless, he was maddened by Ever's intervention, and swung about on him, savagely.

"What in hell d'you mean by that?" he demanded.

He was a big, powerfully built fellow, and constant riding had made him lean and fit, so that the expanse of his shoulders loomed out wide. Yet after enduring Timberline's glance, it was easy to meet the gaze of this fellow called Al.

"This is a fair fight between a man and a horse," said the boy. "It's not murder!"

"No?" said Al. "And this ain't murder, neither!"

He had dropped his gun back into the holster that hung conveniently far down his thigh, ready for a quick draw. Now he reached a pile-driving fist straight at young Everard Winton's face.

It was a very great mistake to start the punch at all. It was a still greater mistake to telegraph the punch by pulling his hand far back of his shoulder. Ever simply stepped inside the drive of the punch, and dropped his crooked elbow into the hollow of his arm.

Al stepped back with a curse.

"You've broke my arm, you young rat!" he snarled.

"What's the matter, Al?" demanded Garry, as though eager to share the trouble with his companion.

"This here——" began Al.

But Clay Winton cut in gently, "Rats have teeth. Don't corner 'em, brothers!"

They looked suddenly aside at the speaker, and saw there what rougher and tougher men than they had seen before—a faint smile, as though Clay was enjoying a curious pleasure. Their own temperatures diminished instantly.

"What're you about?" shouted Timberline. "Out there and catch that red piece of murder! Jump to it!"

They jumped to it, forgetful of their private grievances.

"Thanks," said Everard briefly to his uncle.

"That's all right," said Clay Winton. "You could handle the two of 'em—unless they got to their guns. Only, it's bad business, with Timberline on the lot."

"Timberline won't join 'em," answered the boy with a sudden decision.

"No?"

"No, he won't join 'em. Not after the Pacer's through with him!"

"Why, Ever," said the other, "he nearly rode him the first time. He'll have a good chance, the second."

They had caught the horse again, when Ever remarked, "Why, it's true that Timberline may have learned something about the horse, but the horse has learned a lot more about Timberline."

"Who told you?" grinned Clay Winton.

"The Pacer did," said Everard, and grinned in return.

Timberline had joined his helpers. They muttered to him, and he turned his stern head and looked back over his shoulder. Ever heard him say:

"I'll attend to that later on."

Then he was in the saddle once more.

He sat that saddle for ten amazing seconds, while the stallion tied himself in knots in the air and smote the ground to untangle them. Then over the animal went, backwards, quick as a cat. True, Timberline was out of the saddle and back into it, both feet in the stirrups, as the horse lurched to all fours again. But the next moment the stallion whirled like a spinning top, and at the second turning of the red wheel, Timberline was hurled sidewise again and landed sprawling and skidding, directly in front of the spot where Everard Winton stood.

Flat on his face, and motionless, lay the fallen man, with the stallion wheeling to rush for him. Then something put Everard through the bars of the fence and made him stand over Timberline, while the red streak of murder bore down at him with flattened ears and mouth gaping terribly.

For hideous danger, nothing in the world can compare with the charge of a savage horse. Yet all the while Everard Winton was shouting loudly:

"Don't shoot him! Don't shoot!"

64

And holding up his hands, he awaited the charge.

Just over him, the stallion checked on planted hoofs, reared, obscured the morning sun with his towering crest, and then swerved away instead of beating his forehoofs through Ever's body. Then off he went, at that flowing pace, and stood in a far corner of the corral.

Everard leaned over and raised Timberline's limp body. The man was quite senseless, and there was a streak of blood on one temple. Yet he was not dead. His breast moved slowly as he breathed.

Everard drew him back to the fence; the others pulled him through to safety.

"What made you do that?" muttered Uncle Clay Winton, when his nephew was beside him once more.

"I don't know," said the other. "I can't tell you just how I got inside the corral; I just found myself there."

His uncle nodded, with baffled, bewildered eyes. In the background Everard saw old Harry Lawson, one eye cocked toward the stallion, and a broad grin upon his face. Something had happened that Harry, it seemed, could understand perfectly!

Timberline was sitting up now, and the others heard Al's muttering voice say to the leader:

"The kid, there, jumped through and turned the rush of the Pacer. I dunno how he done it. Looked easier to stop a landslide, but he kept singin' out not to shoot. So I didn't shoot, though it looked a sure thing that the hoss would get the two of you. The Pacer means murder. It looks like the kid had him trained to do tricks!"

Timberline sat back against a fence post, his eyes closed and his jaw set hard.

"Well, he did it quicker than the first time," he remarked.

"Yeah. It was a little quicker," said Al. "But he ain't a hoss. He's a tangled-up streak of lightning, is what he is when he starts to buck."

"He spins with me," said Timberline faintly. "Nobody can stand that, I don't suppose. Not the way he does it."

"He knows the one sure way," agreed Al.

"Call that boy over here."

"Hey, kid!" called Al brusquely. "Come here!"

"Go on," urged Uncle Clay softly.

So the boy stepped over to where Timberline lay.

"Well?" he asked.

The closed eyes of the injured man did not open.

"The Pacer hit me in the bull's-eye, that time," said Timberline. "I won't be riding so well the rest of today. But I'll tell you what—"

His voice stopped suddenly. There was no change in his expression, but it was plain that a touch of pain had checked him.

The boy waited, and presently the other went on, "I'd give something to see you handle that brute of a red devil."

"I had luck yesterday," said young Winton. "Maybe not today."

"I'll make a little bet with you."

"I have no money."

"A hundred dollars to the boots you stand in."

"What's your wager?"

"That you can't stick to him for a full minute."

"I'll take that," said Everard.

It was a little odd, perhaps, that Timberline had found no words for gratitude. A little matter of the saving of his life—that was all! And the boy smiled faintly; the smile that had been on the lips of his uncle not many minutes before.

He turned toward the corral, where the stallion had given up trying to buck off the firmly cinched saddle.

"I use your saddle?" he asked, turning back to Timberline.

"Yeah, that'll be all right."

Everard Winton slid between the bars, walked straight out to the horse, and saw the latter turn quickly around and face him, ears back, nostrils dangerously spread.

But in a moment the great horse lifted his head somewhat, and his ears pricked slowly forward.

"It's a trick hoss!" called the voice of Al loudly. "Look at that! It's a damn trick hoss!"

16

THERE was no struggle. The same recognition which the stallion had given to Ever the day before, it gave again now. Everard Winton mounted, sat still and cautious in the saddle, vainly awaiting the explosion of frantic bucking. With a thrill, he realized that the Red Pacer was docile now. Then he guided the great horse easily around the corral.

He saw Timberline, standing up and holding by an upper rail of the fence, looking somberly forth upon this scene. Ever patted the side of the Red Pacer, and the stallion struck out in a flowing stride. Swerving at the corners of the corral fence, he doubled back and forth like a wolf before the bars of its cage, eager to be away. Ever felt that the rider of such an animal would be as much ruler of the range as the eagle is ruler of the air.

The boy's spirit leaped. Then he swung down to the ground.

"Is that riding him?" he asked Timberline.

"That's riding him," said the man darkly. He added, "Al, give the kid a hundred dollars."

Big Al drew out a wallet, carefully thumbed over several notes and handed them to young Winton as the latter slid between the bars of the fence again. Garry, Timberline's second follower, was already stripping the saddle from the back of the stallion, taking off the bridle.

"Here you are, boy," said Al, holding out the sheaf of money.

A very odd and uncontrollable impulse came over Everard Winton when he heard that word "boy." He looked down at the money and back at Al's face.

"I take money from friends, not from you," he said.

For him it was the only money in the world, just then, but he could not avoid the remark.

"So I ain't good enough to put money in your hand?" said Al.

In the distance, Ever saw the Indian, the same yawning, red-eyed, wolfish smile upon his face.

"Steady, Ever!" cautioned his uncle.

But the words came out in spite of Ever; he could not master them or put them down.

"No," he was saying. "You're not good enough to put money in my hand."

"Am I good enough to put my hand in your face, then?" demanded Al, and a second time he struck, with all his might.

He did not make the mistake, on this occasion, of taking so much deliberate ease in delivering the blow. Instead, he drove a snapping jab from his hip toward Ever's chin.

It seemed to the onlookers—except to the practiced eye of Clay Winton, perhaps—that the blow had landed and knocked young Winton's head sidewise onto his shoulder. Only big Al could realize that he was driving his clenched hand through empty air; for the target had fallen away from him, and his knuckles barely grazed the cheek. Then his arms were caught and held; and he was tied up in secure fashion while Ever asked calmly, over his shoulder:

"Shall I hit this clumsy fool, Uncle Clay?"

"No, don't hit him," said Clay Winton, with equal calm. "Throw him over your hip, but don't hit him."

It was no sooner said than done. Al's fighting bulk struggled vainly. For all his weight and tension, he was caught by hands that seemed to have magic in their touch and was flung suddenly and heavily to the ground. Even his own weight seemed to fight against him.

Al stared up at the calm face above him. He rose to one elbow, and then reached for a gun.

"Drop that!" snapped Timberline's voice.

Al allowed his fingers to slide from the handle of the Colt revolver; then he rose slowly to his feet.

"You'll take your lickings, when they come the way

68

this one did," Timberline was saying. "Don't clutter up my trail with murder, you lanky fool."

There was no answer, though Al's face was black.

Timberline turned to Harry Lawson. "What's the price on that horse?" he demanded.

The other raised five fingers.

"Five thousand is four thousand too much," said Timberline.

Lawson shrugged his shoulders.

There was only a moment of pause.

"I'll take him, though," said Timberline. "Garry, lead the Pacer out. I'm buying him. Al, pay Lawson five thousand."

It was done in a dizzy trice, and the world suddenly began to spin around before Ever's eyes. Then Timberline stood before him, saying:

"Did you make that stallion a trick horse?"

"I never saw him before yesterday," answered Ever frankly.

Timberline stepped back and looked suddenly from Lawson and Clay Winton to Ever. Then he was asking:

"Your name is Winton, eh?"

The boy stared at the great horse as Garry led it out of the corral.

"I'm Everard Winton," said he, in a mechanical voice.

"I'll tell you, Winton," said Timberline. "If you want to ride with me for a while, you can take that horse."

Everard was too amazed to make an answer.

"He would have mopped up the dust of the corral with me, except for you," said Timberline. "So if you want to ride with me, Winton, the Pacer is your horse—every inch of him!"

Lawson's voice broke in, surprisingly: "Then I don't sell him! I don't sell you the hoss. Here—you take back your money!"

He came hurrying forward, holding out the bills.

Timberline merely smiled. "I've paid the money. You've taken it. I've got the horse," said he. "You can't go back on that."

Harry Lawson hesitated. He halted, and his chin thrust out in ugly fashion.

"What's the matter with Winton?" asked Timberline. "Why don't you want him to own the Pacer? He's the only man in the world who can ride him!"

"Yeah. He can ride him. But where'll he take the Pacer, and where'll the Pacer take him?"

"What the devil do you mean by that?" asked Timberline, and then turned back to Everard. "Coming with me, Winton?" he asked.

Ever, in bewilderment, stared at his uncle; and his heart fell when he saw the latter make an almost undiscernible sign of dissent.

"I'm staying with my uncle," said Everard slowly. "I'm thanking you—but I stay with him."

Timberline snapped his fingers. "I've given you your chance," he said briskly. Then he added to his followers, "Saddle up. We're starting. We've got a way to go, before night.—Put the Pacer on the lead, Al. Put a double lead on him, because the big devil looks strong enough to break one line, or to run away with the horse and man at the end of it."

Accordingly, the saddle was replaced on Timberline's own horse. The red stallion was put on a double lead, and the three men re-mounted. Al had not spoken during all this time, but now, reining his horse a little to the side, he loomed huge above Everard Winton.

"I don't forget, kid!" said he sourly.

Timberline, an instant later, remarked, "I'm one down to you, Winton. I'm sorry that you wouldn't take the horse and ride with me. I stop at places you might like to see. But you know your own business—or your uncle knows it for you. Still, the trick I'm down I may have a chance to make up to you before the game's over.—Come on, boys. So long, everybody!"

He touched his long-legged sprinter with the spurs and galloped away in a straight line, the others following more slowly, leading the great red horse between them.

Clay Winton turned on Harry Lawson.

"You played a raw trick there, Harry," he said.

The Indian stared grimly after the disappearing group, paying no attention to the remark, except to say eventually:

70

"Hell is raw, too. And Timberline—he's got it!"

And he grinned, red-eyed. He looked more like a wolf than ever, thought young Everard Winton.

17

LAWSON went back to the rear pasture with no more words, and Clay Winton returned with his nephew, slowly, toward the shack. In front of it he saddled the mustang.

"You think I've let you down, Ever," he suggested. "But I tried to back you up. I offered that crazy half-breed two thousand on the side, if he'd let you have the hoss; but he wouldn't do it. He's got something in his head. I dunno what it is. He's batty, I guess. Plain batty!"

"There's something in Lawson's head," said Everard Winton. "He'd sell that horse to me for two thousand, yet he made Timberline pay five. You noticed another thing: that when he thought I was going to join Timberline for the sake of the stallion, Harry Lawson wanted to cancel the sale. Well, that means something."

"What?" asked Clay.

"It looks," said Everard, "as though Harry really wanted me to have the Pacer, but wanted me to ride him on a straight road, and inside the law. I may be wrong, but that's the way it hits me."

"Perhaps you're right," nodded Clay. "But nobody can understand what goes on inside the head of old Harry Lawson."

"Why didn't you take the hundred that you'd won, fair and square, from Timberline?"

"I don't know," muttered the boy. "I want the money now. I need it. Yet I couldn't take it then."

"Tainted money, eh?" demanded his uncle, rather sarcastically. "Same old story?"

Everard shook his head.

"I don't know why it was," said he. "I had the feeling I wanted to put my hands on that fellow Al. I even wanted to put my hands on him so badly that I couldn't take money from him."

His uncle suddenly laughed. "You remember what old Harry Lawson said? That you're like him—you want the Pacer too much. Well, Ever, all I can say is—about the money—I've seed a bull terrier that wouldn't eat, just because it saw a chance of a fight to windward. We'd better start along, eh?"

"Yes, we'd better start along," nodded the boy. "So you offered Lawson the two thousand?"

"Yes."

"And still he wouldn't take it?"

"I don't understand why not," said Clay Winton.

"Nor I!" muttered Everard.

They reached the front of the house, and Clay Winton was about to mount his horse when he said:

"Here's Harry, coming back from the pasture with a horse towing behind him. We'd better wait to say so-long to him."

The boy made a gesture of indifference. His eyes were continually turning to that point on the horizon at which the Pacer and the three riders had disappeared.

In the meantime, Lawson came up with them.

"We're saying so-long," said Clay Winton, "and thanks for putting us up."

"You wait," answered the Indian.

He passed into the shack and came out again, carrying a saddle and bridle which he put on the mustang he had brought up—a roach-backed, lumpheaded gray mare that looked like a caricature of a horse, except that it had shoulders as beautifully made, and as fine a set of legs, as ever a horse moved by. And it would have been strange to find among the horses of the Indian, expert that he was, a single animal that did not have some remarkable qualities. Lawson stood back from his pony, remarking:

"A hawk, he flies pretty damn fast, but a buzzard, he goes just as far in a day."

He indicated the mustang, to give point to his remark. Then he turned to Ever and added:

"You take this one."

"I haven't a penny to pay for her," said Everard, puzzled.

"You take this one. You pay me pretty good, sometime," replied the half-breed enigmatically, and walked away from the house with a gesture of farewell.

"Is he crazy, Uncle Clay?" asked Ever.

"I don't know," frowned the older man. "I don't think so. It's just that his brain, it don't work like other brains. He's got something inside his head, though. He didn't want you on the back of the Pacer—and yet he likes you. That's plain, or he wouldn't give you this hoss, and him down on his luck so far. A hoss all rigged out, too! I dunno what to say about it, Ever. Almost seems like he don't think you'd have good luck on the Pacer."

"I remember what he said about raw hell and Timberline having it," agreed the boy. "He's a little crazy, all right. Hold on!—Here they come back, the three of 'em. And by thunder, Uncle Clay, they've lost the Pacer!"

For three riders were coming at a round gait, through the gap in the hills that had swallowed up Timberline and his companions, with the led stallion. Clay Winton shielded his eyes, and stared for a long moment.

"Not the same three," he said. "They ride different. There's one of 'em slopes to the right in the saddle, and none of them three that just left rides like that."

The riders came on rapidly.

"I'll tie up the gray mare and leave her here for Lawson," said Ever.

"Tie her up? Don't you do it," said his uncle. "You tie yourself to her and take her along."

"But it's too much," said Ever.

"Nothin's too much to take, when an Indian gives it," answered his companion. "They got reasons, always, behind their gifts. They give because they wanta give or because they think they oughta give."

"No, I can't take the mare," said Ever flatly.

"You better had, Ever. If you wanta make that Indian happy, you take his hoss. He means it. Somehow, he's all wrapped up in you, and you're the first person I ever seen that he give a damn about. You take that mare of

73

his and don't answer back about it. You can pay him for her, one of these days."

Ever glanced toward the distant horizon, sighed, nodded. Vast leagues separated him from the destination of the men who had bought the Red Pacer, whatever that might be. As yet, it was totally unknown to him.

"I'll take her, then," he said. "But I'm beginning to think that it's a queer world, Uncle Clay."

"The older you get, the queerer you'll find it turnin' out," said the other. "There's only one thing to remember, all the time: keep your head up and play your cards close to your chest. That's all!"

His nephew looked up to him with a quick cant of the head; then he smiled. "I'll remember," he murmured.

Then he turned to regard the three riders, for Clay Winton exclaimed:

"Why, there's a man-hunt on! That's old Sheriff Darrow, or I'm mistaken. Yeah, that's Lew Darrow, and he looks as if he meant business."

He frowned as he said this; but presently he shrugged his shoulders. The boy was already in the saddle, as the sheriff came up with two companions.

Everard knew all three men. One member of the sheriff's posse was Jud Waley, who rode for Rudie Berner's father. The other man was Ray Collins, a drifter who made headquarters in town and who knew how to waste time as well as any man in the world.

Both were such fellows as any sheriff would be glad to have along on a trail that promised danger; they rode well and they were well known as good shots. Their courage had been tested in that fine, white heat which the West, and the West alone, can furnish to temper the souls of men.

"Hello, Clay," said the sheriff. "Hello, Ever. Ain't you far from home? And what's that I seen of Timberline, ridin' off with the Red Pacer? He says he bought the hoss. Know anything about that?"

"He bought the Pacer, all right," said Everard sadly.

"And what's this about you ridin' the hoss?" asked the sheriff.

Ever shrugged his shoulders, with a joyless face.

74

"Timberline may tame him," said the sheriff, "but doggone me, it'll take time for even him to ride that red devil. Clay, can I have a word with you?"

"What about?" asked Clay Winton.

"Something private, old son."

"Sure," said Clay, and reined his horse to a little distance, so that he was beside the sheriff.

Whatever the conversation was to be about, it did not take Everard more than a glance to understand that it was serious business. For Darrow's companions edged their horses after their leader, and unmistakably, they were ready for anything to happen.

The sheriff's voice came out louder, no doubt, than he had intended it. Fast riding had made him breathe hard, and his words were audible to Ever's strained ear as he said:

"Clay, I'm arrestin' you in the name of the law!"

"What's the matter, Lew?" asked Clay.

"I'm arrestin' you," said the sheriff. "Anything that you say from now on might be used agin you in the court. Understand?"

"I understand that," said Clay Winton. With a wonderful calm, he looked into the sheriff's face. "What's it all about?" he asked.

He was almost cheerful. Many a time, Ever had admired his uncle's perfect poise in tight pinches, but never had he admired him as now.

"I wouldn't mind tellin' you, Clay," said the sheriff, suddenly producing a gun, "only I'm gonna have to ask for your weapons first!"

Revolvers appeared in the hands of Collins and Waley, also. Waley leveled his at the boy.

"Got a gat, Ever?" he asked.

"What's that to you?" demanded Everard.

"It's whatever I say," said Waley. "I'm a sworn-in deputy."

He grinned faintly as he said this.

Clay was unbuckling his gun belt and passing it over to the sheriff, who received it with his left hand.

"Give 'em your gat, Ever," he called back over his shoulder.

"Give me your gat. Your uncle says you got one," insisted Waley.

Ever raised his voice.

"Sheriff Darrow!" he called.

"Aye?" said the sheriff.

"Are you arresting me, too?"

"No," said the sheriff.

"I'll have that gun," remarked Waley, thrusting out his chin.

"I'll see you in hell first!" said Everard firmly.

His voice, his words, surprised even himself. He found himself staring into Waley's face; he felt a contraction of the muscles in his cheeks. Perhaps it was a smile. Yet he was angry. He was angry, in a sense, as he never had been before.

"Why, you runt of a sawed-off brat!" shouted Waley angrily. "Gimme your gun!"

"Hey, Ever," called the sheriff, "you gotta give up your gun when it's asked for. Ain't Waley told you he's a deputy?"

"Well—" said Everard hesitantly, it seemed.

Suddenly he slipped a leg over the back of the saddle and dropped to the ground, putting his mustang suddenly between him and the others. Waley found a gun muzzle staring at him.

"If you fellows want my gun, come and get it!" said Everard Winton.

18

"HEY THERE!" exclaimed Jud Waley. "Round him up on that side, will you? I'm gonna teach that high-blooded kid something about what it means to give growed-up men his lip."

"I've got a dead bead on you, Jud," said Ever calmly.

"And I can shoot straighter with a rest than you can free hand. Call Collins back!"

"Wait a minute, Ray!" exclaimed Waley. "By the jumpin' thunder, he means it! He means murder! There's murder in the blood of these Wintons, is what there is!"

The sheriff cried, "What's all that nonsense back there?"

"The kid won't give up his cannon," said Waley. "I aim to make him!"

"Have you got a warrant for me?" the boy demanded.

"Son, don't you go and make a fool of yourself," urged the sheriff.

"Ever, give up the Colt!" exclaimed his uncle. "Are you trying to get yourself into hot water on account of me?"

"I'm playing my own game," said the boy. "Waley, you turn that gun another way. You hear me? Drop the muzzle of that gun!"

He did not raise his voice. He did not need to. And the thrill of liquid ice ran through the blood of Jud Waley as he heard the command and lowered his weapon, saying as he did so, "I don't like the look of this, Darrow. You ain't gonna let him get away with a bluff like this, are you?"

"The Wintons don't bluff," said the sheriff calmly. "Bluffs don't run in their blood. I dunno just what to do, here. I can't call it resistin' arrest, because I ain't arrestin' him. I ain't got a warrant for him."

"Let him alone," said Clay Winton. "I can handle him, mostly; but when I can't, nobody else can—and take that from me! Leave him be, Darrow, unless you want hell to break loose."

"I don't," answered the sheriff hastily. "I don't want to push any lad to the wall till I have to. You know me, Clay. I never fought in my life till I had to; I never fought without bein' scared to death—scared to death of a jackrabbit, even. But I got to make a livin' sheriffing, in spite of the devil and my bad nerves."

It was a characteristic speech; it was characteristic of the sheriff that he was able to laugh as he spoke.

"You haven't told me the charge, Lew," said Clay.

"It's the Green River business," said the sheriff.

"Green River business?" repeated Clay Winton.

The boy, listening, found the world swimming in black and red before his eyes as he heard the name, but his uncle was perfectly cool and collected.

"You know—the bank robbery," said the sheriff.

"Can't say I do," said Clay Winton.

"Can't you?" grinned Lew Darrow. "Well, maybe you'll be able to remember it a lot better, later on. I ain't here to try the case. I'm only gonna make the arrest and take you in."

"Green River—Green River?" repeated Clay, with the same admirable poise. "Lemme see—well, I remember a yarn about the robbing of a bank, there, seven or eight years back. Is that what you're talking about?"

"I wouldn't wanta arrest you for a job that you didn't remember, Clay," said the sheriff, still grinning. "Yeah, it's the Green River bank job. Only it was just four-five years ago. That's all. Remember it any better, now?"

"Oh, it's all right," declared Winton. "You have to pinch *somebody*, now and then, I know. I don't mind standing the rap, only why the devil should you have started in my direction? What would make you think I'd rob banks, Lew? You know that's not my business."

"Sitting on your rear and taking it easy is your business, Clay," answered the sheriff. "But you know how it is—a lot of jurymen might be pretty curious to know how you made enough money to retire on."

"Why, everybody knows that I made it out of mining," said Clay Winton.

"And kept your hands soft all the while?" asked the sheriff.

With that Ever saw his uncle straighten. He had heard that expression before. Red lightning struck across the brain of the boy, too. It was his mother who had developed the theory of the soft hands. It must be she who had put the sheriff on Clay's trail. Who else would be apt to remember that his uncle's hands had been soft, four or five years before?

He looked hard at Clay Winton, and one burning glance flashed back at him from his uncle's eye. Their mutual understanding was perfect; and the boy, out of the depths

78

of his wretchedness, felt that he could fathom all the workings of his mother's mind. To strike his uncle from his side, to win her son back to his home because of her own sheer loneliness—those had been her motives, perhaps?

Bitterness and savage grief consumed him. All that had gone before was as nothing now; and in one stroke he grew mature. His father could not have had a hand in this thing—against his own brother. Such a thing could be in the nature of no Winton, not even Ned Winton. But his mother—

He heard Clay Winton saying:

"That's all right, Lew. You're doing your job, and I don't hold it agin you. Are we starting along?"

"Yeah, we're startin' along."

"We're startin', Ever," repeated the uncle.

"I'm not riding the same trail, then," said Ever.

"Where you bound to, brother?" asked Lew Darrow.

"Over the hills and far away," said Ever evasively.

"Good luck to you, then!" said Lew Darrow. "But ain't you got a home waitin' for you?"

"Not now," said Ever.

His teeth clicked as he made the answer.

"No? Not now?" repeated the sheriff.

"I've got a horse and a saddle and a gun. That's home enough—and furniture, too."

He smiled at the sheriff and the sheriff frowned in return.

"I won't be paying rent for the roof over my head, either," remarked Everard.

"I'm sorry you're cuttin' loose on your own," remarked the sheriff. "I'm mighty sorry. So-long, Ever. Good luck to you agin!"

"Thanks," said Ever.

He walked out from behind his horse and wrung his uncle's hand.

"Good-bye, Uncle Clay," said he. "I'm not seeing the last of you."

His uncle lowered his voice, but he could not lower it enough to keep it from the ears of the others. They followed too closely.

"Good-bye, Ever," he said to his nephew. "If you do what I want you to, you'll go back home and stay there—make your mother happy and your father happy. They're people as good as you'll find anywhere. Maybe you have little differences with 'em about some things, but in the long run they'd die for you, and you oughta be ready to die for them. Understand me?"

"I'm trying to understand," said Ever.

"And no matter what you do, remember one thing."

"I'll try to remember," said Ever. "What is it?"

"Don't worry about me. Nothing is gonna come out of this arrest. The sheriff, here, is doin' the best he knows how, but I'm not worryin' about anything."

"Innocent men always win out—unless they're framed," suggested Ever.

"Of course they do, Ever. And that's what I bet on, d'you see?"

"I see."

"So-long, Ever," called Ray Collins, and the group moved off.

"So-long, Ray," he answered.

"So-long, Ever," echoed Jud Waley cheerfully in his turn.

But Ever made no answer this time.

Jud Waley turned suddenly, and stared back at him.

"Wait here a while, Waley," said Ever, "and I'll say something to you besides good-bye."

Waley, with an oath, swung his horse around.

"Here, you!—Jud!" shouted the sheriff.

"He can't give me none of his back talk!" said Waley.

"Leave him be," ordered the sheriff.

"I got a mind to stay right here and dress him down," remarked Waley.

"You come along," said the sheriff. "You're workin' for the law now, and not for yourself."

"Oh, damn the law! That kid can't give me no lip," decided Waley.

"Can't I?" said Ever, walking forward with the same smile that had been on his face before. "I can, though. I'm giving you lip now. I'm telling you that you're a yellow rat. You hear me, Waley?"

"Damn you!" shouted Waley in a fury.

"Hold on!" cried the sheriff. "Ever, what're you up to, you young fool?"

"I'm trying to work up a chance to defend myself," said Everard, "but there doesn't seem to be much hope. You don't pick the right kind of men, sheriff. Coyotes is all you go in for—just coyotes, like Waley."

He expected an answer to that, but to his surprise, and then to his sudden horror, he saw fear freeze Waley's face.

The deputy suddenly turned his horse, muttering, and rode on after his companions.

Ever swung about. He saw that Harry Lawson was leaning against the corner of the shack, with the same red-eyed wolfish grin upon his battered face.

19

AN OVERWHELMING impatience forced Ever to exclaim, "Lawson, what's the matter? What are you grinning about?"

The Indian looked him up and down, shrugged one shoulder, and disappeared through the dimness of the doorway. Winton stood for a moment gripping the reins of the gray mare, stunned by the sudden realization of his predicament as if by a great flare of light.

His duty was toward his uncle, he felt, but what he could do to help Clay Winton was a puzzle to him. Perhaps when he defied Waley it had been merely a futile gesture to prove to Clay Winton that he was willing to fight. But how *could* he fight? Not only was Clay Winton disarmed and helpless; he was now in the hands of three practiced gunmen.

What remained to attempt? Ever turned toward the shack and called out:

"Lawson! Oh, Lawson?"

The Indian came to the door of the shack. His felt hat was pushed to one side of his head, giving him a half rakish appearance; he had a short-stemmed pipe gripped between his broken, yellow teeth.

"Yeah?" he queried.

"You hear what they arrested my uncle for?"

The Indian nodded.

"What would the sentence for a bank robbery like that be?" asked the boy.

Harry Lawson held up ten fingers, closed his hands, raised five more.

"Fifteen years?" exclaimed Winton in horror.

Lawson nodded and turned again, in his curt way, into the interior shadows of the place. He could be heard rattling at the stove.

Fifteen years! That length of time would be quite sufficient to thin and whiten Clay's hair, bow his shoulders and bend his head. He would be fifty years old or more when he came out; and inevitably the prison mark would be upon him forever. That must not be.

Ever could see only one possible solution. It was a very vague and distant one, to be sure, but it made him spring onto the mustang. Without a word of farewell to Harry Lawson, he spurred toward the gap among the hills.

He was at a considerable distance when he turned in the saddle; and looking back, he saw that Lawson was standing in the sun at a little distance from the house, swinging one arm to beckon him back.

He checked the mare to a trot. But on second thought he decided that there was nothing Lawson could say that would be of help. So he put the mare to a canter again, and loped on through the rolling lands on the trail of Timberline.

Two hot and dusty hours Ever put behind him before he overtook his quarry. The mare was red with dust, save where sweat blackened her. Then he saw the three riders. Garry was mounted on the Red Pacer; the other two were leading the horse on long ropes. The stallion

82

submitted to that leading, though his ears were flattened. He was awaiting his chance.

As Ever came up, the group halted. He rode straight up to Timberline.

"Changed your mind?" asked Timberline with his usual terseness.

Ever pointed into the distance behind him.

"Lew Darrow and a couple more," he said, "picked up my uncle and packed him off to jail. If you'll help him out, I'll be your man, Timberline."

Timberline grinned. "They'll have your uncle in jail before we could reach him," said he.

"Yes, they will," said Ever, and waited.

Timberline lifted his head higher.

"You want me to break him out of jail, eh?" he asked. Winton nodded.

"And that buys you?" asked Timberline. "That and the Pacer buys you, eh?"

"It does," said Everard Winton solemnly.

"What's he in for?" asked Timberline.

"Bank robbery."

"What job?"

"The Green River Bank—five years ago."

Timberline whistled. So did Garry.

"That was a beauty!" said Garry enthusiastically.

"Well, if he's got the loot," remarked Al, "he can buy himself out."

"Did he really rob that bank?" asked Timberline.

"That's not my business," said Ever. "My job's to help him out of jail."

"Not admitting anything, eh?" said Timberline.

He looked at Ever again and nodded, as though confirming his previous estimate of the boy. Then he added:

"When they pick up a fellow for a big job like that they watch him, you know. They watch him the way a cat watches a mouse."

"I suppose they do," said Ever.

"What does he mean to you aside from blood?"

"We've been pretty close," answered Everard.

"If it came to shooting, would you join in gunplay for him?"

"Yes."

"How are you with a gun?"

"I'm good with a gun."

"He teach you?"

"Yes."

"He's a cool one," agreed Timberline. "He seems to know what he's about. But this is a pretty big job that you're asking out of me, Winton."

"I know it is."

"How do I know that I'll get back from you as much as I put out?"

"You take a chance on that."

Timberline shook his head. "You ride with me, you're useful a couple of times, and then you slide out from under. I've had that happen before. Besides, you don't mix with my other men. You started trouble with Al in the beginning."

"He talked down to me," said Ever. "That's all. He'll admit that."

"I'll admit nothin'," answered Al. "I'll take and break—"

"Aw, shut up, Al!" said Garry, his companion.

Al was silent, glaring.

"Make your case," urged Timberline to Ever.

And Everard answered, "Making trouble is your business. I can help you make it. I can ride, I can shoot, and I'm not a quitter."

"How do you know you're not?" asked Timberline sharply.

"Because I've taken my beatings," said Everard.

"Well," murmured Timberline, "you're too young. I'd be a fool to take such a chance for you. A long chance! How long would you stick by me if I managed to do this job for you?"

"Until you said that you had enough of me."

The eye of Timberline glinted.

"It's a long chance—a fool's chance," he muttered, still eying the prospective recruit.

Then he snapped his fingers.

"Garry!" he called.

"Yeah?" drawled Garry.

84

"Climb down off that horse and let the kid take the Pacer. He seems to need that horse, and the horse seems to need him. We're going to try to crack open the jail and get Clay Winton out for him—and after that, we'll see what lies in the cards."

20

IT WAS several nights later that a voice, quietly calling, brought Mrs. Winton with a gasp and a cry from her kitchen and out onto the back porch. The screen door slammed behind her with a loud and jingling crash, and she saw the glimmering form of a lofty horse in the starlight. A man was standing at its head.

"Ever?—Ever?" she stammered.

He came to her to the end of the reins that were hooked over his arm.

"Steady, Mother," he said. "Don't make a fast move or this horse will be off like a hawk. It's the Pacer."

She caught Everard in her arms and drew him to her with all her might. She tried to speak. She could only weep with a stifled sobbing against his breast.

With his hand he caressed her.

"Is Father likely to have heard?" he asked.

"He ain't here, Ever," she answered. "He's down talkin' to the lawyer. It ain't much time that he spends in the house, now, since—since—"

She broke off, then added, "He'll spend his money and his soul to get Clay free. He thinks that it was me that set the sheriff on Clay. Your father sort of hates me now, Ever. He hates me—you're gone from me—and I dunno why I keep on living."

"*Did* you talk to the sheriff?" he asked.

"If you thought that I had, you'd despise the ground

that I walked on, like your father despises it now," she said.

"Mother," he said, "I *know* that you talked to Lew Darrow. But in spite of that I've come to see you—to tell you that no matter what you do, you're as close to me as my blood."

"Are you meaning it, Ever?" she asked, suddenly lifting her head and a cold sense of awe came over her.

"I mean it with my whole heart," said he. "The other night I sneaked away. I'm sorry for that. I've had a chance to think it over, since then, and I know that no matter what you've done, you weren't thinking of yourself—you were thinking of the rest of the family."

"I was, Ever," she told him. "And God bless you for understanding!"

"If you had it to do over again," said he, "you'd act differently, I imagine."

"Differently? I'd crawl on my hands and knees to the sea and back, if that would set Clay free!" she cried. "But now you're here, ain't you come to stay? Ain't you here for good, Ever?"

She caught the lapels of his coat and held him, straining up on tiptoes the better to study his face through the darkness. To him she seemed thinner and older. He was now a man, and she was suddenly afraid.

"I'm tied up with other things," he answered her carefully. "The moment I can come, I'll be here. You can be sure of that. But I have some other things to do in the meantime. You can remember the rest though. The moment that I'm free, I'll come back, and as nearly as I can, I'll try to be what you and Father want me to be."

"We've changed!" she protested quickly. "Ah, we've changed a lot, Ever. We were pretty hard and sure, before; but that's all changed. What we want is you. That's all we want. We ain't young any more, and it's an empty house and an empty life, without no child in it. We want you back, and then you can do what you please. You can go where you please; you can be what you please.

"If it's more schoolin' you want, you can have it. If it's life far away from us you can have that—if only you'll be with us a part of the year. But there's been dreadful times for me, Ever, settin' at the table and seein' your father as cold and hard and silent as a stone. He'll never forgive me for what I've done. He'll never forgive me!"

She began to weep again.

"If he doesn't," said Everard Winton, "he's wrong, and you tell him that I say he's wrong. He may understand. He and you and I, no matter where we are, are all tied together. Blood holds up, Mother—and God forgive the first of us to forget it!"

"What you're sayin' breaks my heart, Ever," she told him, "because it makes me think of Clay, down there in the jail."

"Have you seen him?" asked Ever.

"I went and seen him. He—he forgave me as free and kind and gentle and simple as anything you ever heard. I've been a bad woman, Ever. I never knew how bad till I took and looked into your uncle's face and seen his blue Winton eyes, with no meaness in 'em."

"It's the best thing he's ever done," Ever said, "and he's done good things before this. Mother, I've got to go."

"Not yet, Ever!" she moaned, clinging to him harder than ever.

"Some one's waiting for me," said he. "I'm going away for a long time, perhaps. You may not hear from me. And what you do hear may not sound the best. But I want you to think, in spite of anything, that I'm trying my best to do what's right."

"Whatever you try you'll do," she said.

"May I go now, Mother?" he asked.

"I made a vow," she answered, "while you were away. I made a vow that I'd never say no to you in the rest of my days. If you have to go, it's all right, Ever. Somehow, I feel that there were mountains raised up between us, black as night and high as the stars, and that now they're down— Good-bye, Ever. We'll never have the mountains between us again. And with them out of the way, what difference does distance make?"

He took her in his arms and kissed her; then he swung into the saddle. She saw the sheen of the horse slide away through the darkness, tilt up over the fence and disappear.

It was not long afterward that he stood with Timberline, under the shaggy darkness of the pine trees that filled all the rest of the village block that had been reserved for the jail and the other county buildings. Of those structures, only the jail had been erected; it was the only building for which there was a pressing need!

"Al and Garry will stay back there with the horses," Timberline was explaining. "You and I do the inside work. Is that right?"

"That's right," said Ever. "Whatever you say is right —for me."

"Good!" said the other. "As soon as the bright light goes out inside the cell room, we start."

"What's the news in the town today?" asked Ever.

"Couldn't you find out?"

"No, I didn't show my face."

"They've got a case against your uncle. They turned up the cashier of that Green River Bank, and after those five years he still remembered your uncle."

"Was he sure?"

"Pretty sure—at first. And then he asked to have Clay's mustaches shaved. They did that, and after the mustaches were gone he took his oath that Clay Winton was the robber, all right!"

Ever sighed.

"That makes it pretty final, I suppose?"

"It's so final that it's finished," said Timberline. "Didn't you even see the newspapers?"

"No."

"The newspapers have him as good as in stripes, already. That's the way with newspapers. They tell the juries what to think even before the juries are picked out and put together."

"There's nothing left, then, but breaking the jail," said Ever.

"Nothing left," agreed Timberline.

He was extraordinarily cheerful about it. He went on:

"The folks in this place seem to have a good deal of sympathy for Clay Winton. They say that anybody who can keep his face shut and live quietly for five years, after a job like that, deserves to go free, almost. And I agree with 'em."

"There's the light!" exclaimed Ever.

The stronger illumination that shone through the one window on that side of the jail had now gone out; in its place was what at first seemed to be solid darkness; but afterward it turned into a faint glimmering.

"We start now," said Timberline.

He stepped forward as he spoke, and Ever accompanied him closely.

Ever was wonderfully aware of every nerve in his anatomy. It was as though a search light was playing upon him, with the danger of bullets striking through the light. He remembered one other thing; the Colt revolver which he had received from his uncle. It had the sights filed away, so that they might not interfere with a fast draw; the trigger was gone; the spring was set so the weapon could be fanned. If the pinch came, he wondered if he could use it at a human target.

21

BENEATH the barred window of the jail Timberline stopped.

"A tree's no stronger than its roots, Winton," said he. "I'll take a pry at the bars up there and see what happens."

He was up to the ledge at once, active as a cat, and working the end of a small crowbar into place beneath one of the rods. A little shower of loosened mortar and cement fell down. Ever heard a small grating sound.

Something was held down to him; he took it, and found it to be one of the curved window bars.

Timberline leaned above him.

"Could almost do it with my bare hands," the man murmured. "This is going to be a joke, Winton!"

A joke to get through the window, perhaps—but what about the inside of the jail?

Bar after bar was handed down to Ever. He laid them cautiously to the side so that they would not jangle one against the other; would not present another and even greater danger if it proved necessary to return through that same window and leap down in haste.

Then Timberline slid feet first through the naked gap of the window.

Every muscle, every nerve of Everard Winton grew as hard as ice, brittle with extreme cold. But in another moment he was at the same opening. Shame gave him warmth. It was for his own flesh and blood that this thing was being ventured, and yet Timberline had laid out the plan of attack and was working alone!

At the window, Ever looked through into an obscure interior that was lighted from one dim source that he could not see, as yet. He put his head inside and saw Timberline standing back against the wall, just beside the window. It was a good eight foot drop, from the sill of the window to the floor inside. A hard business, too, to climb up that smooth inner wall and out, once a man was inside.

However, Timberline had already committed himself. Ever went through as the other had done, feet first, and dropped to the floor. Then he stepped to the side of his companion.

"A hard job to get back through that window—for the one who's last," whispered Winton. "How can we do it?"

"We'll know how to do it when we have to," said the other. "One thing at a time. But let's try to spot that cell where your uncle is stored away."

They had no chance to begin their search at once. A brighter light moved toward them, and voices. Timberline glided instantly through the open door of a cell. Ever followed.

"Damned bad luck!" murmured Timberline.

He slid to the floor and lay flat upon it, face down-

90

ward, his head pillowed on one arm. In his free hand gleamed a bit of steel. It might be time for shooting, before ten seconds had passed. Ever implicitly followed his companion's lead.

Lying there in darkness broken only by that vague shimmer of light overhead, he regretted intensely that they were shut within the narrow limits of the cell. A push against the door would snap the latch and make them prisoners.

A mad idea came into his head that his companion was betraying him into captivity—that it was an arrangement between Timberline and the sheriff to catch up another of the Winton clan.

The idea grew like a fire in him; he was on the verge of leaping to his feet as he heard the sound of voices, approaching.

Then, "Close up those doors, Pete," said one, with an air of authority.

It was the sheriff's voice, like a confirmation of Ever's suspicion. He drew in his breath hard, gathered himself to leap—and found the door flung shut with a loud clanging before his face.

It was all he could do to keep himself from springing up and shouting at the top of his lungs. He controlled himself; a shudder shook him from head to foot. Other doors were slammed in rapid succession, steel clanging against steel.

"That's the luck of the devil!" murmured Timberline, with a wonderful calm. "Now they'll find the bars off the window, and they'll trap us like rats. Rotten luck—rotten luck. We can't play this off as a practical joke, either!"

They heard the sheriff saying, "Now, Jerry, keep a brain in your head, will you?"

"Sure," said Jerry. "We always been leavin' the doors of the empties open, till just lately. I forgot about 'em, tonight."

"It ain't a time to do any forgetting," said the sheriff. "You be on your toes, Jerry."

"Sure," said Jerry. "Sure, I'll be on my toes."

"How's that fellow Richards?" asked the sheriff.

91

"He'll be all right. He's just got a hangover and the shakes. But he's all right."

"The poor devil's an old-timer," said the sheriff. "I reckon he's got a long record behind him."

"Gonna lock him up?" answered the guard.

"Nope, not me," answered Lew Darrow. "He's only a poor bum now, no matter what he used to be. I'm going to let him go, when he's sobered up. I'll throw a scare into him—and turn him loose. I'm sorry for the old-timers, Jerry. The heart's been cut out of most of 'em."

"Aye!" said Jerry. "The heart's been cut out of most of 'em. Richards, he just lies and shakes whenever anybody comes near him."

"He's like a dog that's been kicked too often," said the sheriff. "There ain't many that can stand a few stretches without losin' their nerve."

"Him in Number Nineteen ain't gonna lose his nerve," suggested Jerry.

"No," agreed the sheriff. "He won't lose his nerve. But look what he is—look at the blood that's in him. No, he ain't gonna lose his nerve. How's he been this evening?"

"Aw, he's all right. He never asks for anything. Never complains. Most of the poor soggy bums we get are always yammerin' about the chuck. The food ain't good enough for 'em. But it don't bother Winton. He takes everything, all right. He's a man."

"He's a man," said the sheriff.

"They got it pinned on him now, I guess," said the jailer.

"They got it nailed into his heart," answered the sheriff.

"What'll he get?"

"Anything. You can't tell. Likely something big. Enough to spoil his life for him." He added, "Now, you keep your eyes open. Make a round every half-hour, or so."

"Look here," said Jerry. "You think that they're gonna try to cut Winton loose from the jail?"

"He's got a kid nephew," declared the sheriff, "that looked like business, to me. If he sets down on his haunches and don't try his hand to get his uncle loose, I'm a fool and don't know a man when I see him. No,

92

that boy's gonna try something, and no mistake. That's the way I read his hand."

They receded, their voices growing dimmer, and Timberline nudged his companion.

"They got an idea about you, Winton," said he. "But it's a good thing to have a reputation with the county sheriff."

He even chuckled a little as he said this.

Then he rose to his feet and went to the door; and reaching his supple hands through the bars, he began to fumble at the lock from the outside. Winton heard light scratching sounds. He held his breath.

Presently Timberline straightened and stepped back from his examination.

"Can you do it?—Can you pick the lock?" asked the boy.

"Shut up," advised Timberline savagely, but in a whisper. "It's working backward, damn it—it's working backward that kills the business!"

He cursed in the same whisper, and set to his task again.

Hours went by.

Ever thought himself caught like a rat, dragged into court, charged, condemned, and sent to the penitentiary. He felt the cold steel belly of the barber's clippers run over his scalp. He looked down and saw his limbs clad in stripes. He served weary years in prison. He came out bowed, bent and gray before his time. He was a marked man. Old companions despised him. His father's ranch had passed into other hands. Father and Mother both were dead. He had only their stilted, scrawled letters to remind him of them.

This life flowed through the mind of Everard Winton in that slow passage of the time. It was no more than a dream, say, but it was a dream that seemed real.

And then there was a light click; a soft, sliding sound. The door had opened under Timberline's hand and his pick-lock!

Winton leaped to him.

"Steady me!" gasped Timberline.

Winton gripped him by the shoulders and found that

93

he was shaking and shuddering from head to foot. His head fell weakly over on one shoulder. He drew in his breath.

"I couldn't have stood it for another ten minutes," muttered Timberline. "I tried to read the mind of that damned lock until I thought that there was no mind in it!"

Rapidly, he grew better. He pulled out a handkerchief and wiped his face.

"My God, I need a drink!" he whispered to himself, not to Ever.

"We'll get out of here and come back tomorrow night," said Winton.

"I wouldn't come back into this hellhole again for ten thousand uncles of yours—and be damned to 'em!" muttered Timberline. "We'll do our job now or we'll never do it."

"It's all you, Timberline," said Ever in a burst of admiration and of gratitude. "I'm nothing—I'm only in the way."

"Let me tell you," whispered the other. "Back there in the cell, except for you, I'd have lost my mind. Come on. We'll find Number Nineteen. That's his cell number, I guess."

They went on down the corridor, beneath the window, where the missing bars had evidently not been detected by either the sheriff or the guard. They turned the corner and saw before them the light which illumined the interior; a lantern was bracketed against the wall, lighting irregularly both short corridors of the jail. They saw the glimmering steel faces of the cell doors. It was a good jail; it was worthy of the pride which the town had invested in it —the pride and the hard cash.

Just to the left of the first corner they found the number they wanted. Ever stepped to the door and whispered:

"Uncle Clay!"

Something stirred inside the cell. Then, almost in Ever's face, came the answering whisper:

"Ever, you young fool! Get out of this place! Do you

94

want to go to prison along with me? Get out of here—and get fast!"

"Shut up!" warned Timberline. "Stop talking and let me work."

He dropped to his knees.

Would it take longer than the first door? If so, the dawn would be on them—the broad daylight! Already it seemed to Ever that when he stepped back and looked down the first corridor toward the unbarred window, he could see the sheen of gray dawn beginning.—No, that was only his imagination, now drawn to the breaking point.

He stepped back and leaned over the form that kneeled on the floor.

"Easy—easy—so easy!" he heard Timberline whisper, and the intent worker looked up, his face shining with sweat—and with silent, triumphant laughter.

Then the bolt gave, with an audible click, and the door opened under his hand.

Inside, Ever saw his uncle's shadowy outline standing ready. At the same time, from the front corner of the room, another door opened and Jerry's voice said: "Scrub up the floors and then come back here and I'll give you a shot of coffee. Then—"

His voice broke off in the midst of this command; then it rose again in a high-pitched, almost feminine scream:

"Help! Help! Help!"

The three cries burned through Everard Winton's brain. They froze him in his place so that he could not move.

Already, his uncle and Timberline had turned the corner, running at full speed, bent far forward. He had even time to note that each of them carried a gun. Timberline had armed the prisoner.

But he himself could not stir.

"Shoot, Bud, shoot!" cried Jerry.

And he opened fire himself.

In his hand, Ever found his revolver. It had come automatically to his fingers; automatically, too, it was leveled at the two jailers. And yet he could not fire. It was as though his thumb was struggling to lift the weight of a ton!

22

ALL of his senses were so speeded up, at this moment, that it was as though the motions of the two jail guards were frozen forever in snapshots, presented in a slow, gradual series to his mind. He could see the guns drawn, and then raised. He could see the bending of the bodies, as the jailers took aim. Still he could not fire!

Swift bullets brushed the air about his face; leaving penciled strokes of red danger, as it were, across his mind. And suddenly he was able to use his own gun.

How many seconds had elapsed since the two guards entered the cell chamber?—Four or five, perhaps; but they were strung out like a whole day in his mind. Everything about his nerves and his wits and his senses had been raised to a hysterical degree of speed. Motion that seemed slow to him, at that moment, would have been lightning fast to almost any other man. But he could always take the swiftest and most fluid movements apart and remember them.

His eye became a slow-motion picture camera. He could tell, for instance, how Jerry's gun had stuck a little as it was being drawn from its holster. He could see the blond fellow stumble, as he jerked out his Colt—stumble and stagger a bit to the side, with the violence of the gesture.

So, to Ever, the few swift seconds were a large and thoroughly mapped country.

Other men were awake in the cells now, and were raising a clamor which rang from one thin steel wall to another and made the whole place reverberate like a boiler factory. Some of the prisoners were howling simply from excitement or with fear. Others were aimlessly beating at their walls or at their doors.

In the midst of this turmoil, Ever was able to fire for the first time. He took deliberate aim—perhaps the hundredth part of a second—to tell himself that he would select Jerry, instead of the other target.

He took another fraction of an instant to decide that he would fire low. He had no doubt about striking his target. He was not even excited about that. He had flicked a squirrel out of the lofty branch of a tree more than once, with a quick revolver shot.

He was perfectly cool. There was nothing strange to him about this situation; it was as if he had been through it a thousand times before.

So he fired.

It seemed to him that as Jerry howled out and dropped his gun and fell forward on his face, grasping at his injured leg with both hands—it seemed to him then that he had seen Jerry fall like this before.

The fat fellow, when he saw this catastrophe, turned with a shriek of fear and fled for his life.

Ever walked around the corner of the block of cells and stood below the unbarred window.

Timberline's face looked back inside, and Timberline exclaimed:

"Jump for my hands! You've been taking all night. What's the matter with you?"

Ever looked up and measured the jump. There was a fan-shaped cornice, a foot above the top of the windows, made by letting the stones of the arch project a little beyond the surface of the wall.

"Back up, Timberline," said he, "and I'll manage it, all right."

"You are a fool!" exclaimed Timberline. "Well, have it on your own head. I tried to help you!"

The head was withdrawn.

Ever backed up a step, then bounded high, caught the sill of the window, swept himself up from this by a strong armhaul, gripped the narrowly projecting rise above the top of the window, curled up his legs, and shoved them through the window hole. An instant later he had dropped through to the safety of the outer night.

It was the deadest hour, that which precedes the dawn;

but already men were awakening about the town. From the houses he could hear excited voices. Doors and windows began to slam open. Such a town as this would rouse quickly, and when it aroused, it was capable of terrible action. Not a man in the village would be unfamiliar with guns.

He was thoroughly possessed by an odd sense of joy. It had been rising in him from the moment when Jerry and the second guard entered the cell room. He could not name the feeling. It was not like the effect of liquor; it was something more. It was a direct, unearthly intoxication of the brain.

Timberline grasped him by the arm.

"Why the devil are you standing here? Start!" he demanded.

"Oh, it's all right," said Ever.

They were fleeing before him to show him the way, his uncle and Timberline, and he followed them.

Gunshots barked behind them; voices began to bawl across the open night. One man was screeching:

"They're gone! The jail's been cracked. Winton's gone! —Turn out, everybody! Hosses! Hosses!"

Well, they would have horsemen out, of course; and all those horsemen would ride like mad. But Ever would be on the Red Pacer's back!

Had he been recognized?

He could remember, now, that Timberline had cautioned him to pull the brim of his hat down over his face. He had pointed out that a man who wore his hat in this fashion, at night, was as secure from recognition as though he had a black mask strapped across his eyes.

But Ever had not followed that injunction. He had worn his hat normally. Perhaps the brim had even blown a little upward from his face, as he ran down the corridor. And it well might be that Jerry had seen him clearly. But he could not worry about that now—he could not worry about anything. It was with Ever as with the young wolf that for the first time runs with the pack and strikes down the kill.

They pressed through trees, struck across the street, and turned sharply down an alley.

They came to the rear of the town. The center of it was a volcano of sound; and here and there were sudden volleys, as though excited townsmen were firing at every shadow.

A little shack stood at the edge of the town, and as the three shot past, the door opened and a broad beam of yellow lamplight swept out to clutch the Pacer like a great, pale hand. Instinctively, Ever ducked his head. But what good was that? Even if he had not been recognized, the Red Pacer had been seen and was not likely to be mistaken. By the Pacer's own light, he seemed to shine out among other horses.

Ever jerked about in the saddle, a revolver in his hand, and saw the tall figure of a man standing in the doorway, staring after him.

Well, chance would have to handle that danger as it might. He put up the gun and rode on. For he felt withdrawn from the rest of the world, raised above the common level of its people.

They came to the poplar thicket where Al and Garry were waiting with their horses.

Al, his face drawn as if with pain—perhaps it was the strain of waiting and the excitement—leaped into his saddle. Garry followed suit.

The others were already bolting away. Only his uncle remained behind, waiting. Clay's restless horse—the same gray mare mustang that Harry Lawson had given to Ever —was turning in uneasy circles anxious to be away with the rest.

"Come on, Ever!" Clay Winton shouted.

He turned the mare and gave her her head, so that she bolted after the others. But the red stallion, without even breaking the flowing current of his pacing, held his own and overtook her, going past with a lordly stride!

23

On the shoulder of Banner Mountain a fire burned, of wood so carefully selected that hardly a wisp of smoke rose in the air of the late afternoon or blew away down the wind. It was hardly more than a wisp of that mist which the warmth of the sun was drawing up from the earth, and it was as readily dissipated in the wind. Under the embers potatoes were roasting slowly, coming to mealy perfection. Beside the fire sat Timberline and Clay Winton.

The latter stood up, walked to the edge of the mountain shoulder and looked down upon a small natural meadow which he could see through a clearing in the woods. There was the great red stallion striding, with Clay's nephew in the saddle.

"He's still at it," said Winton. "Still workin' the Pacer —still teachin' him tricks."

"The Pacer comes to his whistle now," observed Timberline.

"Not to any other whistle, though," remarked Winton. Unconsciously he raised his hand toward the place where those long, drooping, yellow mustaches had once been. The law had removed them, in the course of its investigations. Clay frowned when he found that there was nothing for his hand to stroke. He felt that his face was naked, after having found security for so long.

"That horse won't come to any other man," agreed Timberline. "He never will, now. Ever's spoiled him for good."

"Or made him," differed Winton.

"Put it any way you want," said Timberline. "He won't last long to ride the Pacer, anyway."

"No?"

"No," said Timberline, "he won't."

"You mean he'll get tangled up so deep that the law'll go after his scalp?"

Clay frowned.

"Partly that," said Timberline.

He settled his shoulders more comfortably against the stump that supported his back, like a chair. Then, staring through the clear mountain air, he looked down the ragged, tree-covered sides of the mountain and to the valley beneath, where an irregular silver stream was running. It was for moments like these that Timberline lived, almost more than for moments of high action.

Winton argued, "You got Ever wrong. He's all right."

"Of course he's all right," said Timberline. "Hell, he's better than all right! He's a champion—a champion gunman, is what I mean."

"He's sowing his wild oats, that's all," said the uncle, frowning again.

"Sowing 'em? Yes—and watch 'em grow, too. There'll be a harvest that'll fill a lot of barns with worse than wild fire."

"He's got the bit in his teeth and he's running a little wild, that's all," argued the uncle.

"You can put it that way if you like," said Timberline.

"Look here," said Winton. "Ever never would have kicked over the traces, but for me. He wanted to help me, the same as any good boy would. He wanted to help me—and he did. And now he'll go back and settle down to a steady life." He added, "That's what I wanta talk to you about."

"Go ahead and talk," said Timberline. "I'll listen, all right."

"He's to work out the Red Pacer and what you did for me, until you tell him that you're through with him," said Clay. "Well, when will that time come?"

"I don't know," said Timberline, shrugging his shoulders.

He turned his clear, coldly dark eyes upon his companion, and waited.

Said Clay Winton:

"You've got him. I'll offer you a substitute."

"What?"

"Myself."

"Go on and explain that."

"You want somebody you can rely on. You want somebody who'll be at your back in any sort of a pinch. Ain't that your idea?"

"You've named it. But go on."

"Well, it's like this. You've made your bargain, and Ever means to stick to it. There's no doubt about that."

"I don't think there is."

"All right. But you'll find me a lot more useful than Ever. I can shoot about as straight. I can ride about as far. Besides, I've been through a lot more than he has. I've got an experienced head; one that would be useful to you in some of your schemes."

"As a matter of fact, you'd have too many ideas," said Timberline. "I want somebody who's straight. The kid's straight. I want somebody who's afraid of nothing. The kid's not afraid of the devil on wheels. I want somebody who's tied to me; and the kid's tied to me because I gave him the Pacer and because I helped you out of jail. That makes him perfect, as far as I'm concerned."

Winton was lost in thought. "You gotta think of another thing," he said.

"What's that?"

"You've gotta remember that he's chuckin' his life away. I ain't gonna talk about the breakin' of his mother's heart, and his father's. That won't matter. But I say that he'll be throwin' himself away. He's meant for something better."

"He'll never go back; he'll never go straight," answered Timberline.

"What makes you think so?"

"Because he's too much like me."

"He's not so much like you, Timberline."

"It's in his eye," answered Timberline. "A tame life is no life for him, after this. He's got the juice of the wild in him. Trouble is what he'll hunt, from now on. I see it in him every day. You wouldn't be the same. You're a cool fellow, and you're older. You're a grand fighter, it's

102

true. You've got a head on your shoulders, too. But did you see Ever when he came out of the jail?"

"I saw him," said the uncle gloomily.

"He was laughing, wasn't he?"

"Sort of hysterical, I'd call it."

"Then you'd call it wrong. He was just happy—and that's the sort of a man I want."

"You won't let go of him, then?" asked Winton, facing full at his companion.

"No, I'll never let up on him. I need him. Maybe the days will come when he'll need me, too."

"Then—stand up!" commanded Winton, in a changed voice.

"What's the matter?" asked Timberline, leaning forward a little, his face suddenly both formidable and studious, like that of a wolf when it scents prey down the wind.

"Stand up," repeated Winton quietly.

Timberline rose without touching his hands to the ground.

"If you won't take me in his place, then you'll take neither of us," said Winton.

"Guns, Clay? Is that what you mean?" asked Timberline.

"That's what I mean. I won't let him go to hell because of me—and you."

"You've thought it over?" asked Timberline curiously and without fear.

"I've thought it all over," said Clay Winton, with an equal calm. "Anyway it turns out, I win."

"How do you make that out?"

"If I kill you, he can't follow you no more. If you kill me, you'll have to try to kill him afterwards."

Timberline frowned as he saw the full beauty of the scheme.

"I hate to think you're such a low hound, Clay," said he.

"I've been a low hound before, maybe," said Clay Winton. "But I'm not bein' a low hound, now."

He added: "You go for your gun and fill your hand. You can make the first move."

Timberline studied his opponent.

"I'm a bit better with a gun than you are, Clay," said he, "and you know it. You really want to die?"

Winton extended an arm and pointed down the slope of the mountain.

"I want him set loose," he answered sternly.

A new idea came to Timberline.

"Look here," he said. "Al and Garry will be back by the evening, and they'll bring all the news there is to get. Suppose that the kid was recognized, the other evening in the jail. He lingered around long enough for 'em to see him. What if he was recognized?"

Clay Winton drew back a little.

"Luck couldn't be that much agin him!" he declared.

"Wait and see," said Timberline. "If they spotted him, it's no good to send him back to his ranch. You'd simply be sending him to a life in jail."

Clay considered, his face very dark.

"Breakin' into a jail," he muttered, "and then helpin' a prisoner loose. That's two counts, and two long ones. Worse'n burglary by a whole heap. Then—shootin' down an officer of the law. That's worse still."

He jerked up his head.

"We'll wait till we get news," he said.

"We're friends till then?" asked Timberline cautiously.

"Aye, I suppose so." Winton stalked off among the trees.

24

THE CAMP FIRE glowed like a great eye with multiple red pupils, sending out dull rays through the darkness, gilding the rocks, and dimly touching the foliage of the trees. It fell on Clay Winton's ominous face.

Clay's nephew, and Timberline, sat farther back,

finishing their coffee. And now, as Timberline rolled a cigarette, Everard Winton lifted his head and whistled softly. A whinny hardly louder than the whistle made answer.

"Ah-ha!" murmured Ever triumphantly. "Hear him, Timberline?"

"He'll be singing scales for you in another day or two," suggested Timberline, with a smile.

Ever laughed happily. He lay back on the pine needles, his head pillowed in his hands and his eyes drifting past the dark tops of the pines and toward the chilly, bright multitudes of the stars.

"Think of the rest of 'em!" he murmured.

The two older men were watching him, one openly, one covertly.

"The rest?" asked his uncle finally.

"All the others who are down there. Everybody who's not up here. *Think* of 'em!"

"They're getting on pretty well, I guess," said Clay. "They've got their families around 'em, those men. They've finished their day's work. They've had their supper. They've got a snug night before 'em."

"The men are sitting out on the verandas," said Ever. "They've got on slippers, to rest their feet, perhaps. Now and then a mosquito comes along with a song and dance, and spears 'em. But they're too tired even to fight back. And tomorrow'll be a dead ringer for this day.

"Out in the dust of the streets the brats are either tumbling about or chasing each other. Somebody bangs a tin piano and hammers out a thousand-year-old tune, with a lot of halts and pauses in it. Somebody's baby begins to squall. And back in the kitchens the women are sloshing the dishes or the tins around in a lot of gray, greasy water, and wondering why God put 'em on this sort of earth."

He paused, waited for an answer, got none, and continued.

"No, they're not even wondering. They're submitting to everything that comes to 'em. If they started wondering, they'd get up and break away. They'd leave the whole thing cold behind 'em. They'd pack and start off with

105

fishing rods and rifles, and they'd make a living in the hills. That's what they'd do!"

"Even the women?" asked Clay.

"Yes, even the women. They can be human beings, too. Look at Mother. She's worked hard, but she's still straight as a string. She still has a young step. She can ride a horse like a wild Indian. She can shoot a deer at four hundred yards. She's a hand with a shotgun, too. And by one look at a stream she can tell the pools and the white water that the fish will like. She can tell better than you or I can, Uncle Clay. She ought to be up here like we are, free. It's living down there in the dust— down in the lowlands, hitched to the ranch and to milking cows and to dishwater and to mending clothes—that's what kills women like her."

He was silent again. He began to breathe deeply, his eyes closed.

"He's dropped off," muttered Timberline presently. "He's got some ideas, that kid."

"I'm not asleep," said Ever. "I was just inhaling this air. I've been so long on the ranch that I'd forgotten that air could taste like this—right down to the bottom of the lungs. Feel it?"

"I feel it," said Timberline quietly.

There was a short, low whinny from the brush.

"That's the Pacer!" exclaimed Ever, and he bounded to his feet.

"Well, what of it?" asked Clay Winton. "Gonna go and tuck the baby in with a blanket, maybe? Afraid he'll catch cold?"

Ever paid no attention to this mockery.

"That's his danger signal," said he. "There's something near us."

Timberline stood up in turn.

Ever stepped out into the darkness; and they heard him speak softly to the horse. Then, after another moment, another horse snorted in the distance, down the mountainside.

"It's all right, Ever," said Timberline. "Probably just Al and Garry coming in."

"I'll make sure," said Ever in a guarded voice.

Clay Winton was tense, with an excitement that grew greater and greater as human voices presently sounded from below.

"We'll know, in a minute or two," he muttered.

"Aye, we'll know," said Timberline.

Then Garry and Al came in. They brought with them a cargo of food—chiefly flour and bacon and coffee, with a few luxuries such as tinned jams, and a final can or two of tomatoes.

As the packs were undone and the contents arranged in five parcels to match the five men, Ever, who had met and escorted the pair up the slope, stirred the fire and put bacon in the pan. The coffee began to murmur in the pot.

Clay Winton, in the meantime, had found the newspapers that were brought up; and fumbling among them, he found news that kept him silent for a long moment.

"Well, what is it, Clay?" asked Timberline, at last.

"Bad!" said the uncle.

He read aloud, giving the contents partly in his own words, partly in direct quotation.

"They rode all over the face of the hills. We went and mysteriously disappeared, it looks like. . . . Got a reward offered for me now, boys. That'll warm things up a little. Yeah, it'll warm 'em up a pile. You'll be glad to have me along with you yet, Timberline."

"We can stand that, Clay," said Timberline.

Clay Winton continued, "This is for you, Ever."

"All right," said the boy, turning sharply.

"Well, listen.—'The jailer, Jeremiah P. Huntington, declares that he recognized the man who fired the shot that struck him on the right leg, halfway between the hip and the knee. He was unwilling to give testimony—' Hello, think of that!"

"Why wouldn't he wanta give testimony?" demanded Garry.

"He says he could of been shot through the heart, as easy as through the leg.—Wait a minute, here's some more. They got him to talk, finally. The damn lawyers, they could make a saint talk!—Here's some more of Jerry, the jailer."

Again he read aloud:

" 'Finally the jailer swore that he had recognized the face and the figure of young Everard Winton, the son of Mr. and Mrs. Edward Winton of Savage Creek, respected members of this community. This startling information causes great disturbance of the many friends of the Wintons, and it is hoped that Mr. Huntington may have made a mistake.

" 'Young Winton, however, is missing from his home. It appears that he had left it to go to the ranch of Harry Lawson. He was seen there, in fact, with his uncle, Clay Winton, the escaped prisoner, at the moment when Sheriff Darrow made the arrest. Harry Lawson, when questioned, declared that after the arrest had been made, and the sheriff had returned toward town with the prisoner, young Everard Winton told him that he was going to go into the hills for a short hunting trip.

" 'Mr. Lawson pointed out the direction in which young Winton had ridden. This trail has been followed, and it may lead to something.

" 'Mr. Huntington was perfectly convinced and positive in his testimony, and he says he had a good look at the face of young Winton. An air of probability is given to this testimony by the fact that it is well known that Everard Winton was his uncle's constant companion. It is a sad thing to reflect that—' "

Clay Winton broke off his reading and allowed the paper to flutter from his hand to the ground.

"Well, you're in the soup, brother!" said Al to Ever.

"Shut your face, you fat-headed fool!" snarled little Garry to his bigger companion.

A dead silence held the group, all at once. The fumes of burning bacon wafted unnoticed from the frying pan.

25

THEY STOOD side by side in the gray of the next morning
—Timberline and Ever. The day was gray above and gray
below. High clouds sheeted away the sun and most of its
light; low-driven masses swallowed up the bottoms of the
ravines, the rivers, and the plain beyond. They lived in a
world that was bounded by two seas of mist, and films of
the grayness curled up among the pine trees near at hand.

The leader was pointing.

"You know where Bentonville is, Ever?"

"No."

"Heard of it?"

"Just that it's a gold rush town."

"That's what it is. Could you get to the Benton River
from here?"

"Yes, I might wander a little, but I could get there."

"You get there, then," said Timberline. "I've heard
there's a fellow there I want to get in touch with. He's
Carson Jimmy—some people call him Jimmy Carson.
Ever hear of him?"

"I have. Some sort of a big crook?"

"He's all sorts," said Timberline. "I'm *some* sort of a
crook myself; but he's *all* sorts. Understand?"

"Of course I do. That is—he's an all-round bad one,
eh?"

"That depends on what you mean by 'bad.' Whatever
he is, he's a *good* crook. That is, he's successful."

Ever nodded, frowning a little at this definition.

"And now that you're with me," said Timberline crisply,
"I expect some good crooked work out of you, too.
Understand?"

"I understand," said Ever.

"Go hard against the grain?" asked Timberline, watching him with brilliant eyes.

"It's all right," said Ever. "I'm your man, for anything you mention."

"Well then, you ride down to Bentonville. When you're in the town you'll be in a little danger, but not much. Men aren't likely to recognize the Red Pacer. They've heard of him, and some of them have seen him, but they haven't seen him bridlewise, and under a saddle."

"He'd look different now, I suppose."

"He looks different—and he *is* different. And if you make him do a few tricks, nobody'll dream that he's the maneating Pacer."

"I follow you."

"When you get to the town, you'll follow your nose down the main street to the Sentinel Hotel. Get a room there, and ask for Dolly Gray."

"I'll write it down."

"Don't write down anything! Never write down anything while you're working with me. Writing things down is what hangs men."

"Jimmy Carson—Bentonville—the Sentinel Hotel—Dolly Gray.

"I have the names."

"That's the way, Ever. Lodge 'em in your head. If you forget, it means riding all the way back here to see me, and you wouldn't want to do that."

"No," agreed Everard Winton.

"Dolly Gray isn't her real name—it's Dorothy Gray Siddenham, or something long like that. But the boys call her Dolly Gray for the short of it, and because it fits her. I'll give you an idea of what she is, and tell you why afterward.

"Before the boom hit Bentonville, the Sentinel Hotel was just a crossroads place, and it was run by Dolly's father. The boom came, the business got big, and Dolly's father ran into a chunk of lead, one evening in his barroom.

"Dolly nursed her father through, but he got tuberculosis lying on his back. She hired a nurse and sent him off to the mountains to a resort, while she stays at home and

110

runs the hotel to clear her old man's expenses. Makes you think that she's one of these meek and mild martyrs, eh? But you'll see you're wrong when you meet her. Dolly's only eighteen, but she grew up young. When she's a year older—because wiser she'll never be—I'm going to marry her. That's what you're to tell her."

"I'm to tell Dolly Gray that you intend to marry her in another year."

"That's it. She'll laugh, but she'll give you a good room on account of it, and she'll keep you out of trouble. Nobody in Bentonville can do that as well as she can."

Ever nodded and Timberline continued:

"Then you go to call on Carson Jimmy—or Jimmy Carson, any way you choose to put it. The point is that Jimmy does things on a big scale—and so do I. I think it's about time for us to work in double harness together, Jimmy and me. He may have heard of me, but he's not likely to know me well; and he's likely to pretend that he dosen't know me at all. That's where you come in. You show him that no matter what he thinks, I'm *worth* knowing."

He laughed as he said this, and a flare of light came into his eyes.

"Worth knowing?" repeated Ever.

"Yes, worth knowing. So worth knowing that he can't get along without me. When you've convinced him of that, you can tell him I'm willing to make a deal with him, and that we'll work the town of Bentonville together. While the rush is on, it's worth running!"

"I'm to make him put a high value on you. But how am I to do that?"

"Don't ask me," snapped Timberline. "If you're worth your salt to me, you're up to harder jobs than this. You go down there to Bentonville and just try your hand."

"Very well," said Ever. "I'll go down there and teach Jimmy Carson that you're on the map."

"That's exactly what you're to teach him. Like the idea?"

"I'll do my best," said Ever evasively.

"If anything goes wrong and Carson Jimmy doesn't want to play ball with me, you can tell him that I'm on the

111

other side of the fence. Bentonville is always in need of a bang-up good new deputy sheriff or a town marshal or something like that. Since Carson showed up, there are likely to be more vacancies than officers. And I might slip into an empty spot, with you at my side and some of the other boys along."

He laughed again and snapped his fingers.

"As a matter of fact," he continued, "I don't give a damn. Wherever Carson is, the game is sure to be fast and the stakes high. And that's what I want. *With* him or *against* him makes very little difference. So long as I'm sitting at the same table or fighting in the same ring."

"To enforce the law? That would be a joke—the law wants me and wants me badly," said Ever.

But there was a grin on his face.

"Of course it would be a joke," said Timberline. "A good joke, too. Nobody is apt to spot you, though. A mining town makes its own horizon. Wall Street could burn and smash, and a good rush town would never hear of it for a year. Now, I've told you everything I want you to know. It's a big job, but I hope to give you still bigger ones before I'm through with you. Get on your way, Ever. My idea in sending you is to play up the size of my hand. If Jimmy Carson doesn't know me, he has to figure me pretty high, when he realizes you're one of my men."

Instinctively, Everard unbuckled his belt, drew it tighter by a notch, and slipped the loose end back through the guard.

"I'll try to play up," said he.

"Are you ready to ride?"

"I'll say so long to Uncle Clay and start now."

"Clay's gone up to the creek to try to catch some trout for breakfast. Never mind saying good-by to him."

"I'd better say good-by to him."

"No, you'd better not. I'll tell him that I sent you away on an errand. If you stop to talk to him, he'll get bluer than ever. He's almost blue enough for suicide right now."

"Perhaps you're right. I'll start, then."

"Start fast, and go easy till you get to Bentonville. Then burn up the town." He added, "Got any money?"

112

"I'll manage."

"No, you won't," said Timberline. "If you represent me, you can't be a piker. You need money—and here's some! So long! Now get the Pacer and start!"

26

EVERYTHING seemed almost easy to Ever except the money that lay in his pocket. Stolen money—and the Wintons were not the people to deal with that stuff. Or had it been stolen in fact? Perhaps it was only the proceeds of one of Timberline's more honest exploits.

He conned the matter over as he passed down into the level of the lower mist and reached the brilliance of sunshine among the foothills.

He hit Benton River in the early afternoon and came into Bentonville in the heat of the day. He had had a glimpse of boom towns before this, and Bentonville was like many of the others. It was simply a scattering of tents, lean-tos, shacks made of boxwood or flattened tin cans, with rude thatchings of grass and pine branches for roofs, as likely as not. In the streets were a thousand people, each a different type. From the four quarters of the land they had come, some to hunt fortunes in the ground, others to hunt their luck in the pockets of those who had dug wealth out of the rock.

Ever's heart began to rise as the stallion took him at that flowing stride along the street. The Red Pacer was not a red stallion any longer; he was gray from head to foot, except where the sweat had worked through in little rivulets. But dusty or not, he was enough to make men stop short and look once and then look again. Once the horse was recognized, might not recognition of his rider follow? What did the law know? And even if the Pacer were not known, how long would it be before pictures of Ever, as a criminal wanted by the law, were in the hands of the officers thereof?

Ever felt like a gambler who sits in at a game where the stakes are as high as life or death, but he was glad to be there.

The Sentinel Hotel was a fairly large building, rising out of the half-story level of the rest of the town. The original structure had been a two-story affair, and wings had been added to it to accommodate part of the rush population. Sheds further extended its possibilities for receiving guests. Behind stood a great barn with shelving roofs to take in the livestock. Altogether it looked like a flourishing concern, the Sentinel Hotel, and as Ever put his horse in the stable he wondered how an eighteen-year-old girl could possibly manage it.

He went into the lobby, which had been enlarged to meet the prosperous times by knocking down the partitions of several adjoining rooms. At one time or another during the day all the population of Bentonville flowed through this lobby.

To the little one-armed man who acted as clerk Ever said, "I want to see Dolly Gray."

"Everybody else does, too," answered the other, with insolent impertinence. "What you want to see her for?"

"I'll tell her that," said Ever.

The clerk frowned, hesitated, finally rose and led the way.

"Aw—all right," said he. "Come along. But she's busy."

He went to a door at the side of the lobby, knocked on it, and then pushed it open.

A red-headed girl with a face as tanned as leather looked up from behind a table loaded with stacks of papers—hotel bills and accounts, perhaps.

"This fellow wants to see you," said the clerk.

He closed the door behind Ever, and left him looking into a pair of seagreen eyes. Dolly Gray had folded her hands behind her head and was pressing back against them, like one whose neck aches from too much bookwork.

"I don't know you, do I?" she demanded.

114

"No," said he.

The matter of a new name for him, strangely enough, had not entered his mind before.

"I'm Bill Smith," he added.

"I place you right away," said the girl. "Bill Smith—born way up the Mississippi—age between fifteen and thirty—height, average—eyes, average—no marks of identification. Are you a brother of Bill Jones, by any chance?"

He smiled. "Timberline asked me to call on you," he said.

"Oh, did he?" said the girl. "Haul up a chair. How's old Timber, anyway?"

"He's all right," said Ever, bringing a chair nearer to the table, though he did not sit down.

"He wasn't all right the last time I knew him," she said, with meaning. "You know him, Bill?"

"Why, yes. I know him a little."

"Nobody knows all about him," she said. "He's spread his history over too much ground for that. What's the news from Timber?"

"He's sending word to you that he'll be marrying you in about a year."

"Did he send that word?" said she, without smiling. "That's all right, too."

"After I had told you that, Timberline said," went on Winton, "you'd take care of me and keep me out of trouble."

She leaned forward and rested her elbows on the edge of the table. It was characteristic of her that over her face came those rapid changes of expression that are usually seen only in a man's face. Beauty is a thing that is kept undistorted. We see no more of it than the mirror has taught the owner to reveal. But Dolly Gray was different. She had a boy's careless freedom.

"So you want to be taken care of?" she asked.

"I'm only repeating what Timberline said," he remarked. "In a town like this, I suppose everybody wants to be taken care of."

"Are you one of Timber's men?" she said.

"I'm one of his friends," said he.

115

"You're new in the business," said she shrewdly. "What's the game this time? Crooked or straight?"

"I'm to see Jimmy Carson," said he.

"Carson Jimmy—Jimmy Carson, eh?" she answered. "Crooked business, then. Aren't you pretty young to be calling on Carson?"

"I have a calling card with me," he said, moved by a strange impulse.

"Have you? What is it?" she asked.

"Five fingers, all on one hand," said he.

She was not amused; she was not even very interested. She merely looked him up and down, gravely.

"Going to present 'em to Jimmy Carson? Well, I'll tell you where he lives."

"That's what I'd like to know."

"Second floor, Number Twenty-one. Just step up and knock. You'll find he has some friends with him. Make yourself at home in the Sentinel. Anything I can do, let me know."

She stood up. He walked to the door.

"Look here, Bill," she said suddenly.

"Yes?"

"Aren't you pretty young to be mixing around with all these big, rough men? These Timberlines and Carsons, and what-nots?"

"I don't know," said he. "Do I look young?"

"Just out of the cradle," said she. "Second floor, Number Twenty-one. You'll find him there."

"Thanks," said he.

He opened the door. She called over her shoulder to the clerk:

"Fix up Bill Smith, Shorty, will you?" And then her voice sounded softly behind him: "Think it over, Bill—or Joe or Harry or whatever your name is—and don't be a fool!"

The door closed in his face as he half turned. He went back to the desk and found that one-armed Shorty was waiting for him with a key in his hand.

"Here's Number Twenty-nine," said he. "Best thing we got vacant. Go up and let yourself in, and if there's anything you want come down and say so."

116

Ever climbed the steps to the upper hall, found his room, and let himself in. It was a perfectly plain room, and small, but it was on a corner of the building, and it had two windows. The southern one looked over the street. He leaned on the window-sill for a moment, with the heat pouring upon his head, and stared at the constant procession of riders, pedestrians, wagons of all sorts. There were no sidewalks in Bentonville. A huge freight wagon went by, lurching from side to side, putting down its tires into chuckholes and making the dust spurt out like water. Little dust clouds followed it and blew away down the street. It was a new town; it was a place where anything could happen; and he was glad that he was in it.

Something was in his mind; he hardly knew what. An emotion, he discovered, rather than an idea. He decided that it was the girl. Her direct, green eyes, her husky voice, remained with him. There was something behind both her eyes and her voice. For instance, she had neither simpered nor blushed when he had told her that Timberline intended to marry her within a year. He might have been speaking to a post.

He felt a little ineffectual, remembering her; he felt weak and useless and ill at ease. He had a great desire to do something that would bring him vividly to her attention.

He went to the washstand, poured some water into the granite basin, washed his face, scrubbed the grease of the reins off his hands, dusted his clothes, rubbed up his riding boots, and retied his bandanna. When he felt that he was fit once more, he settled his sombrero on his head again and went down the hall to Number Twenty-one, which was at the farther corner of the building.

Voices came through the door and he paused for a moment, his hand raised to knock.

A little man only a few inches over five feet suddenly came up beside him with a rapid step.

"Who are you?" he asked with an air of authority.

He had a pale, peaked face. He wore a cap with a deep visor, and his eyes glimmered and twinkled through the shadow which this headgear cast.

"I've come down here from Timberline," said Ever.

"Don't know him!" said the little man curtly.

"He knows you. Isn't that enough?" asked Ever angrily.

"Not enough for me," said the other.

He pulled the door open, stepped inside and slammed it in Ever's face. The latter, stunned and enraged, heard the same voice continue inside the room. All the other voices were now quiet.

"There's a chestnut stallion down in the stable. I just seen it. Real red chestnut with a white stocking. Get that horse for me, Buck."

Said an answering voice, "Who owns that plug, chief?"

"Don't ask me! I told you to get me that horse. He's something I could ride."

Everard Winton turned and went hastily, almost guiltily, back to his room. There he sat down, lighted a cigarette, and waited. He felt both stimulated and at ease. In all probability something was about to happen.

He took out the revolver which Clay Winton had given to him, spun the cylinder, tried the action, and replaced it with one swift, sure gesture beneath the pit of his left arm. He felt cooler and more than ever content with life, as he leaned back in his chair again. He did not need news print to occupy his mind during the interim.

Before many minutes, a hand rapped on his door.

"Come in," he called.

The door opened and a big fellow with a sun-reddened face came in.

It was the voice of Buck, who inquired, "Are you Bill Smith?"

"I'm Smith," said Winton, rising and coming politely forward.

"My name is Buck Waters," said the other, holding out a great paw.

"Glad to know you, Mr. Waters," said Everard.

"Glad to know you—and glad to know your horse, too. You own that chestnut son of a streak of sunlight, don't you? Out there in the stable?"

"I own him," said Ever.

"I'd like to," said Buck. "That's why I'm takin' up your time. Wanta sell?"

Ever shook his head.

"Sit down," said he. "Here are the makings. Glad to talk horse to you, but I won't sell."

"I know what you mean," said the other. "You wouldn't want to take two or three hundred for him, eh? What did you pay for him, might I ask?"

"You might," said Ever. "I didn't pay for him."

"Raised him, eh?"

"In a way." And young Winton smiled a little as he thought of the wild skies and the north winds that had fathered the Red Pacer on the open range.

"Well," said Buck Waters, "I ain't a piker, brother. I won't sit down, but I'll offer you a flat five hundred bucks for that horse. He fills my eye."

"Does he? He fills mine, too. And five hundred doesn't fill my hand."

Buck frowned a little.

"What price would you make?" he asked.

"I'm not putting a price on him at all," said Ever.

"Come along, come along!" said Buck. "Everybody's willing to sell a horse—for a price. I'll pay you the right price. You name it!"

Winton shook his head.

"I'm glad you like him. But I'm not selling. I'm not naming a price."

Buck grew beet-red with impatient anger.

"I guess I see how it is," he explained to himself, though in a loud voice. "You raised that hoss from a colt, and you think he's the only one in the world. But I'll tell you—I'll give you a thousand dollars."

A new idea came to Ever.

"You're one of Carson's friends, aren't you?" he asked.

"Sure I am," said Buck.

"Does he want the horse for himself?"

"Why, maybe he does, at that," agreed Buck, greatly surprised.

"Well," said Ever, "I don't mind talking the thing over with him in person."

"Don't you?" said the other doubtfully. "Well, come along down the hall with me."

They went down to Number Twenty-one, where Buck pushed the door open without knocking.

"You red-faced lump of beef!" snarled a voice. "Whacha mean by openin' that door without giving it a rap, eh?"

27

Buck drew back half a stride. "Why, I was gonna tell you about the horse," said he.

"Aw, well, come in them. Whacha pay for it?"

Buck pushed the door wider and stepped inside. Ever followed him. Littly Jimmy Carson, his cap still on his head, stood up suddenly from his chair and pointed.

"Where'd you get that?" he demanded.

"Why, he's the guy that has the horse," complained Buck.

"Take him out," said Carson. "I won't talk to him."

He sat down again and turned his back on Buck and Winton. He was giving his attention to a stalwart with a dark, foreign face. The man's head was almost without a back to it, and it was lodged on top of an immense column of a neck. This man favored the two who had been checked at the door with a sour grin and looked back at Carson again.

"The chief's on the rampage. Something's gone wrong," declared Buck, turning to leave the room.

But Winton stepped on past him.

"That's all right, Buck," said he. "I've a few things to say to your chief."

Slowly, controlling his rage, Carson Jimmy turned his head. The fingers of his left hand, which hung over the back of his chair, sprang in and out from the palm like the legs of a struggling spider.

"Back out of here, Smith, you fool!" said Buck, in a murmur. "The chief's mad!"

"Why, that's all right," said Winton, his voice cheerfully raised. "If he's mad that doesn't matter to me. I'm just a messenger."

Carson rose to his feet again and turned, very slowly. He said, with a world of dangerous gentleness:

"Oh, you're a messenger, are you?"

"Yes," said Winton. "I came down from Timberline to see you."

"Oh, you came down from Timberline, did you?" said Carson, his voice still gentle, and his left hand working.

"A left-handed shot," thought Ever to himself. He continued: "Timberline gave me a message for you."

"Oh, he gave you a message, did he?" said Carson.

Madness flashed from his eyes, which jerked their glance back and forth across the room like lightning before they settled again on Ever's face.

"You see, chief," whined big Buck, "I offered him a thousand flat. But he said he wanted to talk to you—"

"You hulk of a half-witted jackass!" said Carson, drawing his lips back from his teeth as he spoke the words.

He stopped, gasping for breath, his lips working rapidly over things which he was unable to get out. Then:

"Get out!" he yelled.

He pointed an arm like a gun at Ever.

"Get out!" he repeated. "Fargo—Buck—throw him out. Break the fool's back. I don't care!"

"You'd better move," said Buck, laying a hand on the shoulder of Winton.

Fargo, the man with the foreign face and the wrestler's shoulders, loomed suddenly on the scene.

"Out!" he growled, barking the word, and reached suddenly in with a wrestler's hold.

Ever planted a jolting left on the root of Fargo's nose, slid from under Buck's hand and met that gentleman's charge with a right hook. It was a neat blow, a prized invention of Clay Winton, and a very deft variation of the classic punch. It started low and looked like an uppercut flying wide, until it turned in a high loop and dropped toward the face. Upon Buck Waters' outthrust jaw, as he charged in, it was a stunning blow. His own charge gave an added weight to the punch. He kept right on charging

121

with his legs and falling with the rest of his body until he had rammed himself into a corner of the room. There he lay still.

But Fargo had not been seriously hurt by the blow he had received. It had merely caused him to change his mind. Shifting from his idea of a wrestling hold, he swung for Ever's head, with a slungshot in the tips of his fingers.

It was a well-aimed blow, but it hissed over Ever's ducked head. Straightening, the boy pumped a brace of uppercuts into Fargo's chin, and found the effect as ungrateful as pounding a stone wall.

Again he dodged the fateful slungshot, and gave a right hook, with all his weight behind it.

Fargo grunted. He stood still and brought into his left hand a revolver that looked to Ever as big as a cannon. So Ever struck again, sliding his left foot forward, rising on his toes with the beginning of the punch, and dropping on his heels as it landed. Exquisite timing put all his one hundred and seventy pounds into the whiplash finish of that blow.

Fargo's face withered and wrinkled into ten thousand lines. The gun fell from his hand and slithered down his leg to the floor. He began to sit down, with buckling knees. He tried to right himself, and began to stagger back with little rapid steps. Then his legs gave way completely and he sat down heavily against the wall.

Winton picked up the fallen gun, but found himself covered by Carson. There was a grin on the face of the little man now, however.

"The pair of big bums!" said he. "The pair of big hams! They couldn't handle a kid like you, eh? Put that gat away before it hurts you, kid."

Winton obediently laid the gun on the table.

"I came to talk. I didn't come to fight," said he. "Timberline—"

"Oh, damn Timberline!" said the other. "What about that stallion? What's your price?"

Winton frowned.

"I'm the same price as the horse," said he.

The other lifted his eyebrows. Then he grinned again. "Well, that's pretty good, too," said he.

Fargo got to his feet, swaying.

"Hey, Fargo," said the chief, "leave go of that knife, will you, and take hold of Buck and drag him out into the fresh air? The kid went and poisoned him!"

28

BUCK, if not poisoned, seemed at least overcome with drowsiness. Fargo half jerked and half helped him to his feet, and then out of the room. As the door closed on them, Jimmy Carson said:

"That was all right—and right is what I mean! A mean wallop you pack in that hand. Who taught you to slam that hook across the shoulder?"

"An uncle of mine taught me."

"What's all this about Timberline?"

"You never heard of him?"

"Maybe I did, somewhere. He's one of these birds that's maybe inside or outside of the fence, or else roosting right on top of it."

Ever shrugged his shoulders.

"He plays the game for the sake of the game," said he honestly. "He doesn't much care what the game may be."

"That sounds like something, maybe," said Carson Jimmy, "but it don't mean anything to me. What game you talking about?"

"Oh, I'm talking about anything that happens to get his eye. Anything that amuses him is his game. That's why he sent me down to talk to you."

"About what I still don't understand?"

"He says the layout you have here in Bentonville ought to be the sort of show that he would like. He wants to take part in it."

"Oh, he does, does he?" said Jimmy Carson. His eyes squinted to points of light. Then he demanded, "I'm to ask him in, am I?"

"That's the idea," said Ever.

"Well, it's a *bright* idea," said Carson Jimmy. "It's one of the brightest that I ever heard. This bird hooks in from the outside and prongs into my business. I just ask him in, out of a clear sky. That's all there is to it, eh?"

"Then he puts his shoulder to the wheel and makes things hum for you," suggested young Winton.

"Oh, he makes things hum, does he?" snarled Carson.

"He does. He's the sort of a fellow who can, too."

"And suppose I tell him I don't want him with me?"

"That doesn't matter much to him," answered Winton. "It's just that he wants a hand in the game. He'll go with you, if he can—and if he can't, he'll go against you. Understand?"

Jimmy Carson rose to his feet.

"I'm *trying* to understand," said he. "This bohunk of a Pole of a Scandinavian dishwasher of a Timberline—he says that if he can't be for me, he'll be against me, eh?"

"That's the main idea," said Ever.

"Blackmail, or I'm damned!" exclaimed Carson, with virtuous indignation. "I never heard of anything like it in my whole life."

"Neither have I," answered Ever frankly.

"He'll be down here with his whole gang, will he?"

"Either on your side or to enforce law and order," said Winton.

"He'll enforce law and order, will he?" said the little man, fairly grinding his teeth.

"That's the idea."

"Tell him he can be damned—and all of his men along with him, the blackmailing double-crosser!"

"He never double-crosses," said Winton. "He's just telling you beforehand what he'll do and which side he'll be on. That's square."

"He wants a flat lump for pulling out, eh?" snarled Carson. "Well, just for curiosity, you tell me how much he wants on the nail to buy him off."

Winton said, with real conviction, "You couldn't buy him off with a million. It's not the money that he's after—not so much that, anyway. It's the game that he likes."

"Tell that to Sweeney!" said Carson Jimmy. "I ain't that much of a fool to believe that kind of rot."

"All right," said Winton.

"He'll be down here with his gang, then. And you're one of his men?"

"Oh, no. I'm just the roustabout," said Winton.

Carson Jimmy grinned.

"I like 'em young, and I like 'em modest. Tell me, kid, can you sling a gun half as good as you can make your hands talk?"

"You mean, can I use a Colt?"

"That's all I mean to say."

"I don't know," said Ever. "I've only shot at a man once."

"Oh, only once, eh? Just beginnin' to pick up seeds, are you? Well, the point is, did you hit him?"

"Yes."

"So he stayed down?"

"So that he stopped shooting back, anyway."

Carson Jimmy laughed and twisted himself first to one side of the chair and then to the other.

"Something about you that I sort of take to, kid," said he.

"Thanks."

"The fact is," went on Jimmy, "I could always use a good man with my crowd—and I could take you in, maybe."

"You couldn't," answered Ever. "I stay where I am."

"Roustabouting, eh?"

"Yes, roustabouting."

The good nature faded out of the small, narrow face of Carson Jimmy.

"I'll tell you what I'll do," said he. "I'll make a deal with you for that stallion you ride around. I'll make you a deal for fifteen hundred flat. Don't tell me you'd be fool enough to turn me down on that. I'm a complete fool to make the bid. But I kind of like to think of a little runt like me sittin' up there on the back of that big whale —that big red whale! Fifteen hundred right on the nail, boy. You'll never get another offer like that!"

"It's too late," said Winton. "I've made my deal already. I can't give up that horse. I may need him, one of these days, to run away from you and your crowd."

Jimmy Carson stared—then broke into a hearty laugh.

"That's all right, too!" said he. "But get out of here, lad, before I change my mind about you. I'm good-natured now, but I can feel something comin' up inside me. Get along—and watch your step. Fargo and Buck may wanta talk to you before you get clear of town."

He crossed the floor with Winton.

"I'll watch my step, and thanks," said Ever.

"About Timberline—I'd welcome him down," said Carson Jimmy. "There ain't been any town marshals in Bentonville that have held down the job more'n a coupla days at a time. And besides, me and the boys need exercise."

"Timberline will be glad to hear that," said Ever.

He stepped out into the hall, waved his hand, and walked rapidly into its gloom.

At the next corner he almost ran into Dolly Gray, running up the steps. She paused and nodded to him.

"Did you put that lump on Fargo's jaw?" she asked. "Did you skin up big Buck Waters's face for him?"

"What's happened to them?" he asked vaguely.

"Well," said the girl, half smiling. "I don't suppose you know." She hurried past him and started down the hall, calling over her shoulder, "Getting any more uncles out of jail—Bill?"

He had headed toward the stairs, but now he stopped short and whirled around, to find that she had hardly taken three steps and was standing there poised, to look back at him.

"What's the idea of saying that?" he asked her.

"I went out to the stable to see that red horse," she said. "And I've seen the Red Pacer before, on the open range. Nobody ever forgets him—Bill."

She smiled faintly as she used the false name.

"You spotted me through the horse?" he asked.

"Of course. We get the newspapers even in Bentonville, though most people never read 'em. But one of the three men, after the jail-break, got away on the Red

Pacer. Other people will be recognizing you before long, if that's what you're asking."

"I don't know anything about a jail-break, no matter what horse I'm riding now."

"As far as I'm concerned," she said, "don't worry. I have a couple of uncles of my own that won't stand without tying. Besides, this place keeps me too busy to let me do much talking."

"Thanks," said he, and as he said it he looked deep into his future—for he thought he was seeing it in the green of her eyes. "Can you tell me where I'll find the town marshal?" he asked at last.

"In bed," she answered. "Down the street to the second corner on your left, second house on the left. If you want to call it a house. That's where he's trying to get well."

"Did Carson do that to him?"

"Nobody in Bentonville knows anything about it," she answered.

In the phrase that Carson Jimmy loved, he replied, "That's all right, too!"

And he went down the stairs and through the lobby to the street. Hardly ten steps were needed as he crossed that room, but he used his eyes enough to realize that he had become a marked man in town.

People turned their heads suddenly and stared at him; he felt their eyes. Stepping out onto the street, he remembered that, after all, the partitions in the Sentinel Hotel were not of the thickest.

He was a marked man. Being already marked, how long would it take Bentonville to learn about him all that the girl, for instance, knew? Perhaps it was simply that she had put things together more deftly than most. The red stallion had helped her, no doubt, to identify its rider. Perhaps that fellow who had seen him pass through the shaft of lamplight, the other night, had been able to identify both horse and rider.

With long strides, he went down the street in the direction the girl had indicated. The future would have to take care of itself. In the meantime, he must keep his wits about him. Two such men as Buck and Fargo represented a world of enmity. As he walked, he turned

his head now a little to this side, now a little to that.
Wonderful how wide a range the eye can cover, when a
man cares to use the very corners for purposes of obser-
vation. It was almost like having eyes in the back of his
head. And still, as he stepped along, he felt that the
murmur from the lobby of the hotel was following him.
He knew that two or three men had stopped and turned to
look at him with great curiosity.

He turned the corner to the left, and stopped at the
second house. It was a makeshift of tent-cloth, tin cans,
boxes, and logs, with a brush thatching for a roof. There
was at least a sort of door. He rapped at it and a woman's
voice called out:

"Who's there?"

"Friend," said Ever.

The door was pulled open a few inches, and he saw the
broad outlines of a woman's face in the shadow.

"Know this gent, Danny?" she remarked.

"Never seen him," said a weary voice.

"Came down to see you from Timberline," said Ever.

"Aw, let him in, Ma, will you?" said the man's voice.

The door was pulled wide open and, together with a
shaft of sunshine, he stepped into an irregularly shaped
room with a dirt floor. There was a cot in one corner,
upon which the wounded man was stretched. His face was
lost behind a cloud of unshaven red hair, so that it appeared swollen and nebulous. One had to search for his
features, except the eyes and the forehead.

"Who are you, and what's the crooked news from
Timberline?" asked the man on the cot.

29

"My name is Bill Smith," said Ever.

"Well, well, well!" murmured the deputy marshal.
"And all the time I was taking you to be John Jones!

Shows the way that a man's memory'll go back on him. I'm Dan West. What you want with me, brother?"

"I'm from Timberline," said Winton. "He told me to come here and look up the town marshal."

"I'm all that's left of him," said Dan West.

"Don't be wastin' your strength makin' jokes, Danny," advised his wife, curtly. "They ain't funny, either."

"Timberline," went on Ever, "thought that there might be quite a crowd in the town, and that Carson Jimmy was likely to be the larger half of the crowd."

"Timberline is a bright feller," said the marshal. "What else does he think?"

"He wonders if you need a few deputies to quiet down the town? He'd like to be the first deputy himself."

The other shook his head.

"It's a mighty fine idea—mostly," he said, "but not here. Timberline's got a big name for himself by quietin' down some little circuses along the range, but he never ran into any circus like this here one. Never in his life. They'd get Timberline by the nape of the neck and pull him apart in no time."

"That would be his gamble," said Ever. "Do you want him in?"

"Want him in?" exclaimed Mrs. West. "Who would we better want in, I'd like to know? Guns are all that can talk to guns—and the cowardly, mankillin' hounds that fill up this town, beginnin' with Fargo and Jimmy Carson and—"

"You've said enough, Ma!" suggested her husband, gently.

She was instantly silent. She began to stare with some apprehension toward the visitor.

"That's all," said Ever. "If you'll have Timberline with you, he'll come."

"Mind you," said Town Marshal West, heaving himself suddenly up on one elbow, "I'll have him if the game goes straight. They tell some stories about him that ain't any fairy tales for the young, the way I remember 'em. Understand? I'll have him if he'll play straight with me!"

"Oh, he'll play straight as a string. The mopping up of

Mr. Carson Jimmy is what he's most interested in. So long, marshal!"

"So long—Bill Smith," said the marshal, grinning faintly.

Ever left the hovel and returned to the hotel stable.

It was late in the afternoon and there was not much of the daylight left to him.

But he judged that he could ride the stallion back to the mountain camp by midnight.

In the hotel stable he saddled the horse, led him out to water at the trough, bridled him, and mounted. A stable boy leaned on the edge of the trough and looked down at the reflection of the drinking horse and then up to the dusty reality.

"Say, chief," he remarked, "that ain't the Red Pacer, is it?" He spoke in a confidential murmur.

A little chill of apprehension ran up Everard Winton's spine. Two people in the town had spotted the horse already; how much was known about the rider? He merely answered:

"The Pacer's a man killer, isn't he, son? And this is a pet horse. So long!"

He waved and then sent the Pacer off, not at that smooth, ground-devouring gait which might be a tell-tale, but at a gallop.

Earlier on the morning of that same day, and a scant hour after Ever had started downward through the mountain mists, Clay Winton had come striding back into Timberline's camp with a long and weighty line of fish.

"Ever!" he sang out. "Oh, Ever! Give me a hand cleaning these—"

"Ever's out on a job for me," said Timberline.

"He's what?" snapped Winton, jerking back his head.

"He's out riding for me," repeated Timberline.

The fish slithered into a shining heap upon the pine needles, with a motion like that of life.

"Where'd you send him, Timber?" demanded the uncle.

"Why," said Timberline, "you know how it is, Clay. We can't have two bosses in any one camp. I mostly run this outfit to suit myself."

Big Al looked up with a satisfied but faint grin on his

face—satisfied because he enjoyed any prospect of trouble between others, and faint because he did not wish to call to himself the attention of either of these formidable men.

"You run any outfit okay—any outfit that'll have you for its boss—" suggested Winton, "but you don't run that boy down hill where you and me and the rest have gone, Timberline!"

"What I do with him is my own business," declared Timberline.

He was perfectly calm, and while he talked he continued to break up small brushwood, preparing it for the fire. It was dry, and fed in small bits it would make little or no smoke when they wished to cook.

"I guess the time's come," said Clay Winton finally.

"For what?" asked Timberline.

"It's you to run him to hell—or me to stop you," said Clay Winton.

"What are you talking about?"

Timberline dropped the brushwood from his hands and turned fairly about.

"You done me a good turn, Timber," said Clay Winton. "You helped me out of jail—and that was part of the price that bought in Ever."

"The kid?" said Timberline, a sudden sneer crossing and distorting his face. "Why, I picked him up for the price of a horse. He was cheap enough to come by."

He had been speaking gently before this, but now the devil jumped from his brain into his face and left him glaring, hunting the mischief that he would otherwise have avoided.

"He was cheap, was he?" said the uncle.

"I said it—cheap," said Timberline. "I say it again—cheap! Like all the Wintons—cheap—cheap—cheap! What about it?"

"What about it? Why, nothing much, except that one of us has to die right now, Timber." Quietly.

"Maybe. I'm ready, Clay. I'm sick of your damned mooning around about that kid. What is he, anyway? What about him? To hell with him—and with the rest of the Wintons! I'm sorry I put myself out to get him, but

131

now that I have him I'll keep him. I'll use him for the dirtiest jobs I know. Understand?"

"Why," said Clay Winton, "I understand perfectly. Are you ready to shoot, Timber?"

"I'm ready—and past ready."

"Just stand up and let a handkerchief drop for us, will you, Al?" said Clay, softly.

"How about it, chief?" asked Al.

"Sure. Do what he says," said Timberline. "If he gets me, you'll be kissing his foot, the same way you've been kissing mine. So you might as well do what he tells you to do."

Al, without protest against these insults, stood up and drew out a bandanna from his trousers pocket.

"Ready?" he asked.

"Ready!" the two answered.

"Wait just a minute.—Here's Garry," said Al. "He'd die if he didn't have a chance to see it. Hey, Garry—they're gonna have it out about the kid."

"*Hai!*" shouted Garry, and stood at the edge of the trees, frozen with excitement and joy.

"I count to three, and a little later I drop the bandanna," said Al, and a grin now convulsed his face. His eyes shone; his nostrils were dilated.

"All right," agreed the two.

They stood on the balls of their feet as though about to jump at one another; their arms hung loosely at their sides, though their hands were empty.

"One—two—three," counted Al.

The handkerchief fluttered down.

Before it had struck the ground, two guns exploded. Timberline's hat jumped from his head. Clay Winton spun around and dropped on his face.

30

WITH his left hand, Timberline brushed the hair on his head.

"Take a look at him, Al," said he.

"Better give him another slug, chief," suggested Al. "He nearly brained you with that one."

"He might have got me, if he'd tried for the body. But the Wintons always play the long chances," said Timberline. "Do what I tell you. Pick him up!"

But Clay was already turning and lifting himself, on one elbow. He sat up and faced Timberline.

"You'd better finish the job, Timber," said he. "If you don't, I'll do you in one of these days."

"That's all right—when the time comes," said Timberline. "Are you badly smashed?"

"Glanced off the ribs and up the left shoulder, that's all," said Clay.

"Look here, Winton, you're as good as dead, aren't you?"

"Yeah. I'm dead," said Clay, fearlessly regarding the gun in Timberline's hand.

"Then play dead when Ever comes back to camp, will you?" asked Timberline. "Keep your hands off him. I could tag you out and make sure of you now, but I don't like that sort of a game. Will you keep your hands off the boy when he comes here to camp?"

Clay hesitated. "Well, I'm as good as dead," he said, "and dead men don't talk. Only—Timberline, what's the line that you're wanting him to follow?"

"Nothing that I wouldn't do myself."

Clay made a wry face, but nodded.

"Beggars can't be choosers," said he. "I'll keep my hands off."

"You had a gun accident," remarked Timberline. "That'll be the story."

"That's it," agreed Winton. "I was cleaning a gun and forgot one chamber. I'm always warning him about that."

"You fan your gun. Does the kid do the same?" asked Timberline.

"He does the same—but he's a lot faster," said Clay Winton.

"And straighter?" asked Timberline, almost anxiously.

"No, not straighter," admitted Winton honestly. "But straight enough. Not every fool plays for the head."

"You're right," said Timberline. "Now let's have a look at that wound and try to patch it up."

All of this had happened before Ever returned to the camp that night. He rolled into his blankets, awakening in the morning without a hint that anything had gone wrong. His uncle he found propped up in blankets near the fire, looking haggard, and with a bandage wrapped around his left shoulder and arm.

"Hello, Uncle Clay!" he said quietly, for the others were not yet up. "What's happened?"

"Made a fool of myself cleaning a gun, that's all," said his uncle. "Remember what I've told you about bein' careful? Here's a lesson for me—an *old* fool. Don't you ever be a *young* fool, Ever."

"How did it happen?"

"Cleaning the gun, I tell you. Forgot one chamber. Don't ask me any more about it. I'm tired of thinking about it. The bullet scraped my ribs, and I'm lucky to be here talkin' to you. Give me a drink of water, Ever."

The others in the camp, at breakfast time, worked perfectly together in backing up the story of the cleaning accident. Al told a complicated yarn about a cousin of his and a tragedy he'd had with a shotgun while climbing through a fence. One leg was so damaged that it had to be cut off.

It was not till after breakfast that Timberline asked for Ever's report from Bentonville. Ever gave it to him briefly.

"I took a room in the hotel. It's still mine. I saw the girl. She's hard-boiled, but she's all right. She spotted the Pacer and me. It may have been guesswork.—I tried

134

to see Carson Jimmy, and he slammed the door in my face. But he'd seen the horse in the stable and he tried to get it out of me. That brought me back into his room. I had a fracas with a couple of his friends—Fargo and Buck Waters—and after they went out he was willing to talk. He wanted to buy the horse, but he couldn't have that. And then he said for you to go to the devil with your ideas. I went to see the town marshal next. He's in bed, laid up with a gunshot wound. He'll be glad to have you come in and talk business with him."

He paused.

"That's all?" asked Timberline.

"That's all."

"It's a good deal, for half a day's work or less. When did you get back here to camp?"

"Midnight."

Timberline's pleasure shone for an instant in his eyes.

"What happened with Fargo and Buck Waters?" he asked. "I know those fellows. Tthey're among Jimmy's best."

"We had a fracas," said Ever. "Carson told them to throw me out. I had the luck and stayed. He had Fargo carry Buck out of the room."

"Did he need to be carried?"

"He stumbled after I hit him, and the floor bumped his head and finished the job."

Timberline smiled again.

"What did you think of the day?"

Ever looked swiftly up to the sky and narrowed his eyes.

"The best day I've ever had in my life," he decided.

"You told Dolly Gray what I told you to tell her?"

"Yes."

"What did she say?"

"Nothing."

"Not a word?"

"No. It was just as though I had read something out of a newspaper."

Timberline no longer smiled.

"How did she look?" he inquired anxiously.

"Busy."

135

"Loosen up, Ever," said the leader. "Tell me some more about her."

Ever hesitated.

"There's nothing much to tell you," he said.

"Yes there is. Dolly Gray is always worth a little conversation."

Said Ever, "I'll tell you one thing—if you don't mind."

"Tell me anything you've got on your mind."

"The next time you've got a message for her, send somebody else."

"Why?"

"I'd rather talk to her about myself than about you."

Timberline started. Then, looking Ever up and down, he chuckled.

"You like her pretty well, eh?" said he.

"I like her too well," said Ever.

"It's all right," said Timberline. "We don't have to start shooting for her until she says the word. I haven't a label on her. She's not mine—just yet."

"She's a long way from that, it seemed to me," agreed Everard Winton.

"It seemed to you, did it?" asked Timberline rather sharply.

"That's what I thought."

"All right. Saddle the Pacer. We're starting for town right away—you and Al and I. Garry will stay up here with your uncle."

Timberline went over to Clay Winton as the others made their preparations.

"You heard him talk?" said he.

"Yes, I heard."

"Well, what did you think?"

"I thought he'd put ten years on his back in one day."

"He's grown up overnight," said the leader. "And he'll grow up a lot more before I've had him much longer. Whatever I make of him, he'll be a man."

"What sort of a man?" said his uncle. He sighed, and stirred in his blankets uneasily. He went on, "Now—when I'm needed as he never needed me before—I have to lie here like a fool! Listen to me, Timberline. Do your best by him. No Winton ever dies alone; he pulls down others with him!"

31

IT WAS late afternoon when they got to Bentonville and moved down the main street abreast. It was the sleepiest time of the day, and few people were in the street. But after they had passed along several blocks, Timberline said calmly to the men with him:

"That was Buck Waters' face in the second-story window, back there. He had one good look at us and faded. You don't need to be surprised, boys, if things start moving around here before long. We'll get to the town marshal as fast as we can."

Straight to the house of Marshal Danny West they went. Mrs. West actually grinned with pleasure when she saw Timberline.

"We kind of didn't believe the young feller, yesterday," said she. "But here you are as big as life, Timberline—and bigger, too. I never was gladder to see anybody in all my born days!"

She ushered the three into the room of the wounded man, and West looked them over with a somber eye of pleasure.

"It's straight, then, Timber, is it?" West demanded. "You gonna take a hand now in cleanin' up this place?"

"We're going to take a hand," agreed Timberline. "If you want us, that is."

"Am I a fool?" countered the other. "Of course I want you—and want you bad. Gonna be deputies? All three?"

"That's the idea, Danny."

"Good!" said the town marshal. "I'm glad to have you all. I hope you've got some more men, too, up your sleeve?"

"Why, Danny," said Timberline, "this isn't a war. It's only a town fight. Isn't that the idea?"

"You'll think it's a war before you're through with Carson Jimmy," said the marshal. "He's more poison than ever, and he's got all the thugs of Bentonville in the palm of his hand, I mean to say."

"They all follow him, eh?"

"They love his shadow on the ground, you'd think," said Danny West. "The little devil is faster and straighter with a gun than he ever was before, too."

"Is that what they say?"

"Well, I'm in bed, ain't I?"

"Did he do that to you?"

"Nobody but little Carson Jim himself! Oh, he's a beauty, he is. He could of killed me, but he didn't want to. As I lay there on the ground he says to me: 'I don't want to be killing any more fools like you, brother,' says he. 'You keep just enough alive to hold down the job and don't swear in any more deputies. I'm tired of killin' deputies.' That's what he says to me, damn him!"

"Have you sworn in any more lately?"

"There were four town marshals in three weeks," said West, dolefully. "I was the last. Nobody wants to be sworn in as acting marshal, with me laid up. They seem to be against it, somehow."

He made a wry face.

"Where's the book?" asked Timberline. "Swear us in, brother. And hand out the badges."

"There's only one thing," said the town marshal.

"What's that?"

"There's a sort of a whisper and a rumor goin around the town that Smith there, ain't Bill Smith at all. That he's young Everard Winton that the law wants so bad!"

"Why, Danny," said Timberline, "don't you believe that he's Bill Smith?"

"He's anything that you call him, Timber," said the other, chuckling. "Far as I'm concerned, he can be the devil—so long, as he takes a whack at Carson Jimmy for me. Only—they say that the county sheriff has heard about him callin' in Bentonville, and that the sheriff may

138

be headin' over this way. I dunno what it all means, and I don't care. I'm just tellin' you."

"Thanks," said Timberline. "We'll take care of ourselves. Now we want those badges, Danny."

It was a brief ceremony, and perhaps the words hardly lodged in the ears of any of the others as they did in Ever's mind as he found himself promising to uphold the law at the risk of his life, to enforce the commands of his superiors, and to be fearless in the performance of his duty.

Then the badges were distributed, and in each instance they were pinned inside the lapel of the coats.

When that was done, Timberline drew himself up with a sigh of relief. "Is that all, Danny?" said he.

"That's all," said the town marshal. "Timber, you know you're steppin' in as deep as your neck?"

"I've heard of Jimmy Carson for years," said Timberline. "Always heard good things about him—straight with a gun and crooked with his tongue. He's lied his way out of more tight places than any other man in the country. And where lying wouldn't do, he's shot his way through. Isn't that right?"

"That's right," said the marshal, shaking his head with a sigh.

"Very well, then. I wouldn't be anywhere in the world except right here in Bentonville, playing the game with him.—So long, Danny. Wish us luck!"

They went out in the blaze of the sunshine.

"Now, boys," said Timberline, "we've been spotted. There's no doubt about that. Jimmy Carson is ready. Buck has told him we're here. We've probably been shadowed to the marshal's shack, and Carson will know perfectly well what that means. We have our work cut out for us. We're three men, and he has thirty, probably. The town is afraid to stand out against him.

"That all means that you boys will have to watch yourselves. Carson is a spider that has sucked the blood out of bigger wasps than we are, and thrown the empty hulls out of his trap. Now, then, mind yourselves—and step lively!

"Al, you look into the Second Chance saloon, over

there. See what you see and listen to what you can hear. I'm going down there to the Bill Laforge saloon and do the same. Ever, you've got the worst job of the three. They may be gunning for us, back there at the hotel; but you go and try the trap and see what it's like. There's trouble in the air, so watch yourself. Guns will be gossiping before night, or I'm a liar. If you have to shoot, shoot to kill. You're an officer of the law just now."

He chuckled a little as he said this, and then turned and hurried off down the street, accompanied by Al, stepping large and long beside him.

Everard Winton went back to the hotel. He did not need the warning of his leader that every step he made in the town was highly dangerous now. And as he rode along he kept turning his eyes a little from side to side, as he had learned to do the day before. If danger came at him undetected, it would have to spring from the very ground at his feet, he felt.

One block was protected from the sun by what appeared like a semi-arcade; that is, the roofs of the buildings extended over the sidewalk like an awning, and made a dim tunnel of shade. The very brilliance of the day made that shadow all the deeper.

To sharpen his nerves the more, Ever was aware of many eyes resting keenly upon him. From every side, men were walking more rapidly to keep up with him, or were slowing down to see him pass. It was the beginning of the gathering of a crowd.

Only in one place was there quiet. That was in front of Dick Borrow's saloon and gambling house. Only a day or so before a brake had been discovered on Borrow's roulette wheel. And though the people of the West, and particularly those of a mining camp, are of a forgiving and a forgetting nature, it was too soon for them to forget that brake. They could surmise that the other gambling institutions were as crooked as this one of Borrow's; nevertheless they were keeping away from his place for the time being. As a result, Borrow had been forced to throw all the blame on his best dealer, fire the man publicly—and bribe him privately—and lower the price of his drinks. Business would return, but this was an

140

interim. Hence, in place of the usual roaring crowd at this time of the day, there was only a group of a dozen or so in Borrow's when one of the lot, clad in a short cotton dustcoat, disengaged himself from the others and looked for an instant thoughtfully toward the back door of the place.

At that back door another man had appeared for an instant, waved an arm, and disappeared.

He of the dustcoat set his teeth, after the single look backward, and then he glanced toward the rather lofty tent roof, as though for further confirmation. That roof was one of Borrow's main attractions, for the height of the ceiling promised a superior coolness.

Shrugging his shoulders, the man in the dustcoat walked straight to the swinging doors, thrust them open. He stepped out and quickly to the side. Straight before him was the Red Pacer.

Tossing his coat open, the fellow whipped a sawed-off shotgun to his shoulder and leveled it to fire.

It was quickly done, but from the instant he stepped through the saloon door, he had been spotted by Ever, and no shotgun can be maneuvered with the speed of a revolver.

As the dustcoat was thrown open, revealing the shotgun hanging by an ample leather noose from the stranger's neck, Ever west for his Colt, jerked it from the spring slip beneath his left arm, and fired, hip high.

Both barrels of the shotgun roared in reply. The double charge sang in the air, high above Ever's head, and the gunman turned with a yelp of pain and sprinted back through the swinging door, peeling off the dustcoat as he ran through the doors. His frightened cry rang behind him.

To have gone after him on foot would have been the natural thing—if one cared to chase a poisonous rat such as he into his underground den—but Ever did not dismount. Instead, he turned the stallion and sent him plunging in pursuit. Under the awning they shot, and lying out along the side of the horse, his arm stretched well to the front, beyond the head of the stallion, Ever dashed open the swinging doors. The Pacer lowered his crest, and into the saloon itself they ran!

He of the shotgun had dodged through the group of men inside and started at a reasonable pace for the back entrance. The yell of the others told him that something extraordinary had happened.

Turning his head, he saw the monstrous apparition of the Pacer and its rider, heard the wooden floor giving up thunder as the armed hoofs struck it, and whirling again, with a screech, he flew for his life.

But he was far too slow to escape that red thunderbolt. The shadow of the danger fell upon him. He turned with a wild cry, a knife in his hand and his face contorted with desperation. Ever laid the barrel of his Colt along the other's head, shot past him, and dropped to the floor as he checked his stallion. Then he returned to his quarry.

The whole business had taken perhaps four seconds, and the staring men in the saloon merely had a glimpse of a very scared man being lifted in strong arms and flung rudely over the saddle, after which the Pacer, carrying that senseless burden, was led out to the street.

The crowd was gathering fast. Strange things had happened in Bentonville before this, but none quite so strange as a horseman pursuing a criminal into a saloon.

Half the crowd rushed into Borrow's place to make sure of what had happened inside, and they were shown by the delighted Borrow the marks of the hoofs on the floor, and the long, black grooves and splintered places where the stallion had checked his rush.

The other half closely surrounded Ever on his way to the jail with his victim.

The bullet from the revolver had creased the latter's shoulder muscles, that was all; and the blood ran slowly down, drop by drop, into the dust of the road.

Not until they reached the little, squat façade of the jail did the wounded man recover his senses; and then only to be walked into captivity.

The jailer opened the door an inch, with a gun in his free hand.

"What's this?" he growled.

For three times that jail had been rushed, before this

day, and various had been the schemes for getting the front door open.

"This," said Ever, in a voice that some of the crowd would remember all the rest of their days, "this is a snake that bites in the dark. It's a poison snake. Got a place for it in here?"

"Who are you, anyway?" asked the jailer.

"I?—Oh. I'm Deputy Town Marshal Bill Smith," said Ever, "and here's my badge."

The jailer gazed, blinked, and thrust the door wide. The prisoner entered. And a loud cheer roared upward from the throats of those in the street. Perhaps a full half of them were rascals as black as one could meet in a year's hunt, but no matter what their profession, they had to applaud law and order when it arrived in Bentonville in such a form as this.

They scattered slowly, talking in small groups as they went off. It seemed, in fact, that a new day might be dawning for the town.

32

EVER remained at the jail long enough to hear the name of the prisoner he had brought in. It was Sidney Williams. The jailer already knew him and said to him grimly:

"You been due for a tumble for a long time, brother, and now you gone and collected it. Maybe you'll stay put for a while."

Sid Williams was a pale-eyed blond whose lack of color made him seem quite featureless, but there was plenty of expression in the sneering smile with which he heard this.

"Lemme tell you something, guy," said he to the jailer. "I got people behind me. I'll be out of here in a coupla days. And when I am out—" here he turned savagely on

Winton—"I'm gonna have your scalp. You hear me talk?"

"When you get out," said Ever slowly, "you tell your friend Carson that I'm after him with both hands and no gloves."

He left the jail and went to the stable behind the hotel.

The little freckle-faced stable boy came running out at the sight of the horse and the rider.

"Hullo, Mr. Winton!" he called.

Ever tapped him on the shoulder as he dismounted. "My name's Bill Smith," he insisted.

The boy grinned.

"Sure it is," said he. "Your name is anything that you want to make it, around here. That sneak of a no-good Sid Williams—jimminy but I'm glad that you slammed him!"

Ever went into the hotel. Twenty or thirty loud voices were instantly stilled, and twenty or thirty pairs of eyes focused upon him. A tremor of self-consciousness came over him and then departed. He went to the desk, got the key for his room, disregarding the broad and welcoming smile of Shorty.

"Where's Dolly Gray?" he asked.

"She's back in her office," said Shorty. "Go and rap."

Ever did as he was told.

"Come in," called the girl.

He entered and shut the door swiftly behind him, stepping away from it. Bullets can be fired through the thin panel of a wooden door almost as effectively as through the open air.

"Hello," said he. "Shorty told me to come and give the door a rap."

She tilted back in her chair and folded her hands behind her head, as she had done once before.

"Hello, Everard Winton," she said.

"My name's Bill Smith," he insisted.

"Is it?" said she without smiling.

Her glance wandered slowly over him.

"Your name is going to be Dead Man in a few hours, if you want to know what I think."

"They're after me," said he. "I know that. They nearly tagged me a few minutes ago."

144

"Then what brought you here, where they can lay hands on you?" she asked. "Got another message from Timber?"

"When I give you another message," said he, "it will be from myself, not from Timberline."

Her green eyes remained entirely grave.

"I won't ask you what you mean by that," she said.

"I wish you would," said he.

"How old are you, Everard?" she asked.

"I'm old enough to know the color of your eyes," said he.

"That doesn't mean anything," she answered. "How old are you in years?"

"I'm on the bright side of thirty, still," said he.

"You're on the bright side of twenty," she suggested.

"You're a mile wrong," said he. "I'm a ton older than you think. What about yourself?"

"A girl is always ten years older than a man," said she.

"You think you're gray-headed, because you're running this little hotel," said he.

"You think you're grown up," she answered, "because you tagged that sneak of a Sid Williams and batted Fargo on the chin. Is that it?"

"I'm old enough for you, Dolly," said he.

"You're only a baby!" she told him. "But I like children," she added. "Sit down and rest your mind for a while. You look as though you'd been thinking quite a lot."

He did not take a chair. He went over to her and sat down on the edge of the table, watching her face closely.

"Does everybody in town think that I'm Winton?" he asked.

"Everybody knows it," said she.

"And the horse?" he asked.

"Everybody knows that it's the Red Pacer."

"The devil!" said he.

"It used to be a devil—they say you've tamed it."

"How thick is the air in town—for me?" he asked her.

"So thick that you'll choke in it if you stay here long."

"I'm a deputy town marshal."

"I've heard about that, too," she said.

"Great Scott!" murmured Ever. "Is every bit of news posted in this place the minute anything happens?"

"We have underground wires," replied the girl. "And it's not far from here to the jail. You showed your badge to a couple of hundred men."

He sighed and then frowned.

"I'm going up to my room," said he.

"Remember one thing," remarked the girl.

"What's that?"

"Outside of the town police, there's a county sheriff in this part of the world."

"Is there?"

"Yes."

"Has he been around?"

"You never can tell where he'll be. He generally comes where he's most wanted."

"*I* don't want him," said Winton.

"Sure you don't," she smiled. "But you've made yourself an outstanding case."

"How's that?"

"Well, fellows don't pry their uncles out of jail every day in the year."

"I wasn't alone there," said he. "All I did—"

He paused, with a deprecatory gesture.

Said the girl, "All you did was to shoot the jailer and then jump out through a hole in the wall. I know all that you did."

"Who's the popular boy you call the sheriff?" he asked.

"Rance McDonald is all he's called," said she.

She waited, as if sure of getting a strong reaction.

He shook his head.

"I never heard of him, Dolly," said he.

"I knew you were young," said she, "but I didn't think you were *that* young. Around this part of the world the kids learn about Rance McDonald before they know their A.B.C.'s"

"Study was always hard for me," he answered. "Well, I'm going upstairs. So long, Dolly."

"You'd better say good-by," she replied tartly. "I don't expect to see you again."

"Is Carson in?" he asked.

"You'd like to call on him, I suppose?" said she, staring.

"I might leave a card," said he.

"Don't be foolish," Dolly Gray pleaded. "You're a good hand, Everard, but you're not good enough to handle that glass of poison."

"Thanks." He went to the door.

"Leave Carson alone, will you?"

"Say 'please,' " said he, grinning.

"Oh, run along!" she replied. "You ought to be in kindergarten!"

He went out into the hall, looked swiftly and carefully about him—for guns might appear in the shadows of any corner—and then went up the stairs to his room.

He opened the door with care equal to that which he had used in climbing the stairs; and as he burst the door wide, he saw the form of a man seated in a chair.

A gun was in Ever's hand, instantly, as he sprang back. But then he saw that this was old Harry Lawson, his arms folded, his head lying over on one shoulder, sound asleep.

33

HE CLOSED the door and touched the shoulder of the Indian. Harry Lawson awakened.

"Hello, Harry," said Ever.

The Indian grunted, inclined his head forward on his chest, and went to sleep again.

Ever stepped to the window and looked out and down the street. He was spotted almost instantly by a dozen people. Hands were pointed towards him; a little crowd gathered.

Already he had become the object of so much interest to the people of the town! He smiled a little grimly as he turned back into the room.

"Hey, Harry!" he called loudly.

Harry Lawson started up from his chair with a revolver in his hand. His red-stained eyes blinked at Ever, then he caused the gun to disappear in his clothes again. He nodded at Ever.

"Pretty hungry," he declared.

"All right," said Ever, "and you'll have something to eat, too. What brought you into this part of the world, Harry?"

"I come take the Red Pacer," said the Indian.

"Oh, do you?" murmured Ever.

He stared at the strange, square face of Harry Lawson. The latter nodded. He was not smiling.

"You see, Harry," said Ever, "I still want the Pacer."

"Pretty soon you die," said Lawson. "I take the Pacer." He was quite unmoved in saying this.

"What makes you think I'm going to die, Harry?" asked Ever. "I've no intention of dying."

Lawson shrugged his shoulders.

"Pretty soon you die," said he. "I take the Pacer." Then he added, "Now we eat?"

Ever had his back toward the door. As he turned toward it, it swung soundlessly open, and in the dimness, against the hall twilight, he saw a man standing, covering him with a firmly held revolver. After the speeches of Lawson, it was too pat— like a sudden effect in a melodrama. He was about to die, said Lawson, and instantly the man with the gun appeared, as though to explain the manner in which death would come.

"Just hoist your hands, kid," said the newcomer. "You, too, Lawson."

Lawson did not "hoist" his hands. Instead, he drew back against the wall, his face unperturbed, as though to signify by his withdrawal that he was outside this case and not involved in the fate of Everard Winton in any way. The stranger paid no more attention to him; he merely watched the gradual rise of Winton's hands. Breast-high—shoulder-high. There they paused and fluttered and seemed to fight against being lifted further. But finally they were up to the top of his head. And all the while his grim eyes kept drilling into the face of the gunman. The latter said:

"I'm McDonald, the sheriff. I'm arresting you in the name of the law. I reckon you know what for."

He stepped inside the room, hooked the door shut with a backward swing of his heel, and then gradually advanced on Winton.

Slowly Ever said, "You'd better stand where you are, McDonald, till you tell me what you want me for."

"Don't make a fool of yourself, kid," said the sheriff hastily. "I've got you covered. Don't make no funny move. I don't wanta tag you with no lead, but if you make me shoot, I'll blow you in two."

"Stop where you are," said Ever. "Or you can have your chance to start shooting right now!"

The sheriff paused, both amazed and angry.

"What's the matter with you?" he snarled.

He was a true son of the desert—lean, leather-skinned, the outer fringes of his hair sun-faded to white. Like the birds and the animals of the desert, there was nothing to him but skin, sinew, and bone.

"What's the matter with you?" he repeated, with irritation. "You don't think you can burglarize a jail and let loose a crook and shoot up the jailers and get by with it, do you? Turn your back to me, kid, and then shell out a coupla guns and drop 'em on the floor. I'm gonna give you a chance to be decent—but if you won't take things easy, then take 'em hard. And be damned to you!"

He stepped forward again.

"One more step and the music starts!" said Ever.

The sheriff halted in the middle of the small, hard-woven grass mat that covered the center of the floor.

"You think you're gonna get away with anything?" he asked.

"I'm not trying to get away with anything," Ever said. "I'm just trying to make up my mind."

"About what?"

"Whether I want to spend twenty years in jail—or finish things off right now."

The sheriff obviously tightened his grip on the handle of his gun.

"Kid," he said, "I'd sure hate to drill you, but I've got an idea that you're gonna make me!"

"Maybe," said Ever, his lips barely parting to speak, so hard set was his jaw. "Twenty years of shade doesn't appeal to me. I think I'd rather take it now."

"Who said twenty years?" demanded the sheriff, his voice suddenly changing. "Look here, kid, I'm gonna be rated a skunk if I come in here and shoot you up. The boys'll say that I done it out of meanness. They won't believe that anybody'd prefer being planted in the ground to being planted in prison for a while. But who said twenty years? It ain't gonna be that long. They'll let you off with the smallest they can give. You never done anything wrong before. And what you done wrong was for the sake of your uncle. Why, the whole range votes for you, son. Maybe a couple years—maybe only six months in the can, and the governor'll pardon you out—if he wants to get elected for another term in this here state!"

He spoke gently, rapidly, persuasively, as he put forward these arguments. Ever's hands had lowered until they were resting lightly, now, on the lapels of his coat.

"Get those hands up!" commanded the sheriff, in quite a different voice.

Ever shook his head, slightly, but decisively.

"I won't wear irons!" he said.

Fine, bright sweat stood out all over the sheriff's face.

"Who said anything about irons, kid?" he demanded. "Gimme your word to do what I say and go where I say, and I'll trust you. I'll trust you as free as the air. I know that you're a Winton. Only, for God's sake don't murder yourself by makin' me pull the trigger of this gun! Don't make no mistake. I ain't the kind that misses a mark—not at this here distance."

"So you're going to let me be arrested—without wearing the irons?" Ever asked.

"That's what I said, and that's what I mean."

Ever sighed.

"I'd like to give in," said he, "only—there's something inside of me that won't let me!"

"Kid, you talk like a fool!" snapped the sheriff.

"Maybe I do. Maybe I *am* a fool! I'm not acting this

150

way because I want to. It's only because I *have* to. Pull that trigger, McDonald, or take a step forward, and I'll go for my own gun. I can't give up like a cur before I'm beaten!"

The sheriff looked at him with real agony in his face.

"Why," he muttered, "God A'mighty, settin' right on His throne, wouldn't know what to do in a pinch like this. You fool of a half-witted worthless brat, you!" he finished by crying at Winton. "I'm gonna—"

His speech was cut off at this point.

Behind those red-stained eyes, Harry Lawson had slowly been evolving a thought. He looked down at the rug and up again at the sheriff. Now he leaned over, rolled the edge of the rug until it made a comfortable handhold, and jerked back and up with his whole weight. The rug shot to the side and the sheriff sat down with jarring force on the naked floor. The gun spun out of his grasp and slithered away until it came to rest before Winton's feet.

Ever's own revolver was already out. And the sheriff, giving his head a shake to clear it, scowled at Harry Lawson.

"*You'll* get twenty years for this, you damned half-breed!" he said.

"Maybe so," said Lawson, unimpressed.

The sheriff rose to his feet. He dusted his hands, and his face was pale.

"You've won this here trick, kid," said he. "I was a fool that I didn't drill you the minute you started actin' up."

Winton nodded. He was as grave and as pale as the sheriff.

"Sit down," the boy invited, "and we'd better talk it over."

As he spoke, he put away his own weapon and picked up that of the sheriff, passing it to him, handle first.

The sheriff, a wild gleam in his eye, gripped the recovered weapon as if he were receiving back his damaged honor, made as bright and famous as ever before. Then his face went scarlet.

"I'll sit down," he said. "Doggone me if I don't *need* to sit down. You got me beat, kid!"

Harry Lawson stepped up and held out his hand.

"Gimme money, Ever," said he. "I wanta eat."

A ten-dollar bill was placed in his hand. He left the room at once, with McDonald's eyes rolling rather wildly after him.

"That fool of a breed has his nerve, ain't he?" asked the sheriff.

"He saved my skin for me," answered Everard Winton. "I thought he was a bad luck prophet, a regular buzzard. But he's turned into a friend in the pinch. Sheriff, let's see if we can't make a deal."

"What's in his head?" asked the sheriff.

"I don't know—not exactly," said Ever. "He doesn't know himself, I suppose. But he owned the Red Pacer and now he seems to think that he owns me. He seems to take it that the Red Pacer is going to carry me to hell; and it appears that he wants to get the horse back before I land in the middle of the big fire. Something like that must be in his head. You can't figure out exactly what Indian brains are thinking about."

34

THE SHERIFF took out tobacco and brown wheat-straw papers. He tore out one of the papers, scowled at Ever, snapped the little case shut with violence, rolled his cigarette with a liberal strewing of the thin, golden flakes over the floor, licked the paper to secure it, and lighted his smoke.

He had not spoken during the whole of this operation.

"You've been and made a fool out of me, Winton," said he. "You and that Indian, damn him!"

He sent up vast volumes of smoke; the coal at the end of the cigarette was red hot and half an inch long.

"I didn't make a fool out of you," said Ever. "I hadn't

planned anything. I was getting ready to eat lead when Harry Lawson turned the trick for me. I don't know that you're really so sorry about it."

"You don't know?" said Rance McDonald, his staring eyes filled with fury. "When I come into this hotel, I still got the name of being a man. I walk out again and I got the name of bein' a half-faced bluff that can't take a trick from a twenty-year-old kid!"

"Does anybody know that you came here to arrest me?" asked Ever.

"Why, I come in the back way, not advertisin' myself. Maybe I wasn't see comin' in. But I'll be seen comin' out."

"Well, then," said Ever, "you haven't seen me. That's all. You've been hunting around in the hotel all this time, trying to spot my room."

"How d'you mean that?" asked the sheriff.

"I mean what I say. You step out of here with me in front of you. I run down the stairs like mad. I flash through the lobby as though wolves were at my heels. I get my horse and ride."

"What does that mean?"

"It means that I've seen you and run for it as fast as I could go."

The sheriff frowned, then smiled.

"That'd save my face," said he.

"There's no reason why it shouldn't be saved," said Ever. "Any other man, in your boots, would have dropped me with a slug of lead long before Harry made his little play."

"The Indian has probably started telling the world about what happened, long before this," said the sheriff, darkening once more.

"Lawson never talks," said Ever. "He never says a word, particularly about what he's done with his own hands."

"I'd like to believe that," murmured Rance McDonald, more and more soothed by what he heard.

"You can believe it like the Bible."

"Then I'd better step out," said the sheriff, rising. "Winton, I'm thanking you for this decent break; and I'm sorry that I'll have to keep on your trail."

"That's the fortune of war," said the boy. "But I wonder, McDonald, why you don't go out after fellows like Carson Jimmy, instead of taking after game like me first."

"Carson Jimmy?" echoed the sheriff, with a start. "Jimmy Carson? Lord love you! There's nothing in the world that I want so much as to take a fair crack at him. But it's hard to get anything against him. He's on the watch. He's a fox—always. I know that he's got his hand in every dirty game in Bentonville, don't I? But I can't get at him. I can't bring it home. He's surrounded by a ring of thugs a mile deep. You can't wade through 'em."

"He's trying for my scalp now," said Ever.

"Is he?"

"Yes. A fellow named Sid Williams took a shot at me with a riot gun, a minute ago. I got hold of him and he's in the jail now. If you put pressure on him, he might talk a little about his boss, don't you think?"

"No," said the sheriff. "I don't think so. There ain't much of a chance of that. He knows that if he talks, he'll be loaded full of lead, later on, by some of Jimmy's men. Even if we catch Jimmy in the meantime. It ain't any use trying to pump the men in Carson's dirty crew. They stick by their chief. They have to! If they let go of him, they'll be drowned in lead!"

He shook his head.

"It's no go!" he declared. "Did Carson send that fellow after you?"

"He did. There's no doubt of that. Nobody else in town had a grudge against me."

"The cur!" said the sheriff, in disgust and in anger. "I'd give ten years off my life—the best ten—if I could lay hands on Carson!"

"Timberline's in town," said Ever, quietly. "He's a deputy marshal, now."

"I've heard that. Timberline's another I'd like to snag."

"Well, he doesn't shoot from behind," said Ever.

"Aye—and that's true. He keeps his hands pretty clean."

"He's here to get Carson, and Carson knows it. It's open war. Why not work on the side, then, and see what you can do? I'm in the game with Timberline."

"I'm sorry to hear it."

154

"So am I—in a way. But that's how I stand. I'm for Timberline—and I'm for the law and for you. That may sound strange, but I mean it."

"Where's your uncle?" asked the sheriff suddenly.

"You don't want me to answer that," said Ever.

The sheriff flushed. "I wasn't pumpin' you," said he. "I wouldn't of used the news even if you'd told it to me. I was just wonderin'. Listen to me!"

"Yes?"

"Perhaps we can play this game together. And if you can hang anything on Carson, I'm the man to go after him. I'll get him or die tryin'—if there's anything to get him for."

Ever nodded.

"That sounds good to me," said he. "I'll try to work up something on Carson, then you and Timberline can try to bag him. And after that?"

"After that," said the sheriff, "if you help put that poison Jimmy Carson in the bag for us, we'll see what's what. But I'll still be sheriff, and I'll still have to hunt a wanted man."

Everard Winton stood up.

"I'll go down the hall," he said, "on tiptoe. Then down stairs as fast as I can get through 'em and across the lobby so that people can see me and around the hotel to the stable. I'll jump my horse without a saddle."

"I understand," said the sheriff. "I'm to start right after you?"

"You're only three steps behind me. But crossing the lobby, you stumble into something. Give me ten seconds' head start, and I'll ride out the back door of the barn and slide away. You can ride after me as hard as you want— I'll be on the Red Pacer."

His head went back with a smile.

The sheriff nodded.

"I run you out of town and shoot some lead into the air," said he. "That makes a good show for me. And you running like a rabbit instead of fighting like a wolf— that's not so easy for you!"

"I can stand that. After I'm gone, suppose that you

see Timberline and have a chat with him. He'll be at the hotel before long."

"This here Timberline," frowned the sheriff, "is a tough hombre, but he's a straight shooter. You think I could talk to him on the up and up?"

"I think you could," said Ever. "All he wants is trouble with Carson Jimmy."

He settled his hat on his head, held out his hand, and gripped that of the sheriff.

"Thanks, kid!" said the sheriff.

"Thanks, sheriff!" said Ever, and straightway left the room.

The sheriff, standing at the door, watched him to the head of the stairs. Then he lurched in pursuit, with a sudden shout. He fired a bullet straight before him. It shattered the window at the other end of the hall.

Down the hall, down the stairs, he rushed and into the lobby, which was already filled with a swirl of men, all crying out in great excitement.

He gave his shoulder to the first fellow in his way, stumbled, sprawled, and was on his feet again, shouting, "Stop that man—in the name of the law!"

But not a single soul moved from the lobby to join the pursuit, a fact of which Bentonville, in days to come, was exceedingly proud!

Out from the hotel the sheriff darted, crying, "Where'd he go? Where'd that jackrabbit jump to?"

A staring youngster pointed toward the barn. Of to the stable sprinted the sheriff as hard at he could go, the naked revolver still ready in his hand.

He had gained the front door of the barn when the rear sliding door slammed open and through it went a red flash into the sunlight. A rider sloped well forward, sitting without a saddle on the shining stallion.

Right onward through the barn, past the heels of stalled horses, ran the sheriff, and out into the open, firing as he went. But he saw the Red Pacer already well out of gunshot, pouring over the ground with that wonderfully fluid gait which set him apart from other horses.

Great was the pretended rage and disappointment of

the sheriff; and half a minute later, mounted on his horse, he dashed off in pursuit.

All of Bentonville was not standing still, however. Half a dozen well-mounted men had suddenly appeared, as though drawn by the noise of guns. They joined in that pursuit, making the situation far more serious than the sheriff had intended. One of them was the dark-faced Fargo, now pale with a savage eagerness. And all the rest, as the sheriff could very well guess, were Jimmy Carson's men. It was not for the sake of the law that they would be riding on this dangerous quest!

Twice the posse saw the fugitive in the upper valley. Again, nearly a mile away, the sun gave a red blink on the form of a horse that was scaling a slope to the right.

Then the posse gave up and returned slowly, disappointed, toward the town. Said Fargo, on the way: "Sheriff, he's worth your while catchin', that kid. I know a gent has put up five thousand reward on him!"

35

EVER had been driven so high into the mountains that it was hardly a step to pass on to Timberline's old camp. He left the Pacer near it, and before leaving the big horse, squeezed the animal's nostrils firmly together. That warning would keep him from whinnying for a long time.

Then Ever went on quietly through the thick gloom of the trees until he came out into the clearing, reddened by the sunset light. There was no fire burning now, but that was not altogether strange. It was odd, however, that the lean-to that had been put up for shelter from the weather should have disappeared. No, yonder were the ruins of it.

He stepped out into the clearing with a frown. Something was wrong. The sense of it came more and more heavily upon him, and he felt that hidden eyes were watching him.

He was right. Turning quickly, he saw to the left a hideous face that glared at him with eyes that had little seeing in them. It was Garry, lashed with his back to a tree, swaddled like a mummy in long wrappings of rope.

Ever had him free with two touches of a knife; he had to catch Garry in his arms as the body fell nervelessly forward.

On the ground Garry lay, gasping slowly, staring with swollen eyes in a swollen face at the sky above him. His mouth was open. His breath came in a little, ragged fluttering sound that gradually grew stronger and more prolonged.

"Where's my uncle?" demanded Ever.

Garry, finally, was able to answer, but he only choked out, "Don't—leave me—kid!"

The other sat down cross-legged beside him and gripped his hand reassuringly.

"I won't leave you, Garry," he said. "I'll stick by you."

"My God! My God!" breathed Garry. "They tied me so's I could just barely get wind into my lungs. They tied me so's I was slowly chokin' here—hours and hours—"

He held up a hand to shut away the horror of that experience.

"Who do it?" asked the boy.

"Carson Jimmy. Nobody else would have that much devil in him."

"Was Jimmy here, himself?"

"Yes, Jimmy was here," said Garry, "I seen him. Why, he was the one that wound the rope around me. He wanted me to tell where he could find Timberline. He wanted me to bait a trap for Timber. I wouldn't do that. So he said that he'd leave me here to ripen till I fell. He knew I'd choke before very long. I been there, inside the rope, tryin to make my breathin' small —and small I kept it—and then a craziness would come over me and I'd try to haul in a breath. I'd try so hard that the ropes bruised all the flesh above my ribs. But I never could drag in a big breath. My chest was all squashed in by the pull of the rope. There was no give in it.

"I seen that I was dyin' the worst death in the world. Then you come, kid, an' I blessed God. But when you come out from the trees you wouldn't look at me. I thought you sure would pass on without seein' me. I put my eyes onto you. I willed you to look at me—and thank God, you done it!"

He recovered so much, suddenly, that he was able to sit up, propped on his elbows. His body shook; his voice quavered, also; but he was rapidly regaining control of himself. His eyes no longer thrust out from his face so horribly.

"Now, what about Uncle Clay?" asked Ever.

"Him?" said Garry. "They put him on a hoss and took him off."

Ever leaped up.

"Took him where?" he asked.

"God knows! I don't," said Garry. "They started off that way. It's too dark for trailin' under the trees, now. They took him—"

Back toward Bentonville went Ever like a homing pigeon, taking every short cut. Through the gloom of the long evening and through the darkness that followed, the Red Pacer went on with a wonderful surety of foot and an instinct for the way that no man-raised horse ever could have had. In just such a manner he had made marches by night in those days when men were hunting him hard. So he had gone over a range of mountains, leaving their snow peaks glimmering behind him under the stars while he dropped into an unknown valley.

Tirelessly he went, and brought his rider once more behind the town and to the rear of the hotel.

With the night, Bentonville had opened its throat and was celebrating, as usual. The jigging rhythm of dance music kept a tremble in the air and now and then some one yelled or a chorus of shouts burst out as joy overflowed the throats of a group of celebrants. There was an underlying hum of humanity that was like the noise of bees or wasps.

Ever found the lighted window of Dolly Gray's office,

159

and looked in over the lower sill. She was sitting at her desk with her head pillowed in her folded arms.

He took off his boots, tied them together, hung them about his neck, and climbed inside. From somewhere in the darkness that window might be watched, but he would have to take far greater risks than this, no doubt, before the night was over.

He drew down the window shade, stepped to the girl, and saw that she was sleeping. A half-written letter to her father was partially covered by one hand, to mark the point where weariness had overcome her.

"Dolly!" he whispered.

She lifted her head, frowned, shrugged her shoulders, and then seemed to be in perfect mastery of herself, once more.

"You *want* 'em to get hold of you, don't you?" said she, sarcastically. "You can't keep away from the net, can you, you poor fish?"

"Where's Timberline?" he asked. "Where is his room?"

"Walk right out to the lobby and ask Shorty to show you up," said she.

He shook his head.

"You know that I can't do that—now," said he.

"Why not?" asked the girl. "A little thing like a reward on your head doesn't matter, does it? That makes the game all the sweeter, eh?"

"You're talking like a wife before we're even married, Dolly," said he, with a little chuckle. "But that doesn't matter."

"You get out of Bentonville and stay out!" said the girl, almost sharply. "They're after you like starved wolves, and they'll never leave the trail till they get you—the sheriff and Carson Jimmy. Either one of 'em would be enough, by himself!"

"What room is Timberline in?" he repeated.

She started to renew her protest. Then she made a gesture as of one casting away all concern about a subject.

"He's in the same room that Carson used to have."

"Not sharing it with Carson Jimmy, though?"

"I asked Jimmy Carson to leave the hotel," she said.

"Sorry to spoil your business like that, Dolly," said he.

160

"Is there any way I can get up to that room without being seen?"

"No. Not unless you climb up to the roof from the back yard and climb down from the front eaves to the window!"

He narrowed his eyes at her.

"Is that the only way?" he demanded.

"That's the only way," said she.

"Well," answered Ever, "that way will have to do, then. So long, Dolly."

He stepped to the window.

"Wait a minute! You're not crazy enough to try it, are you?" She stood between him and the window. "Go on," she urged, "and tell me that you won't try to kill yourself in a fool way like that."

His face turned suddenly gray and long, grim lines were cut into it by his emotion.

"Carson's picked up my uncle—Clay Winton," he said. "He's grabbed him and run him off. He left another man strangling in ropes. You understand?"

She stepped back from the window.

"I understand," she said. "I understand—and I'd give my boots to help!"

Her face was as stern as his now.

"You can't help just now," he told her. "But later on, when I've got time, I want to talk to you about something."

"You'll be in your grave before you'll have any spare time," she assured him.

"I'll tell you now, then," said he. "You're grand, Dolly! You're the pick of the lot. If ever I'm out of the shadow of the law, I'm going to try to marry you."

"You haven't a chance," said the girl. "They're going to murder you. You're asking them for it, every day. So I don't mind telling you that you're the only man in the world that I give a rap about. I'm burned up about you —a silly, romantic kid!"

"That's all right, too," said he. "But I'll get older. So long, Dolly."

"You might kiss me good-bye, at least," said she.

"I won't touch you," said he. "Not while I'm in the

shadow of the law. If ever I'm free of that—my God, we'll be happy!"

He raised the shade, dropped through the window to the ground, and turned down the side of the building. She did not watch him go. He saw the shade drawn suddenly down again.

He found that all of his nerves were trembling and jumping. They had always been steady enough before, but now they were terribly uneasy. He was sorry now that he had spoken to the girl. Better to have stolen room by room through the hotel to find Timberline.

He found a drain pipe running up at the farther corner of the building. A man climbing up that would make an ideal target, even against the dim rays of light that struggled back here from the windows of the street. But he put his hands and knees and feet to work. It was a tough job, but he could climb a rope, and a rope was a far harder business than a pipe, after all.

He got to the upper eaves, gripped them, and then used the trick that Clay Winton had taught him, long before, of swinging his body once to the side, violently, and in the still more violent backward swing, of throwing himself up and over the edge of the eaves.

He lay on his side, looking down into the murky well of the night and taking his breath deeply. He remained like this until he was breathing easily, then he resumed his work.

The whole top of the roof was unsafe, the shakes which covered it having been carelessly put on. Many of them slipped dangerously under his weight. He had to sprawl his body out almost flat and move like a wriggling seal. But at length he came to the front eaves, and lay there, prone.

A pair of riders galloped up the street, whooping. A golden, dim shaft of light struck across them. They passed on, the acrid scent of the dust they had raised rising gradually up to Ever's nostrils.

He thrust his head over the eaves. Below him and just to the right was a lighted window which must be Timberline's room, now that the great Carson Jimmy had been expelled from it. But more than the light that glowed

162

from it, he saw just outside it the crouched figure of a man, between the sill and the drainage pipe that ran down from the roof!

36

IT WAS as if his eye were a ray of light, disturbing the eavesdropper. For instantly the man stood up, grasped the pipe, and swarmed rapidly but noiselessly up it. Ever drew back a little, crouching, tense with readiness. It would be a dreadfully uncertain battleground, this slanting roof of the hotel, covered with loose shakes; but it might be that this man climbing up through the darkness was the man he wanted most of all!

So Ever strained his eyes as the climber came over the edge of the roof with catlike sureness. He could make out no features, but something about the shape of the head and the smallness and agility of the body made him certain that this was the very man—Carson Jimmy!

The next instant that slender body was hurled with a sidewise spin at him; the feet struck him heavily in the breast and knocked him clean over the edge of the roof. Only his left hand hooked over the lip of the gutter, and the shock was greeted with an ominous tearing sound, as though nails were pulling loose.

His right hand joined the left. He swung himself strongly to the side, in the pendulous motion that would bring him to the top of the roof. Then a grinding weight stamped down on the fingers of his left hand. That was Carson Jimmy's heel, striving to make him loose his hold.

But already he was on the backward swing, and now he rolled over the edge of the gutter and reached for the smaller man's legs. They evaded him, and he lurched to his feet and saw that Carson was sprinting fearlessly

163

across the rattling shakes of the roof—already almost at the farther side of it. Now he dipped over the edge so suddenly that it seemed he must have jumped down into the thin air.

Carson was gone from his very finger, as it were! And that left him a slight margin to work on; every second would have to be used.

He dropped over the eaves again, gripped the drain pipe, and a moment later was on the sill of the window below, a dizzy position, with the street still so far beneath him that a fall to it certainly would mean broken bones.

But inside the open window, he saw Timberline in the act of shaking hands and saying good-bye to the sheriff.

Ever stepped into the room, and saw the eyes of the sheriff, who was at the door facing toward him, open widely, like the eyes of an amazed child.

"Look!" gasped Rance McDonald. Away from the lighted square of the window and whatever prying eyes might be watching from the street, Ever moved down the wall saying:

"I'm the second visitor you've had this evening, Timber."

Timberline had spun on one heel, bringing a gun instinctively into his hand. Now he remained with the weapon poised, gaping.

"Where the devil did you come from?" asked Timberline.

"From the roof. Give me a rag to tie up this hand."

He showed his hand, the blood dripping from it. Three of the fingers were torn and bruised.

Not Timberline but the sheriff stepped forward, drawing out a clean bandanna; and with expert speed he made the bandage, muttering softly to himself as he did it.

"How did you get that?" asked Timberline.

"Carson Jimmy's heel was on it, a minute ago," said Ever.

"The devil you say! Jimmy Carson?"

"Yes, on the roof. He was down here at the window, listening in. What scheme were you and McDonald cooking up? It's no good, whatever it was, because he heard

164

the whole yarn. I tried to nab him when he came up to the roof again, but it was like trying to handle a snake. Something kept him from using a gun, or I'd be a dead one, now, down in the dust of the street."

"A busy little bee, this fellow Winton," said Timberline to the sheriff, as the latter completed the bandaging. "What have you been up to since McDonald gave you the run?"

"I dropped in at your camp. Carson had been there before me. He got my uncle and took him away, and he left Garry tied so hard with a rope that he was choking to death. Garry's done up for a day or two. I couldn't trail my uncle at night. So I came back down here and found that Carson was already on the job again ahead of me. That's all."

" 'That's all!' " quoted Timberline. "Thank the Lord there's no more! What did Carson do to your uncle?"

"He'll murder him," said Ever, his face white. "Uncle Clay's a dead man now—or as good as dead. Timber—McDonald—have you any ideas?"

"Carson's out of the hotel," said the sheriff. "Dolly Gray asked him to move, after the play that was made at you from the door of the Borrow saloon. I tried to drag some information out of Sid Williams. I scared the rat, but not as much as Carson has him scared. I knew that I couldn't make him talk, and I was right. But Carson's moved headquarters out of town."

"Al's on the trail," said Timberline. "Al can follow a trail like a wolf through the dark—by the scent, you'd say. He'll be reporting any minute, I hope. When we know the hangout, we go for it—that's all—and try to round up the bunch of 'em."

"We've got one gain," said the sheriff. "We've something on Carson. He attacked Garry, your man. He grabbed your uncle, too, though that don't count."

"Why not?" asked Winton, grimly.

"Your uncle's wanted by the law. Jimmy Carson, he just up and grabs the man that's wanted for the fun of it, and starts takin' him to jail. But your uncle tries to make a break for it, and, sorry to say, they have to shoot him full of lead, understand? Your uncle don't count—

165

but Garry is evidence. I wish you'd brought him in with you!"

"I've got to get out of here, now," said Ever desperately. "Already they're laying for me around the hotel. But I'll take the stairs down."

"You can't do that!" said the sheriff. "Carson likely has some of his thugs planted in the lobby."

"The only way I see, outside of the stairs, is climbing down from a window; and by this time the crooks are watching the windows. I'm starting, Timber, what d'you want me to do?"

"If you can get out, you wildcat chunk of lightning," said Timberline, his eyes glimmering as he looked at Ever, "wait around the hotel. You know my signal whistle, don't you?"

"Yes, of course."

"When you hear that, come in. Al will be along before a great while, and he ought to know something. It's hard to throw him off a scent."

"So long!" said Ever and, disappearing through the door, he walked hastily down the hall toward the head of the stairs. He had spent many invaluable seconds in the room with the sheriff and Timberline; and Carson Jimmy's preparations would be electric in their speed, now that he knew his enemy was in the building.

Down the stairs Ever ran lightly, and stepped into the lobby, gun in hand. The shock of that sudden appearance brought a deep, quick grunt from a dozen throats.

"It's all right, boys," said he. "This gun is only a safe conduct for me, if you don't mind."

He saw the big form of Buck Waters draw back into a corner, as he went across the room.

"I see you, Buck," said he. "Don't try to tag me, or you'll be it for keeps."

A short, thick-shouldered form came out of a chair and went towards the door in front of him. That was Harry Lawson, the half-breed. He whirled, half way across the room, and went on toward the door, backing up rapidly, moving his head a little from side to side as he scanned every face.

Buck Waters, in the far corner had a face made ugly

by a fighting expression that was frozen on it; the other men looked more bewildered than hostile.

Ever gained the door, leaped sidewise into the dark of the veranda, and saw Harry Lawson running before him around the corner of the building. They paused beside the faintly gleaming form of the red stallion. Behind them the hotel was in an uproar, but no one ran into the backyard in pursuit. Harry Lawson said:

"You still alive, Ever? Pretty lucky boy! But I get the Red Pacer before long."

He chuckled, as Ever swung into the saddle. Then Harry Lawson caught his stirrup.

"You wait here," he said, and trotted off toward the door of the barn.

Wait there? It was almost as safe as to wait under a tree when a wasps' nest has fallen from the branch to the ground.

And yet something made Ever linger where he was, merely reining back the stallion so that they were more than half buried in the clump of shrubbery.

In the meantime, doors were slamming inside the hotel. Feet beat heavily on the front veranda. The hoofs of horses pounded in the main street, muffled by the thick layers of dust.

Harry Lawson returned, riding a small mustang.

"You come along," said he.

"Where?" asked Ever.

But he received no answer. At a dog trot, Lawson faded his mustang into the dark of the night, and an uncontrollable instinct made Ever follow. To be sure, he had promised to remain near the hotel, but he was drawn irresistibly after the strange little man of the desert.

THEY took the road down the valley, and twice, on the way, Ever strove to pump the half-breed. But he received only grunts in answer.

He was much troubled, not only because he had promised Timberline and the sheriff to remain near the hotel, but also because he could not be sure of the friendship of that oddity among men, white or red, Harry Lawson. It was true that the Indian had twice acted with most unexpected kindness and loyalty. It was also true that he might be willing to go to almost any degree of desperation to get the Red Pacer back into his own possession.

Finally, reining back the stallion beside the dim silhouette of Lawson on the trail, Ever said:

"You know, Harry, this horse is almost part of my flesh and blood, I'm so fond of him. But if you can help me get my uncle out of trouble—why, man, the Pacer goes back to you as sure as fate. Understand?"

"You shake hands?" asked the voice of Lawson.

Fumbling, Winton found the man's rough hand in the darkness, and gripped it.

"All right," said Harry Lawson, as their fingers parted.

The bargain was made and sealed, and Ever suddenly felt that he might be riding the great horse for the last time.

They traveled two or three miles from Bentonville—a distance hard to estimate because of the darkness and the winding of the trail. Then, turning to the side from the main trail, they worked through dense brush, and from this came out among lofty trees. These again gave place to what had once been a handsome clearing, but was now a growth of shrubbery, ten or a dozen years old. It filled up the space which the giants of the forest bordered. In the center of this space stood a house which, even by starlight, appeared to be bowed and broken by time. But from two windows gleamed light, as from two unevenly placed eyes.

"Is my uncle there?" he asked Lawson.

"I hold the hosses," said Lawson. "You go look."

He dismounted as he spoke, and took the reins when Ever sprang down to the ground.

"If you hear guns, Harry," said Ever, "and I don't come out to you again right away, you'll know that you're free to take the horses back to Bentonville. The Pacer will belong to you then. In that case, you'd better find the sheriff and tell him exactly what has happened. Tell him I gave you the horse, and he'll believe you. If I don't see you again, good-bye, Harry. You've backed me up when I needed backing."

He held out his hand. Lawson sail calmly:

"You go along. Look what you see."

Ever patted the wet neck of the stallion, turned, and began to work his way carefully through the brush towards the lights.

Two figures strode suddenly toward him through the darkness. He sank to the ground.

"What's that?" muttered a voice.

And another answered, "Nothing. I didn't see nothing."

"I thought something moved out here."

"The wind in the brush, I guess."

"Yeah. I guess. Where d'you think you heard the voices?"

"Over yonder."

"It might be the chief comin' back."

"Yeah—and it mightn't. Rance McDonald is a smart man. So's Timberline. I guess they're both agin us, now."

"They might as well be agin the devil as agin Carson Jimmy."

"Yeah, and they'll find that out, too. Come on—and look sharp."

They moved ahead, at right angles to the spot where Ever had just left Harry Lawson.

He could breathe freely, now, but not too freely. For

he had just had a sufficient testimony of the care with which this house in the woods was guarded. He began to wonder how many men were working under the leadership of Carson Jimmy. The man's organization, it was said, was very flexible; but once a man had been employed by him he was subject to call again at any time. So, at need, a crowd could be made to spring out of the ground by the will of Carson Jimmy. And every one was a tried man.

Ever went carefully, feeling his way, making sure that no twig crackled under his foot fall as he came close to the first window. The shutters had been closed, but many of the slats had been broken out, and the whole affair sagged clumsily from the crumbling hinges.

He was about to look in through one of the gaps when an outbreak of gunshots came from the valley. But the noise died out in a second or two, and again silence covered the valley. It was cut by the whispering of the wind.

Inside the house voices began to rumble. Ever stepped closer to the broken shutters and saw a lantern standing on a table. By that light, moreover, he made out two men sitting up from their blankets, one blinking and one rubbing sleepy eyes. They were mere youngsters, though they were older in appearance because of a wealth of unshaven beard.

"What was that up the valley?" asked one.

"It wasn't up the valley. It was down," said the other.

"You're crazy! I heard it."

"I heard it too. You're a crazy loon."

"I gotta mind to sock you for that."

"You better bust your hand on a brick wall than on me," said the other.

"Aw, go back to sleep and shut up!"

They both settled down in their blankets again, one of them groaning at the hardness of the boards.

Ever passed on to the next window, and found this one unshuttered.

Inside a different scene met his eyes. On the hearth of a fireplace wood was burning with a cheerful crackling. Another lantern was pegged against a wall, and under it, a rifle lying across his knees, sat Fargo. At the center table a man in a blue flannel shirt, his sleeves rolled up to his elbows, was playing solitaire. His back was to the window, and therefore his face remained unseen.

But neither of these figures was of the first importance to Ever. What counted was the tall figure seated beside the fire, thoroughly secured, foot and hand, with strong ropes. For that man was Clay Winton! Once more the Indian had been mysteriously right.

Said the man in the blue shirt, "Lookit, Fargo."

"Look at what?" growled Fargo.

He lifted a hand, as he spoke, and softly massaged the purple bruise on the side of his chin.

"Look at what's the use of settin' over there when we might be havin' a game of seven-up."

"The chief told one of us to keep on guard."

"The chief ain't here."

"Somebody would tell him, though, if things wasn't done to his likin'."

"Yeah. A lot of lip is shot off around this camp," said the man wearing the flannel shirt.

"Get Jerry or Mike to play with you," suggested Fargo.

"Jerry and Mike is corked."

"Go on, Bud, and get Mike. Mike'll always wake up for cards—if they's any money in the game."

"Mike's dead to the world, too," said Bud. "He wouldn't play. They rode a long way to get here. What would the chief want so many men for? He's got a regular army."

"Why not?" asked Fargo. "Ain't Rance McDonald on the job, and Timberline?"

"Timberline is a mean card to play, all right," said Bud.

"He's a mean card to handle," agreed Fargo.

"Then there's the kid—young Winton—that they all talk about so much."

"Him? *I'll* handle him when the time comes," said Fargo angrily.

"Last time you met up, *he* done all the handling, didn't he?" asked Bud.

He turned. The watcher from the window could see

the big jowl of the man, wrinkled by a grin as he stared at Fargo's bruised jaw.

"He got in a lucky sock at me, that was all," said Fargo.

"Oh, was that all?"

"Yeah, I'm tellin' you!"

"All right," said Bud. "Leave it that way. He ain't any brother of mine. But how about it, Winton? Could your kid nephew handle Fargo in a level go?"

Clay Winton turned. "Ever could eat a couple dozen like Fargo," he said.

"You lie!" exclaimed Fargo, jumping to his feet. "There never was a Winton born that I couldn't lick!"

The prisoner regarded him with lackluster, indifferent eyes, and made no answer.

"A lot of fatheads is what the Wintons are," declared Fargo, his heat increasing. "But there'll be one less Winton before many hours, I reckon."

"Maybe you're right," said Clay.

"Unless you got sense and write the letter that he wants," went on Fargo.

Clay shook his head.

"Ever's life is about spoiled because of me, anyway," said he. "I ain't gonna be bait to any trap for him."

"Well, it don't make any difference," said Fargo. "The chief's got a specimen of your writin', and he'll forge the letter!"

"He can't fool Ever," said the uncle.

38

THERE was one way for Ever to deliver his uncle. With the muzzle of his revolver resting on the sill of the window, the boy meditated upon it. He could shoot down Fargo and Bud, leap through the window, cut his uncle's bonds and attempt to hold off the rush of Mike and Jerry from the next room. Even if they were disposed of, which might not be so easy, there would still be the two men outside the house to consider—perhaps more than two. He could not tell how completely the place was guarded.

But the primamry obstacle that confronted him at once was the important fact that he could not shoot down a human being in cold blood. Hardened rascals they both might be. But murder he could not do.

He turned and faded rapidly back into the brush until he stood beside the Indian and the two horses again.

"D'you hear me, Harry?" he murmured.

"Hush up—they're mighty near!" whispered Lawson.

Ever put his lips to the ear of the breed.

"Ride back to town—take both the horses with you. Find the sheriff. If you can't find him, find Timberline. Tell them they may need a dozen men. Bring 'em out here on the run, and make them soft-foot it into the house, yonder. They'll find plenty to do. Tell them my uncle's there. Tell them that six other men, at least, are on hand. Hurry, Harry! Ride like the devil as soon as you're out of earshot!"

The Indian tapped him once on the shoulder, as though to give silent notice that he understood, then he faded back into the trees, with the two horses. Ever stared after him until his eyes ached.

A moment later, the clatter of hoofs stopped on the trail; and presently there was the noise of a considerable body of horsemen breaking in through the underbrush toward the old abandoned clearing. Ever wondered if these new arrivals were connected with the outbreak of gunfire that he had heard not long before, and he hurried back with all the speed and the silence that he could manage, to the window he had just left.

He was in time to see a strange procession enter the room. There was Mike and Jerry, in the first place, coming blinking from their sleep, and then Timberline, held on the one side by Al, and on the other side by the great Jimmy Carson in person. Behind them hurried two more rough-looking fellows.

"Here's your friend Winton," said Carson to Timberline. "Winton, here's your friend Timberline."

He stood by, rubbing his hands together with great pleasure and surveying the two captives, while Timberline was forced into a chair and lashed to it firmly.

"Sorry to see you here, Timber," said Clay Winton.

"The luck's against me," said Timberline. "The luck —and one cur."

He nodded toward big Al. The latter, his face convulsed with anger, strode forward and leaned over the prisoner.

"You call me a cur, eh?" he said.

With the flat of his hand he struck Timberline heavily on the face.

The blow knocked Timberline's long hair awry, but he steadied himself instantly, and looked calmly on at the traitor.

"I wasn't good enough for you, eh?" sneered Al. "You wanted that kid, that Winton. That was what you wanted. Well, you got him, now, and you've got hell, too! He brung it on you. Lay to that—and remember it."

"I'll remember it," said Timberline.

"Back up, Al," said Carson Jimmy.

He advanced with his wonderfully quick, light step, and tapped the big man on the chest. His eyes were afire, though he kept his voice soft.

"You're new," said Jimmy Carson, "and you ain't used to the rules of my crowd yet or you'd know that you'd better jump off a cliff than to lift your hand on anybody around me, till I give the word. But that's all right— that's all right. You'll learn, Al."

"He sold you, eh?" asked Clay Winton.

"He sold me," agreed Timberline, looking with unutterable contempt at Al.

The latter bawled out, "I was tired of your damn highfalutin' ways. And the kid pleased you a lot more than gents that had worked for you for years and done your dirty work and got nothing but kicks all year round."

Timberline still fixed Al with his glance of disgust. He said:

"Clay, that fellow was about to be lynched by a crowd because he was accused of stealing a horse. I got him away from 'em. I've saved his neck since then, too; but I never expected that any human being could pay back such things with this sort of play. Still, he's not a man. He's a cur."

"I fooled you and you're sore," sneered Al, though his color had changed under this steady flow of contempt. "I was too smart for you."

"When he got to the right place on the road," said Timberline to Clay Winton, "he grabbed my arms from behind and Carson came at me. I got a gun out, but I was shooting blind. That was the clever trick that Al played. What did you pay him for it, Carson?"

"I paid him five hundred bucks and a chance to work for me afterwards," said Jimmy Carson. "You didn't cost me much, Timberline."

"You're not through with me yet," said Timberline, with amazing calm.

"No?" said Carson. Then he laughed and pulled out a gun. "I pull the trigger twice," said he, "and I beckon the souls of both of you down to hell. That's how I've got you, Timberline."

He added, to one of the men, "Bring in the sack of stuff. I want to show this rummy that the *whole* game is in my hands."

Out went a quick-stepping little fellow and came back with a tarpaulin sack under his arm, the sort of a bag that might be used for soft dunnage of any kind. He flopped it on the table.

"Your partner, Winton—he could tell you about what's in the sack and who it belongs to," said Carson Jimmy, grinning with delight.

Timberline stared at Winton, and Clay Winton nodded. He kept his voice calm, but his face was white and his haunted eyes were fixed on the tarpaulin bag.

"You know about the bank I stuck up in the old days?" he said. "The sheriff knows about it, anyway. Well, Timber, when I was up there in the camp with you, I was pretty worried about Ever. It seemed to me that I was the chief cause of dragging him to outlawry. It kept weighing on my mind."

He was silent, shaking his head a little.

175

Timberline said, "So you packed yourself across country from the camp, one day. You decided that you'd get what was left of the loot and turn it in to the law, and that when the bank found part of the stolen money back, it might not bear down on you very hard. And if you were back in the law-abiding ranks—well, then Ever would follow you down from the hills. Is that it?"

Clay Winton nodded.

"I hadn't spent very much of the stuff," he said. "I don't think I had much pleasure out of the loot I grabbed, anyway. How could I, when I was wondering most of the time what my brother and Ever would think of me if they ever found out that the cash I was spending was stolen money? It didn't cost me much to live at the ranch. I lay low. I kept to the family. If the bank president cracked open that bag, he wouldn't find very much missing from it. I only spent a few hundreds out of the whole wad."

"He'd give up the whole steal for the sake of his cracked nephew," sneered Carson Jimmy. "It shows the kind of a fool he is—the kind of foolishness that runs in the Winton blood. But when we grabbed Clay, we grabbed his money, too; and now the bank'll never see a penny of it. We've got better things to do with it. We got better ways of putting it back into circulation."

Such an exultation came over him that he literally raised himself to his toes with his laughter; and the sound was like that of a crowing rooster.

"Now, Timberline," he exclaimed finally, "you see I've got you in my hand? You see that the whole game is mine? Your game, and Clay Winton's game?"

"Far as you know," said the amazing Timberline, "a friend of mine may be standing outside that window, at this moment, covering you!"

Carson spun about on his heel, stared at the shattered window through which Ever was at that moment looking, and cursed.

"Kind of gave me a start, Timber," he admitted. "You're a cool devil, Timber, but you ain't cool enough to work on Jimmy Carson. You stood up in the world long enough to make a name for yourself, but you didn't

176

stand high enough. That's the trouble with you. I only needed to reach once, and I got you! I got you for keeps!"

He laughed again, as he spoke.

Then, stepping back and rubbing his skinny hands together, he added:

"Look 'em over, boys. There's two that stood up to me. You've seen what happens to 'em, every time? Here's two more to go the same way. If I only had Rance McDonald and the kid here, the picture would be pretty, wouldn't it? But they'll come next. I'll teach that damn sheriff to reach his hand into my pie!"

"Why, Jimmy," said Winton, speaking gently, "you ain't ever gonna get Rance McDonald. Don't you know that?"

"Why should I know that?" demanded the leader sharply.

"You wanta know why?"

"Yeah. I'd like to know why."

"Because he's a better man than you are, Jimmy. And because Ever is working with him. Oh, they'll have you in the bag before long!"

"Will they? Will they? Will they?" snarled the little man. "Why, I've made fools of 'em already."

"The way you did when the boy ran you off'n the roof of the hotel?" put in Timberline.

Carson Jimmy jumped inches clear of the floor.

"You lie!" he shouted.

"I don't lie," answered Timberline. "He ran you off the hotel roof and you know it."

"I kicked him over the edge of the gutter," screamed the great Carson, in a fury of mortified vanity. "I could of knocked him down into the street to break all the fool bones in his body."

Clay Winton lifted his head a little and laughed.

"You fools!" shouted Carson Jimmy. "I could of—"

"You didn't do it," broke in Timberline. "And that shows that you couldn't. There never was a dirty, cowardly murder that you could do, that you didn't do. You know that. Why not out with the truth?"

Carson Jimmy's rage made his entire body shake.

"I'm a coward, am I?" he whispered through his teeth.

"Why, you know you are, Carson," said Clay Winton, who had begun this badgering.

What it could lead to except the sudden death of those who were conducting the torment, Ever could not guess.

In the meantime, with an anxious mind, he was measuring the distance from this place to town. How long would it take Lawson to ride in; how long would it take the sheriff to gather the necessary men, and bring them out again?

"I know what I am, do I?" said Carson, grinding his teeth as he faced Clay Winton. "You *tell* me what I am, then!"

"Leave him be, chief," suggested Fargo. "He's just trying to rile you."

"Shut your damn mouth!" yelled Carson to Fargo.

He wheeled back upon Clay Winton.

"Go on and tell me, you. I wanta know what I am. You go on and tell me!"

Said Winton, "Why, you're just a dirty little crook— the whole world knows that. You *buy* your murders. You never killed a man in a fair, stand-up fight in your life. You prefer to bag 'em the way you bagged me and Timberline, yonder!"

39

A BUBBLING sound came out of Carson Jimmy's throat.

"You mean that?" he gasped at last.

"Mean it?" said Clay Winton, as though in surprise. "Why, all your men know that."

"You know that, Fargo?" snapped Carson.

Injured vanity had him more than half hysterical.

"He's pullin' your leg, chief," said Fargo. "He's pulling your leg, is all he's doin'."

"You're their pocketbook, that's all," said Clay Winton

to the leader. "But the whole world, it knows what kind of a little rat you are. You never faced a real man in your life."

Carson almost choked with the extent of his fury.

"It's a sort of a joke," said Winton, "to be settin' here—people like me and Timberline, yonder. You know damned well, man, that you'd never dare to stand up to us in a fair fight—either one of us."

"Wouldn't I?" said Carson, his eyes turning green with insane fury. "I'll tell you what—I'll tell you what—"

He turned away from his prisoners and began to take rapid paces through the room, at the same time, it appeared, considering what he would do—how he would prove his manhood.

He paused, turned on his heel. And then, pointing his arm at Clay Winton, he shouted:

"Who met up with Budge Cracken and Lew Halliwell and blew 'em both to hell?"

"Why, man," said Winton, "do you claim that you done that?"

"Who else did? Who else did?" yelled Carson Jimmy.

"Why, everybody knows what happened to them," said Clay Winton.

He lolled his head back and laughed heartily.

"What're you laughin' at?" demanded the leader, stepping close, his terrible left hand working convulsively, as the watcher at the window had seen it work before.

For Carson seemed to be prolonging his own torment, almost as if he was enjoying the exquisite perfection of his rage.

"Laughin'?" said Clay Winton. "Why, I'm laughin' at you, you puffed up little fool of a skinny toad. I'm laughin' as you because that's all you're worth, is laughin' at. Everybody knows what happened to Cracken and Lew Halliwell."

"Does everybody know? Then you tell me what!"

"They got into a scrap with each other and Halliwell knifed Cracken and Cracken dropped, and shot Halliwell while he was lyin' on the ground."

"Damn you!" said Carson, through his grinding teeth. "That's a lie and you know it's a lie. I killed 'em both.

I run the knife into Cracken, and when Halliwell turned, hearin' the body fall, he was just in time to get a bullet between the eyes."

"You wouldn't have the nerve," said Clay Winton, "even to stab one man in the back and murder his pal as he turned around. You wouldn't have the nerve, Carson. You ain't a man. You're just a sneakin' poison snake. Poison is all you work with. There ain't the heart of a house cat in you. Why, the whole world knows that, Jimmy. Don't be a fool and try to bluff any more. Look around at your own men. They're all laughin' at you!"

Jimmy Carson flashed a glance around the room, and it was true that a smile was being hastily swallowed by all of his men. Not that they really doubted his fighting courage. Most of them had seen it demonstrated too many times. It was simply that they could not help enjoying the purple fury into which their famous leader was thrown by the taunting words of Winton.

So, as a matter of fact, Carson saw the disappearing smiles, and if he had been half insane with anger before, he was entirely mad now. He began to laugh in a way that curdled the blood.

"Say it to me once more," he entreated. "Say I ain't got the nerve to stand up to a fiightin' man."

"No. Everybody knows that," said Clay Winton.

"Would you call yourself a fightin' man?" snarled Carson.

"I'm a halfway fightin' man," declared Clay Winton.

"Would I stand up to you?"

"Of course not. Nobody would expect you to."

"Why, damn your yellow heart and lungs and liver!" gasped Carson Jimmy. "I'll stand up to you right now."

"Sure you will," agreed Winton, nodding his head amiably. "Sure you'll stand up to me, now. It's just your style—a fellow tied to a chair is just the way you want him. That's the way you've killed a good many before this day!"

"Set him loose!" commanded the strangled voice of Carson Jimmy.

"Hey, chief! You don't mean that!" exclaimed Fargo.

"Don't I?"

"You wouldn't want to turn his hands loose, would you?" said Fargo.

"You see, Jim," persisted Clay Winton, "all of your men know that you're a yellow cur. Even Fargo knows it. They only work for you because the pay in high. They'd work for a Chinaman, just the same."

"Fargo!" screamed Carson.

Fargo leaped to his feet as though a bullet had torn through his flesh.

"Yeah, chief?" he stammered.

"You hear me?"

"Yeah, I hear you."

"Then jump when I speak to you, you dog! Will you?"

Fargo stood half sullen and half frightened.

"Whatcha want?" he asked.

"I told you before!" yelled Carson Jimmy. "But it's true.—Winton's right. I ain't observed around here, no more. I'm treated like a halfwit boy. I ain't got any rights and no command. You all know better than I do. You damn blockhead! Cut Winton loose from that chair, you hear?"

All protest was checked by this savage outbreak. And the nephew, at the window, at last understood the tactics of his uncle, deep and dangerous as they were.

If it came to a fair fight, might he not win? Was there not a chance? And if he won, the instant that the leader fell would his gangsters really care to continue the fight for that fallen bloodhound, their master? It was very dubious, to say the least.

Even now their eyes were lighting hungrily and with sheer joy at the prospect of the fight that was opening before them.

Fargo, in the meantime, was untying the ropes.

"Cut them, damn you. Cut the ropes and turn him loose!" shouted Carson. "Because I wanta get at him!"

181

40

"Wait a minute," called Timberline. "I ought to have the first call in this."

"*You* want some of the same medicine, do you?" snarled Carson Jimmy.

"I want as much as I can get of it," said Timberline. "But you won't take me, Carson. You'd rather pick on a poor devil who's been shot already, and who's only half himself."

"Leave Winton be," said Carson Jimmy. "Let him go. Here's the best game of all; here's the great Timberline! Ain't the world heard plenty about him lately? Ain't we all been told about what a great man he is? Well, now we're gonna see!—Look here, Timberline!"

"Well?" said Timberline.

"You ain't been wounded, have you?" asked Carson.

"Not a scratch."

"You ain't out of condition in any way?"

"No—as soon as I work out the cramps that these ropes are putting in my arms."

"You'll have a chance to work 'em out," answered Carson. "You're gonna have every chance, the same as me. It's gonna be a square fight. I'll teach you who's your master, Timber."

In the meantime, urged by the angry command of their master, the men had liberated Timberline from the chair. Both he and Clay Winton were now free, hand and foot. But to Winton little attention was given. It had been his prolonged series of insults that had worked up Carson Jimmy to the point of frenzy, but it was Timberline who would do the fighting for them both.

What depended upon this contest Carson made clear. Timberline rubbed arms and wrists to restore the circulation which the grip of the ropes had checked. Carson said:

"Fargo, Al—all the rest of you boys—this is gonna be a fair, free, stand-up fight, understand?"

Fargo took it upon himself to answer that he understood perfectly.

"Well, then," said Carson, "if I drop, what d'you do?"

"Plaster the devil with lead!" said Fargo.

"That's what you call a fair fight, is it?" sneered Carson Jimmy. "Lemme tell you what you'll do, then, if I drop. You keep your hands off this gent, and you let him go. Is that straight? You understand that?"

Fargo exchanged glances with the others; they shrugged their shoulders.

"All right," said Fargo. "Anyway that you put it is the right way for all of us."

"Because," said Carson, "if I ain't the fastest and the straightest shot this side of hell, I ain't the man to lead you boys. You oughta foller Timberline—if he'll have you. I don't ask any favors. All I want is a fair crack at him. And if I drop, he's the king, as far as you're concerned."

Fargo nodded and grunted a few words which Ever could hardly understand.

Now he saw Carson actually place a Colt's revolver in Timberline's hand, saying: "Is that your medicine, Timber?"

"That's the gun you took from me," nodded Timberline.

He sat down on the edge of the table and broke the gun open; examined it carefully, spun the cylinders. It had no sights. The trigger had been filed away.

Carson produced a gun of exactly similar appearance and looked it over in the same way, although taking less time to the examination. Then he said:

"Fargo!"

"Yeah, chief?" answered Fargo.

"If I put Timberline down, whether I'm killed or not, it's up to you boys to finish him off. Take him easy and steady. Don't hurry him none. Let him die gradual, and taste it all the way down his throat. Understand?"

A sudden light flashed across Fargo's brutal face.

"I understand," said he, "Eh, Al?"

The latter was grinning also, and his eyes became fixed like the detestable eyes of a hungry wolf upon the face of the master he has betrayed.

"Ready?" snapped Carson.

"I'm ready," said Timberline.

"One minute," said Carson. "What about Winton, after this little scrap?"

"He goes the way with Timberline," said Fargo. "If Timber wins, Winton goes free with him. If Timber loses, Winton steps right along into the same hell with him. That suit you, Winton?"

Timberline broke in. "I'd rather do my fighting for myself. Let Winton handle himself."

"Any play that he makes is good enough to suit me," answered Winton.

"Then," said Carson, "it's all fixed. I'm gonna walk the pair of you into the hottest part of hell, Timberline. I'm gonna show you how much bluff there is in me. Clear away, there, all of you. Back up agin the wall. Timberline, any special way that you want this little song and dance run off?"

There was no doubt that Carson Jimmy's good humor was returning as he approached the moment of battle. Certainly the little man had no possible doubt concerning his skill or the outcome of the battle.

A grin began to flash on his face, appearing and disappearing suddenly. He was like one who knows a grim and soul-filling secret which involves the fates of many other men, but is a secret unknown to them.

The attitude of Timberline, on the other hand, was grave and sober. For once, the delight of battle seemed to have disappeared from him.

It was not shining in his eyes when he answered the last question by saying, "There's only one proper way to fight: stand back to back; some one counts five; at every count we take a step forward. At ten we turn and shoot; and—we pack the guns out of sight, and not in our hands."

"That'll be hard on me," sneered Carson. "Me, I'm so slow on the draw that it'll be mighty hard on me. You're a regular lightning flash, when it comes to getting a Colt out into action, ain't you?"

"I'm fast enough to beat you to the draw, Carson," said the larger and younger man. "And I'm going to kill you today, with a lot more pleasure than I ever had in any killing before this!"

Carson Jimmy laughed. He was fairly quivering with a savage eagerness.

"You're gonna put me out of the way, are you?"

"I am," said Timberline.

They were pictures of perfect self-confidence, and suddenly the explanation came home to Ever with awe, and a cold tightening around his heart. Here were two men who never had been matched, one because of his union of strength and dexterity, the other because of his uncanny craft of hand, which multiplied the force of a small body.

If ever a swift and silent prayer went up from a human heart, such a prayer rose now from Ever for the victory of Timberline. It was not only that his uncle's life and death depended upon the battle, but because Timberline himself had treated him with an odd degree of kindness and consideration. He had been exploited by the gunman, to be sure, but in a way that was bound to appeal to his pride. Was it not for his sake, for instance, that Timberline was now a prisoner in the hands of this deadly little reptile of a man?

He could not tell which appeared to him the more formidable—the tall dignity of Timberline, or the smaller, feline deadliness of Carson. But on the whole, since his hope was for Timberline, his fear was for him also. He made a larger target for a bullet, for one thing!

They stood back to back, in the center of the room. Timberline's face was beginning to shine; Carson's features were rapidly contorting and relaxing and contorting again, like those of a child engaged in the torture of some helpless creature.

"Ready?" snapped Carson.

Their hands were empty. They stood straight, as though measuring, and Timberline was almost a head taller than the other.

"Fargo!" exclaimed Carson Jimmy.

185

"Yeah, chief?" said Fargo, standing near.

"Got a gun?"

"Here it is."

"You stand there and count to five—while you count, you watch."

"I hear," said Fargo gravely.

"If either one of us tries to turn and shoot before the five is counted out, you plaster him with lead. Got that?"

"Yeah, I understand," said Fargo, thrusting out his jaw.

He smirked a little in his turn. It was perfectly plain that he would enjoy pumping lead into either of the great men, without favor.

The whole gang was enjoying the party. One man was leering with pleasure; a smile half brutal and half idiotic spread over the mouth of another; the features of Big Al were puckered up as though he himself were about to make the desperate effort; and yonder was Mike, looking down at the floor with a bowed head, as though the excitement had overmastered him and he dared not watch what was about to happen.

"Start countin'!" commanded Carson Jimmy.

"One!" shouted Fargo, some pent-up force in him making the word come with a roar.

The two took one step forward and paused, wavering a little to keep in perfect balance, as though the next instant they were to whirl and fire.

Then, steadily, rapidly, regularly, the count proceeded: "Two, three, four—five!"

They turned as though a single force had jerked at them. The guns in their hands flashed in low arcs. Timberline stood straight. Carson Jimmy had doubled over as he wheeled, and with one thunderclap the two guns exploded.

Timberline fell prone on the floor on his back, his arms cast wide, his gun rattling to a distance. Carson Jimmy remained in his crouch, his face tensed with brutal will to destroy. Slowly he relaxed with a horrible smile.

A carnival of yelling began among the gangsters.

"Take 'em both!" shouted Carson. "I've showed 'em who's the master. I've given 'em a fair chance for their lives, and now they're gonna get the hell that I promised 'em! Is he dead? Is Timber dead? I wish to heaven I had the sheriff and the kid here, too. I'd pass 'em through the same route! I'd trim 'em, one by one."

Fargo, on his knee beside the fallen man, suddenly looked up and exclaimed, "He ain't dead. He's alive! Your slug just ran astreak down the side of his head, that's all!"

And Timberline at that moment sat up, with blood streaming down one side of his face.

"That's the way I wanted it," said Jimmy Carson. "I knew that's the way it'd turn out. He's down, but he ain't dead. He's gonna die a lot slower than that. He's gonna die so's you boys can remember him and the way he passed out."

He added, shouting the words: "He's gonna die lookin' at me and knowing who his master is! Fargo!"

"Yeah?" said Fargo pleasantly.

"Grab him, will you? Grab him and tie him and we'll start the music on the pair of 'em, pronto!"

41

EVER came out of the trance which had held him so long. He had to do something, and he knew what. Shooting through the window would accomplish little good. Even if he succeeded in potting both Al and Carson Jimmy, there would be others remaining, and they would make short work of the two captives. What he had to do was to disrupt the meeting of the thugs and sweep them out of that cabin as a whirlwind swoops a mass of dry leaves. He knew how to do the thing, and felt that he had perhaps one chance in ten of succeeding.

He went around to the front of the shack. Half a dozen horses stood there at the racks. And as he glanced them over, he thought of the way the commanding head of the Red Pacer would have risen above the rest of those silhouettes. But the Red Pacer was not there. Harry Lawson had taken him back toward the town. Harry had received the horse as payment for services which still were in part unrendered. If only his way through the night were swift—if only he were pounding back on the return road with the sheriff beside him and a few picked men!

But Ever could not wait. He tried the front door and it yielded at once to his hand. As it opened a crack, he put his eye close and scanned the interior. There was a flood of lantern light which, to Ever, seemed brighter than the full light of the sun. But no one else was in the room, so he pushed the door open the rest of the way and closed it again behind him.

In the next room, he could hear Carson Jimmy saying, "Get those two ramrods and heat 'em up in the fire. I'm gonna show you gents that a ramrod can be used for cleanin' out something besides gun barrels! I'm gonna show you a whole lot of brand new ideas. I learned some of 'em while I was in China!"

As he talked, he let bursts of laughter spring from his lips.

Quick, snarling murmurs came from the other men. They were ready to be beasts, every one of them, it appeared.

Then as Ever was turning from the door, he saw a rapid shadow sweep toward the threshold of the other room, and he knew that one of Jimmy's pack was about to come in on him.

He whirled about and went back toward the wall.

"Hey, hello!" said the voice of a man, entering. "Who the devil are—"

"Hello, bo," said Ever, his back still turned.

And he took off his hat and hung it on a peg on the wall.

"I thought—" murmured the other.

But without completing what he had thought, he picked up something from a corner and hurried out again, the thing he carried clanking like an iron chain.

Ever took his hat off the wall again and paused a moment, drawing in deep breaths. For, while his back was turned to the stranger, he had literally felt the bullets tearing through his ribs, through his heart.

Now he crossed the room, so that he could look through the open door into the adjoining chamber. Timberline was the first to endure the music. They were tying him into a chair, half throttling him with a rope that ran around his throat. The full flare of the red firelight played in his face. But Timberline's eyes were wide and composed. He had thought of death often enough to confront it now unperturbably. Perhaps his calm would be shaken later on. Every devilishness that Carson could devise would be used to break him and make him howl for mercy.

Clay Winton was out of sight. The back of big Al was seen as he bent by the fire, adjusting something in it. One of the other men was on his knees, fanning the fire. And the light washed out from the hearth and receded as the fan passed rapidly back and forth.

On the table lay the bag of the stolen treasure. On the table stood two lanterns—and they were not in line! Even when Ever moved as far over as the room permitted, the lanterns were still out of line. A thin crack remained visible between them. Did that mean that he would have to fire two shots to plunge the room into darkness? Or if he placed one bullet with infinite exactness, might it not shatter both chimneys and extinguish both flames at the same time?

If so, there would remain only the crazy flicker and dance of the firelight. With that, however, he would have to take his chance.

He pulled a gun, leveled it with the nicest of aims, and fired. At the same time, with his left hand he snatched the lantern from the wall beside him and dashed it out. As he fired, he was leaning forward to run, and already he was springing forward when the bullet from his revolver smashed both the lantern chimneys to bits. The farther room was left vaguely awash with the jumping firelight, across which swayed the confused shadows of men running blindly here and there in a wild excitement.

Ever had spotted a big slicker lying across a chair near

the door. He caught it up as he ran, and bolting through the doorway, he cast the slicker straight into the fireplace. In its fall, it spread out its folds like the wings of a bird, so that the entire light of the fire was muffled. The whole room was lost in darkness.

Then Ever, springing to the table, caught the corner of the treasure bag at the first grasp of his hand.

But the sharp, ringing voice of Carson Jimmy was cutting through the air like bullets, "Ever! It's the Winton kid! Block the windows. Block the door! Get the money sack—"

Ever, wrenching on the sack, found that another grasp was already on it. He struck out with the barrel of his gun, and heard it ring on something hard. He heard a gasp, and the bag came away in his hand.

Then a lunging form struck him and knocked him to the floor. It had been but an accidental collision. The other, rolling headlong, was cursing as he scrambled to his feet again. Some one reached for the slicker that momentarily muffled the fire, and snatched his burned hand away again with a yell of pain.

There had been one dim flicker of light, however, and it was enough to show Ever that three men were swarming together in the doorway. But that was his only way out of the room, if he wished to make a quick exit, and so he went for it. He ran low, and then made a long, skimming dive.

There was an excellent chance that he might ram his head or shoulder against the jamb of the door. In fact, he struck his head against some one's shin bone with such force that he thought his skull was cracked.

Floundering bodies tumbled down on him. He crawled forward on hands and knees, dragging the bag with a corner of it gripped in his teeth. Then he was through that doorway and regaining his feet.

A hand gripped his shoulder.

"I've got him!" yelled a voice at his ear.

He dropped to his knees again with such suddenness that the blow which had been aimed at his head glanced harmlessly off the side of his skull, and his pursuers tumbled headlong over him.

Then he was on his feet again, running, reaching for the door. Luck aided him there, for his hand found the latch. He snatched the door open.

The star-spotted sky seemed to Ever to be brighter than a bonfire as he leaped across the threshold into the night. A gun cracked; two more roared behind him. He heard a double load of buckshot crash through the wall above his head. A bullet nipped the lobe of his ear.

Then he crashed the door shut behind him and made for the horses. The first horse would have to be the best horse and the right horse, in a pinch like this.

He put away his revolver and snatched out his knife as he ran. One sweep of the blade severed the lead rope by which the mustang was tied, and the wild little beast was already spinning away when Ever leaped for it.

His right hand caught in the mane. The mustang, beginning to spring away, took Ever vaulting forward with immense bounds. But he managed to swing the treasure bag over the saddle seat. The next instant he was in the air and had hooked one foot in front of the cantle.

So, like a springing panther, he clawed that fleeing beast in the darkness and managed to clamber onto its back.

The branches of trees were sweeping perilously close to his head, by this time. But he got hold of the reins, and with a mighty pull bent the chin of the little horse back toward its chest. Not even a mustang can pitch or bolt when his neck is cramped in.

He was able, then, to guide the horse off to the right, until he came out of the trees onto the blessed hardness of the open road.

But two disasters faced him at once. The first was a pyramid of fire that was trembling in the east, sure sign that the moon was about to rise. The second was a dark rush of horsemen down the road toward him.

He straightened out the mustang on the road toward town. Harry Lawson and the sheriff with his posse should be on the way, now, riding hard to get at the shack in the woods. Unless, perhaps, Harry had simply taken the

Red Pacer and gone his way, content. That doubt sank the heart of Ever like a stone in water.

He had something else to think about, a moment later. Fast and true his mustang was legging it down the way toward town, but the beat of hoofs behind was momentarily drawing nearer, and now the voice of Carson Jimmy was screaming through the air like the whistle of a hawk:

"We've got him! He's gone! He's gone!"

Ever looked back.

It was not easy to make out the forms of the riders, obscured as they were against the darkness of the trees on both sides of the road, but he saw fire flying under the hoofs of the leader, and then he was able to see a small figure on a lofty mount. Carson Jimmy. No one else would be so small, and no one else would ride so like a bunched-up ape. Carson Jimmy was already in the lead.

The road swept around a turn, and the long way opened straight toward the pale, distant glimmering of the lights of the town. But Ever knew that he could not reach them, now. Faster horses were behind him. Oh, for the Red Pacer, to pick up and snatch him away from fear on wings! Compared with the immense river of the stallion's strength, this little mustang was a bobbing, jumping, foolish rivulet.

But if the horse could not save him, how could his wits serve?

Off to the left, the mountains rose jaggedly. Already their heads were illumined like clouds by the rising moon. The tops of the trees were glimmering with the pale light, also. Soon the whole countryside would be awash with that bright silver flood, and the pack could run him then by sight rather than by sound or chance.

He twisted to the left, nevertheless. That was his best chance. To get into the rough country and then to dodge away through the crooked, sharp-cut ravines.

He leaned over the mustang and called for the animal's best speed. But that speed was not enough. When he looked back, it seemed as though Carson Jimmy's horse was riderless, driving on ahead as though an invisible devil were on it. Only by a second glance could Ever see

192

the small body of the man perched in the saddle, twisting a little to the side.

He turned and fired—once, twice, again.

Yelling, mocking laughter answered him. Of course, riding at a full gallop, he could not fire with any accuracy, through such light as this.

A dense grove of trees opened before him. He drove his mustang at the fence of closely growing tree trunks as though they were a thin mist. He swung down low in the saddle, hooked his right foot behind the saddle, took a strong grasp at the mane with his right hand. The treasure bag he had already tied to some saddle strings. Now he could swing down from the back of the mustang, and be carried along like an Indian. He might be brushed off against a tree trunk, but he would not be brained by the sweep of branches close over the back of the horse.

That was how he entered the forest. And the tree trunks went past him with rapid, rushing sounds, like the strokes of fans in his face.

The trees thinned out. He pulled himself back into the saddle and struck off at a sharp angle to the left, again. Behind him he heard the distinct impact of some man who had come to grief—the horrible sound of flesh and breaking bones struck against some solid target—and a yell was choked and gone before it was half uttered.

Then he came out on the farther side of the trees, and saw no rider whatever near him.

42

THE CAÑON opened before Ever like a dark flume through which flowed the shadowy gold of safety. He rushd the tiring mustang down the little ravine, knowing that every instant gained now would be worth an hour hereafter.

But when he was deep in the throat of the gap he heard

193

the iron ring of hoofs down the passing, and turning, he saw by the increasing gleam of the moonlight the running of a great horse in pursuit, and the little, ape-like figure on the back of the monster. Jimmy Carson again—and well behind Jimmy came the horde with a sweep. As they entered the shadows of the pass, they brightened it with a wild yell that pierced the brain and the soul of Ever.

He could not shake them off with a headlong flight. That was clear. And so he rode like mad, now, taking the last strength of the mustang with spur and quirt. He took the first turn to the left again, right toward the face of the mountain. It was a sharp turn. The walls of the ravine shoaled away. He saw before him how the valley pinched out to nothing—there was only a jagged watercourse marked out on the side of the mountain above him. It came down like a fantastic ladder.

Ever untied the treasure sack as he rode, gripped it in one hand, swung free from the mustang, and hit the ground running. A vigorous slash from his quirt sent the weary little horse scampering down the first ravine that opened on the right. Ever flung himself into the shrubbery at the base of the cliff, waiting, drawing his breath hard.

The rout of the pursuit came into view instantly, the little monkey form crouched on the big racer, and then others speeding frantically to catch up with their master. Al, riding with a bold confidence, Ever particularly marked. And the sight of him brought back into his mind the thought of the two prisoners in the distant shack. Surely Carson had left in such haste that he had not ordered their execution. He would not cheat himself of seeing their slow suffering until they were dead. He must, surely, have appointed one or two guards as he went off to chastise Ever.

So hope grew stronger in the heart of Ever as he saw the last of the riders swing out of view. They had come so close to him that the reek of sweating horseflesh was now in the air.

He started to climb, in haste. The way was easy enough for him now. In a number of places the water had gouged away the rock very deeply. In others, the groove was more shallow, and he was in constant danger of slipping from his hold. From a safe coign, he looked down and saw the pursuit scattered through the ravines below him, half in shadow, half gleaming in the moonlight. They went rapidly here and there, searching. They had his abandoned horse, now. And how long would it be before they stopped hunting among the crevices and the holes in the ground and looked up toward the ragged face of the cliff?

When he started to climb again, he gained height rapidly. The work was more and more difficult, but as he gained a position near the brink of the cliff, pausing with both hands occupied and the treasure sack hanging from his teeth, he looked down again and saw a whole body of riders sweeping past the base of the cliff to the left. In a moment they were out of sight.

At that distance, they seemed far too small to be worthy of his attention. Then, as he hauled himself up on the brow of the cliff, he saw that he was on the great shoulder of the mountain, with scattering trees standing here and there, and an outcropping of big boulders that must have rolled down from the summit high above. He could see, on that upper slope, how timber ceased growing, and how the great snowcap glittered in the moonlight, like the pyramidal head of an iceberg afloat in the midnight sky. To his left the rocky ground rose rapidly. To his right it descended toward a narrow ravine that split the mountainside in two. Beyond the ravine, a bare sweep of rock and scattered stones went upward again.

He was safe. And in his safety, he groaned aloud with relief. It seemed right that he should be standing up here on the crown of the world, looking down on the small sections of the badlands beneath him.

Then he heard a strange sound rolling toward him. At first he thought it must be the thunder of an unseen storm approaching among the mountain heights. Then his ear told him it was the distant beating of horses' hoofs. The animals were being ridden up on his left.

He could understand at once. They had seen him from beneath, and one among them had known a horse trail they could follow up the height. Should he turn and try to climb down again as he had come?

No, they would soon be at the verge of the cliff, and then they could shoot him off the face of the rock at their leisure. Neither was there any safety for him among the scattering trees that extended above him toward the snow-line. There was only one hope, and that was a small one.

He turned and flew toward the ravine on his right, the sharpness of the slope giving gigantic length to his strides. As he ran, he saw the slender trunk of a dead tree lying beside the gap. The branches were broken away from it. It looked as though it must have been uprooted far up the slope, having been trimmed off by the force of its fall as it rolled down the rocks. Toward that tree he went.

The ravine's mouth was a good thirty feet across. The tree might measure ten feet more. If only he could throw it across the gap, it would serve him, rotten as the wood was, as some sort of bridge.

He grasped the base of the trunk and lifted. But his hands slid away from their hold, and the mass was not stirred. Then he sprang to the slender tip of the trunk, lifted this easily, and walked down toward the root, shoving up the weight with both hands. The burden grew monstrous as he proceeded. Finally, he could no longer endure the pressure on his arms. He had to get his shoulder under the trunk and inch along, bit by bit, thrusting the wavering tip of the tree higher and higher against the moon-lit sky. And so, at last, the weight eased, suddenly.

He looked up and saw the top of the tree swing through a rapid arc. It was upright, then it whipped forward, while he guided the fall with all the straining power in his body.

Right across the ravine fell the trunk, with a crash of splintering wood. Somewhere in its length it was fractured; but he could not mark the exact spot of the break.

A yell, far behind him, struck cold terror through his heart, and as he turned, he saw the big, familiar silhouette of Al ride over the edge of the slope and come racing toward him with a wild Indian yell.

There was the possibility of missing. To miss his target now, meant to die horribly, a little later, in the hands of Jimmy Carson and his men. So Ever stood up straight, measured the distance with one glance, then whipped up his revolver and fired.

The horse ran straight on toward him, with Al leaning sidewise from the saddle—sidewise and toppling.

He struck the ground not ten yards from Ever, and rolled the rest of the way, his arms and legs flung loosely about, until he skidded to a halt at Ever's very feet. The mustang, managing to turn at the last instant, galloped furiously back up the slope.

Ever gave one glance at Al's torn, shattered, red-blurred face. Then he picked up the tarpaulin bag and hurled it far before him, across the gaping ravine.

He mounted the heavy trunk of the tree, changed his mind, and used a priceless second to jerk off his boots. Far away, sounds of yelling broke over the rim of the hill in a sudden shout that told him what he must do. There was no time to balance himself and creep forward step by step. He had to take that bridge on the run.

So he sprang forward as the bullets began to sing through the air. Under him some seventh sense showed him the white of the flying water, a hundred yards sheer down; the voice of the stream came up to him on a dolorous and mournful note.

He fairly flew over the narrow, rocking bridge. And it was well that he went at full speed, for suddenly the trunk of the tree gave under him with a sharp snapping sound. Only the speed of his going carried him over the breaking place in safety. Beneath him, now, there was the narrowing trunk as it approached the other brink. It seemed to him that he dared not look down; that his flying feet were finding their hold by instinct which would fail the next step and send him hurtling down into the abyss.

And then he made the last long leap and gained the safety of the ground beyond. Only as he leaned to snatch up the bag of money did he give a glance behind that showed him the tree, breaking now under its own weight, less than halfway across, and sagging down rapidly. He saw, in the same glance, the monkey-like form of little Carson Jimmy, rushing down the slope on his huge horse, firing as he came. All the rest of the riders were sweeping down the way.

The width of that ravine was only a stop-gap of a moment. The guns of the pursuit, once they were steadied, would soon pick off Ever as he ran, unless luck were with him.

He ran up that slope like a snipe, dodging this way and that to spoil the aim of the enemy. He ran with his head down and his feet flying furiously. And then it seemed as though a club were raised and that he heard the swish above his head. A violent blow struck the base of his skull; the face of the mountain slope rushed up against him, and the moonlit world twinkled once and went out.

43

THE very force with which he fell shocked Ever back to his senses. And the yells of Jimmy Carson's men helped him suddenly to his feet, with the tarpaulin bag slung across his shoulder. He had been flattened by the impact of a glancing bullet, that was all. But before he had taken three steps, a second shot smashed through the ribs on his right side.

As he toppled, he managed to throw himself behind the shelter of a projecting rock, where he lay curled up, his head down, such agony burning and trembling in him, like flame, that he was sure that this was death.

Blood soaked through his clothes. It began to trickle into the hollow of the rock, a sickening pool.

He pulled off his coat and his shirt, and every move filled his body with perfect anguish. He wanted to call out to the enemy that he surrendered, and that they could have the money bag, so that he might die in peace. But he knew that that was folly. He had made too much trouble for Carson Jimmy; and on the opposite slope lay the dead and battered body of big Al. They would contrive in some way to make him pay for this night's work, if he ventured to give up.

He could hear their voices as they called to one another, busily at work.

Ever struggled to make a bandage for himself. He had to use his left hand almost entirely, for his whole right side was almost paralyzed by the effects of the wound. He managed to cut up his shirt and his undershirt. The bandage was big and clumsy, but strong. And he had to use its strength, for the flow of the blood must be stopped.

He got hold of a shard of loose stone, a long and narrow splinter, and twisted this into the bandage to draw it tight. The pain that he had felt before was nothing, compared with this torment. He felt the broken ribs crush in under the pressure. His eyes bulged outward from his head as though the constriction had been about his forehead. But he had to keep twisting until the flow of the blood had been stopped. As for the fierce fire of pain, that would have to be endured. He might laugh at the memory of that, another day. But this was a different matter, this dribbling away of his blood. It was the loss of life itself, bit by bit.

Finally that leakage was stopped completely, though the grip of the bandage was so powerful that he could barely breathe; and with each breath that he drew, red swords of torment were thrust through and through his body.

When he had finished, he lay gasping. Every time he drew in his breath or expelled it, a sound formed in his throat and shuddered against his teeth. Nausea darkened his eyes.

But he looked out around the corner of the rock and saw the preparations that were going forward. The wits of the great Carson Jimmy had found the easy way to re-bridge the gaping mouth of the ravine. Already, his men had felled a pair of tall, slender saplings, and with their horses they had dragged the trees down to the verge of the cañon. Now they walked one of the trunks into the air and let it fall. And turning, they laid hands on the second to complete the bridge.

And Ever? Well, he had three bullets left in his revolver, and by shooting from a rest, even with his left hand, he ought to be able to hit a target at such point-blank range. Carson Jimmy—he was to be the mark for the gun.

In the meantime, surely Harry Lawson had brought the men of the law out to the shack. If, by the grace of good fortune, they were able to overcome the guards which had been left there by Carson before the latter butchered the prisoners, then both Timberline and Clay Winton would certainly urge the posse to hunt for Ever.

But how would they know the trail? What could possibly bring them over the twists and the changes of the route that Ever had followed? When he considered these difficulties, he accepted his fate. He might be able to kill Carson Jimmy. But he had better save his last shot to end his own life before he fell into the hands of the savages.

When he had made that calculation, he had two bullets to use. Carson Jimmy, the instant the second tree had fallen beside the first, making a narrow but perfectly safe bridge, stepped out upon it, his arms stretched out to the sides to help him balance.

And Ever, twisting himself to the side, steadied his revolver with his left hand. It seemed no hand at all, the weapon was so unfamiliar in the grasp of it. And with every pulse of his heart the agony shook the nerves of arm and hand.

But he drew a bead as well as he could, and then fired twice.

Carson Jimmy leaped backward from his bridge, and raced for cover. His whole party disappeared almost instantly, behind rocks and brush, and with a storm of lead they searched the rock which was Ever Winton's fort.

After a time, the firing ended. But still not one of the crew showed himself. What would they do? They could not guess, of course, that his ammunition had been reduced to a single bullet. They must have considered him as a helpless fugitive, lying behind the rock weltering in his blood, and rapidly dying. They had driven two bullets into him. They had seen him knocked down twice by their lead, and therefore they had reason to expect that the fight was smacked out of him.

So Ever managed to smile as he peered cautiously around the rock.

If only one of those two bullets had clipped through the body of Jimmy Carson! But the man had darted away as though there was nothing at all the matter with him.

The silence continued. Then voices rose in a sudden dispute. The cry of Jimmy Carson came piercingly above the wrangling:

"I'll shoot off the head of the dirty cur that tries to stop me. I'm going across and finish him—or he's gonna finish me!"

And Jimmy Carson appeared from behind a big boulder, vain hands reaching after him.

He stood up straight and walked straight down toward the narrow bridge that had been felled across the ravine. He held a Colt in his right hand. In his thin face the evil lips bared his teeth. And Ever knew, suddenly, that his aim had not been so wrong, after all. Death was already dealing with Carson Jimmy, but with the last of his life he was determined to close with the man who would soon be responsible for his death.

So he stepped out onto the frail little bridge and moved straight on until he came to the center of it. It seemed as though a strong wind struck him there, for his body swayed, suddenly. He put out his hands to save his balance; then his knees crumpled under his weight, and he lurched out to the side.

Even as he fell, the savage fighting instinct was uppermost in the little tiger. He fired one last shot that smashed right against the forehead of the rock that shielded Ever Winton. Then he dropped out of view.

One deep, hoarse shout came from his men. After that, they began to spread out. Ever could see them dodge from rock to rock, from tree to tree, extending themselves far out to the sides. He could understand the reason for this. The moon, climbing into the zenith, gave fairly good light for shooting, and the rifles of the men on the wings should be able to prevent Ever from showing himself at either side or above the rock that protected him. Under cover of that rifle fire, other men could cross the bridge and come hand to hand with the enemy.

It was a good plan. It was so good a plan, in fact, that Ever at that instant surrendered his last hope.

That was when he heard a louder trumpet than was ever blown in brass or iron—the neigh of the Red Pacer echoing from the top of the slope behind Carson Jimmy's men. Ever, venturing a single glance over his rock, had a fleeting glimpse of the great stallion on the brow of the hill, against the moonlit sky, and of a short, squat rider who held the Pacer on a lead and rode a smaller mustang.

Lawson? It could be no other person. And who else could have followed, by moonlight, such a trail? Was he the first, with others behind him? If there were more, they would be excellently situated on the brow of the slope for blowing Carson's men down into the ravine. But suppose it was the half-breed alone?

One glance had been all that Ever dared to venture, and even that brought three rifle bullets whining through the air close about his rock. He lay back, trembling with excited hope.

Only his sense of hearing could tell him what was going on. That was enough. He heard the crackling of rifles. He heard out of the distance a single weapon answering. As though Harry had taken shelter among the rocks and was fighting the gang single-handed.

Well, there could be only one ending to a battle where the odds were so vastly against Harry. Perhaps the Indian was keeping up the fight with the knowledge that more friends were constantly moving toward him from the rear, ready to take up the battle? No, out of the past Ever could remember all the dogged, bulldog determination of Harry, and from the first that strange desire of his to accomplish something for Ever and to save him from harm. Now he was alone on the brow of the hill, and he would stay there until he was shot down or until some miracle saved his protégé. Ever knew all this as certainly as if he had been able to look into the Indian's inmost mind.

And the Red Pacer was up there, too—perhaps with

the scent of his master blowing dimly to his nostrile? There was the engine that might pick up Ever and sweep him away from the danger, and thereby release Harry from his self-imposed task.

Ever, stretched out upon his back behind the boulder, sent the piercing signal whistle through the air, again and again. Then he waited.

There was an instant of pause, when all the guns were still, and then a yell of surprise from many throats, and the ringing of ironshod hoofs on the rocks.

Right up from behind his rock, forgetful of the danger, Ever rose to his knees and saw a sight worth dying for. It was the Red Pacer, shooting down the farther slope, swaying with speed, gathering momentum. Right at the ravine he aimed himself, then lifted from the farther side and hurtled through the air, with the reins tossing above his head, his mane flying, looking huger than life against the sky.

Harry was firing rapidly from the opposite slope, no doubt to hold the attention of the enemy and to interfere with their aim as they opened on Ever and the horse.

But here was the Pacer beside the rock, all at once, halting himself on skidding hoofs, snorting and shaking his magnificent head as Ever grasped the stirrup leather and drew himself up the animal's side. He flung his leg with a last effort over the saddle. And like a great, smooth-flowing stream, the Red Pacer swept away, with the angry bullets beginning to hum about him.

Ever lay stretched on the back of the horse, with the treasure sack dragging heavily down from his left hand. He gave one look to the rear as the Pacer carried him over the ridge to safety, and that look showed him a glimpse of Harry, scuttling away as fast as his little mustang would carry him.

There was life enough in Ever to tie the sack to the saddle strings and then to cut off the reins and bind himself to the stallion. For a touch of the hand or a spoken word would be guidance enough as he headed the horse for the town. Then he entered into an eternity composed of waves of cold, bright moonshine and of incredible agony, contrasted with other waves of thickest darkness, as he fainted and returned to life again and again.

Twice he awakened to find the horse stand still, the way lost. Twice, desperation came over him as he shouted wildly to the stallion and roused himself long enough to discover the right way once more.

Then, after those ages of agony, he heard the hoofs of the horse slumping through the softness of deep dust, and the smell of dust was in his nostrils. He roused, and found that he was surrounded by spinning lights. He told himself that the lights could not be sweeping around the horizon in this wild manner. They must be fixed in place; he was simply dizzy.

Voices came out to him. He saw faces that wavered up and down and began to spin like the lights. Then he closed his eyes. Hands fell on him and lifted him from the horse. Men were speaking his name.

"Take me to Dolly Gray," he begged them. "Take that saddle bag along with me. Dolly Gray has all the brains in the world. She'll know what to do."

They carried him, and their hands seemed to grip nothing but his wounds.

"He's talking, but he's a dead man," he heard a man saying. "He's gotta be dead. Ten men would be dead, from the dose he's had."

"Take me to Dolly Gray," he kept saying.

A small, faint voice was dinning at his ears, making one sound over and over again. He raillied his failing senses and made out that the voice was saying:

"I'm here, Ever. You're going to be all right. You're here with me."

That was Dolly, speaking, and when he heard that he began to relax. He opened his eyes. He said:

"Stop dancing around, and stand still. Stop swinging the lights, somebody. I want to see Dolly."

Everything stopped, for an instant, and in that instant he saw her face, close to his. Her eyes were wild and her mouth was pinched. She looked older by years.

Then everything began to spin again, and he had to close his eyes.

"I want the sheriff," he said.

"The sheriff's here," said Dolly.

A man's voice rumbled, at that, but Ever could not understand the words. Only the voice of the girl cut faintly into his consciousness.

"There's a saddle bag," said Ever. "Uncle Clay was returning the money to that damned bank. I hope the coin chokes 'em! It isn't my job. I'm just finishing the errand for Uncle Clay. You understand?"

"I understand," said the girl. "Everybody understands everything. You don't have to talk, Ever."

"Hush!" said Ever. "Somewhere out in the hills the crooks are chasing Harry, the Indian. He brought up the Pacer for me, and he fought the whole gang till I got away. You've got to send out men—send out everybody."

Her voice was saying something, over and over again.

"Harry is here. Everybody's here. Everything is all right, Ever. Save your strength. I'm going to take care of you. We're all going to take care of you."

"Uncle Clay and Timberline—what happened to them? Tell me what happened to them?"

"They're here. Open your eyes, Ever. You'll see your uncle. Don't you hear his voice? Can't you see him?"

He opened his eyes and stared, but everything was spinning worse than before. "I can't see anything," he said. "Give me your hand, Dolly, will you? Keep a good, tight hold—and—I won't be able to—to get away."

44

In FACT, Dolly Gray kept hold of Ever night and day until the fever had burned itself out of his infected wounds and he lay white as a bone and thin as a mummy, looking weakly out at the world, but with perfect content. For the girl was always sitting between him and the window, and through the window itself he could see the Red

Pacer grazing, with the forested and snow-topped mountains as a fiitting background. And sometimes the great horse came and thrust his fine head in over the window sill. In such moments, sometimes, Ever and the girl and the horse were a silent trio of happiness.

Clay Winton came in and out every day. He would sit whittling, during the short intervals when Dolly was off duty. He told Ever the story of the Green River Bank, and of how the bank officials would not put up a case against Clay, since the money had been returned almost intact. Neither had the sheriff any desire to make the arrest, and the district attorney felt that he would be a fool if he opened a case against a man whom no jury in the country would convict, no matter what the evidence might be.

For the money was safely back in the bank, and, as for anything that the Wintons ever had done to bring the law on them, they had more than made up for it by wiping out of existence Carson Jimmy.

Ever would never forget how his father and mother came to him. Harry Lawson was in the room at the time, sitting as usual with his hat on his head and silence in his throat.

Ever's father stood in the doorway, hesitant, but his mother brushed past, and came quickly to the bedside. She knelt by it and took her son's face between her hands.

"I was wrong—always. I was wrong clean from the start, Ever," she said.

She began to weep.

He put out his hand and gathered both of hers at the wrists.

"You weren't wrong," he said. "You were dead right. Only, I've found enough luck to last me the rest of my days, I think."

"What luck, Ever?" she asked him.

"Dolly," he said. "come over here, will you? Mother, here's my luck."

At that, Mrs. Winton broke into more violent weeping than ever.

"Hell! I better get out of here," said Harry Lawson.

He rose, tugged his old felt hat tighter on his head,

206

and went to the door, where he collided with a tall man who wore a strip of bandage around his head.

"What's all the noise in here, Ever?" called the tall fellow.

"Hey, Timber," said Ever. "Come in here, will you?"

"What's it all about?" asked Timberline.

"It's just this. I'm collecting all my luck together in one room, and you're one of the best parts of it, so I want you in here along with the rest."

Timberline's teeth flashed as he laughed in answer:

"It takes six people to give you luck, partner. But you've been enough luck all by yourself to do for the whole six."

Afterwards, Clay Winton got out of the room and sat on top of the pasture fence, talking with Harry Lawson while the Indian stared at the stallion and Clay whittled at a white stick of soft pine.

"Ever gave you the stallion back, I hear," said Clay.

"That Pacer?" answered Harry. "I won't have him. He'd rather eat me than hay. So I've given him back to Ever."

Clay Winton looked sharply aside.

"Harry," he said, "what the devil has been in you? At first, I thought you hated Ever. Then you give him your horse and you saved his neck for him."

"There was no devil in Harry," said the Indian. "But he saw the devil in the horse and he saw the devil in Ever. He liked both those devils, but two devils together make a pretty hot trail, Harry thinks. He wanted to keep them apart; then he saw they belonged together. A long time ago," concluded the Indian, "Harry looked at Ever and saw something that made him feel young again. After that, he didn't want Ever to go to hell on a horse."